To Helen

Linda M James grew up in Wales but has lived a nomadic life since then. All her varied experiences have filtered into her writing. She has had three novels and two non-fiction books published. Her short stories and poems have been published in many journals, in this country and Vienna.

She has also had four screenplays optioned and three historical screenplay commissions.

She has adapted *"The Day Of The Swans"* into an intriguing screenplay and a film company is now looking for film funding.

Before becoming a writer, she was a model, a singer and an English Lecturer.

Best wishes
Linda M James

D1439223

The Day Of The Swans

Linda M James

Indigo Dreams Publishing

First Edition: The Day Of The Swans
First published in Great Britain in 2012 by:
Indigo Dreams Publishing Ltd, 132 Hinckley Road, Stoney Stanton
LE9 4LN, UK
www.indigodreams.co.uk

Linda M James has asserted her right under the Copyright, Designs
and Patents Act 1988 to be identified as the author of this work.
©2012 Linda M James

ISBN 978-1-907401-77-0

British Library Cataloguing in Publication Data. A CIP record for
this book can be obtained from the British Library.

Designed and typeset in Minion Pro by Indigo Dreams.
Cover design by Ronnie Goodyer at Indigo Dreams

Printed and bound in Great Britain by: The Russell Press Ltd.
www.russellpress.com on FSC paper and board sourced from
sustainable forests

Other books by the author:

Non Fiction

How to Write Great Screenplays
(How To Books)

How to Write and Sell Great Short Stories
(Compass Books)

Fiction
The Invisible Piper
(Pegasus Elliot Mckenzie)

Tempting the Stars
(Pegasus Elliot Mckenzie)

'Be careful of your thoughts, for they will become words.
Be careful of your words, for they will become actions.
Be careful of your actions, for they will become habits.
Be careful of your habits, for they will become character.
Be careful of your character, for it will become your destiny.'

Anonymous

For my students:
past, present and future.

The Day Of The Swans

Chapter 1
ANNA

It was the kind of morning Anna loved: an azure blue sky with a hint of spring budding on the ash trees in Cavendish Square as she walked through the small park towards Wigmore Street. In spite of the diseased smell of traffic; the cacophony of taxis circling the square and the jostle of pedestrians focused on work, all Anna could think of was the previous night. She and Tim had indulged in athletic love-making for hours and they'd both got up late. She smiled to herself as she weaved a path through the stationary cars and taxis; she didn't notice the numerous men staring at her because men had been staring at her all her life. But she noticed Max, her American supervisor, treading carefully up the steps of the clinic in the distance. She weaved around the last car, eager to reach the clinic; determined to discover why 33 year old Kieran O'Reilly was so nervous.

The clinic was a haven after the bustle of the street; such a contrast from her last placement in an NHS hospital with its peeling paint, worn curtains and overworked staff. No wonder the clients felt stressed in such places, Anna thought. She wished she could show Government Health Officials how much more beneficial it was for everyone to be treated in such a tranquil environment.

Marie, the receptionist, was sitting at her desk coping with a number of clients in her usual calm manner. Anna often wondered if Marie was employed by the clinic solely because she sedated the clients with tranquillity.

'Hi, Anna. Kieran's waiting for you in your office.' Marie smiled her enigmatic Mona-Lisa smile before answering the telephone.

'Thanks,' Anna said, picking up a file. She walked along the carpeted corridor towards the small, neat office she had been working in for four months. It wasn't really her office, but it always gave her pleasure when Marie called it hers. Kieran O'Reilly had been her first client after she had applied for a placement in the clinic and had asked to be supervised by Dr. Max Paris after reading his numerous articles in *The Psychologist*. She wanted to be supervised by a man with vast experience and great insight into people's minds. Max had asked her to video some of her sessions with clients so he could watch the way she interacted with them. So far, he'd liked what he had seen, he told her. She only had two months left of her placement and if Max gave her a positive assessment she'd be a fully certified Clinical Psychologist in nine months. She knew her parents would be proud of her; but then they always were – whatever she did.

Anna opened the door of the office and smiled at Kieran who crouched, taut with tension, on the edge of a wooden chair. She had to find a way to make her relax.

'Hello, Kieran. Isn't it a beautiful day?'

Kieran's eyes darted from the ground to the window in surprise and Anna realised she hadn't noticed that the sun was shining.

Anna sat down, unperturbed by Kieran's lack of reply. She hadn't spoken at all during their first session together. This had worried her a lot at the time, but when she'd talked about it with Max, he'd told her about a client he'd once had who didn't speak for three sessions. Then all his problems spilled out of him like an oil slick.

Anna watched Kieran twisting her lank, brown hair around an index finger like a vulnerable child.

'Do you remember me asking you to write a journal?'

Kieran nodded, but didn't make eye contact.

'Did you write one?'

'Yes.'

'Can I read it?'

Reluctantly, Kieran opened the small bag she clutched on her lap as if Anna was about to rip it away from her. She brought out a small cheap notebook and gave it to Anna without looking at her. Her hand shook slightly.

MONDAY

Today Anna told me to write a journal about my thoughts but it's difficult as I don't know what to write about but I have to must write something. But what?

TUESDAY

Very nervous. What can I write about? Nothing ever happens to me.

WEDNESDAY

Didn't sleep last night. Worried about writing the journal.

FRIDAY

Feeling ill. Couldn't write yesterday. Can't write today.

SATURDAY

I went for a walk.

SUNDAY

What will happen when Anna finds out that I haven't written anything?

Anna looked up from the journal and smiled into Kieran's tense face.

'But you have written something, haven't you?'

For the second time that morning, Kieran registered surprise.

13

'You've said you had to write because I told you to. Did you always do what you were told to as a child?'

'Yes,' she answered in a quiet, lilting voice.

'Always?'

'Always.'

'Were your parents pleased about that?'

'Pleased?' Kieran frowned at Anna as if she'd never heard of the word before. 'I think they were, but I don't know.'

It was Anna's turn to be surprised. Parents who didn't show pleasure. She thought how incredibly lucky she'd been to have her parents; parents who showed her how much they loved her when she was growing up.

'So what made them happy?' Anna asked her.

Kieran thought about the question for a long time before answering. 'When I played by myself without bothering them.'

Bothering them? Anna thought. The parents are the problem, not Kieran.

'Didn't you like playing by yourself?'

'No.'

'Why not?'

Kieran's forehead furrowed again. 'I didn't know what to do.'

Anna tried to work out what she meant. 'You didn't know how to play?

'No, I knew how to play, but I needed them to tell me what to do first.'

It suddenly came to Anna. 'You don't like making decisions.'

'I hate making them,' Kieran whispered.

'You preferred your parents making them for you.'

'Yes,' she answered.

'Do you know why, Kieran?'

14

For the first time, Kieran glanced at her before answering. 'Yes. I might make the wrong ones and then what would happen?'

'What do you think would happen?' Anna asked her gently.

'I'd make the wrong ones and then my parents would leave me.'

***

The Italian café in Barrett Street was small and intimate and served good, reasonably priced food. It was hidden down a small pedestrianised area so it was always possible to find an empty table. Lunch had become an integral part of Anna's training. She and Max met there every Thursday to discuss her progress and air any problems she might have. She saw Max through the small paned windows, studying the menu as usual, and yet he always had the same lunch – a prawn sandwich.

He glanced up at her as she sat down opposite him and placed her assessment report on the red and white checked table cloth in front of him.

'Finished it already?' Max smiled at her, his grey eyes creasing in the corners. He looked all of his fifty-one years in the spring sunlight which suddenly slanted through the window. 'That's very quick.' He opened the report and scanned its contents, oblivious to the noise coming from the kitchen. Luigi, the Italian chef was arguing with his wife Alexandra again.

'I think Kieran's got Dependent Personality Disorder. She can't make a decision without her parent's approval, especially her father's. She's still living with them and she's nearly 35.'

She pointed to a section in the report in case Max would miss its relevance. He looked at her pointedly.

'Sorry,' she muttered. Perhaps she was suffering from a dependent personality too. She was desperate for Max's approval.

15

Anna was always amazed by the speed at which Max read. Not only read, but assimilated information and pinpointed any deficiencies in Anna's diagnosis. Perhaps they taught speed reading in America, she thought. She pretended to study the menu whilst studying him, noticing how his eyes narrowed as they raced from line to line. He was nearly at the end of the report before he frowned. Anna tensed. What had she written?

He looked up and her and said: 'So what are you having?'

'What?' Anna hadn't looked at the menu. 'Oh, the same as you.'

Alexandra, the waitress came over, her face relaxing as she saw Max. People always relaxed when they saw him. 'Dr. Paris – it wonderful to see you. Not like him in kitchen.' She glared over at the kitchen door where Luigi was banging every pot and pan they owned.

Anna wondered why Max chose such a noisy place to come to eat.

'We'll have two prawn sandwiches, Alexandra. Tell Luigi to think of his blood pressure.'

'Blood pressure! That man he have no blood pressure! He - a Sicilian!'

'Tell him I know as much about blood pressure as he does about food. He needs to relax if he doesn't want a heart attack.'

'I tell him, but he no listen.' She flounced off to argue with him again.

Max and Anna smiled at each other.

'I wonder why they stay together,' Anna mused. The kitchen now sounded like a battle zone.

'They love each other,' Max answered, staring out of the window.

Sadness shifted over his face like a cloud, but at that moment,

Anna was more interested in what he thought of her report than his sadness.

'So, what do you think?' She tried to sound casual.

'It's detailed.'

'Yes, but do you agree with my diagnosis?'

Max smiled at her. 'Always so direct. Sure you're not American? Yes, I agree. She'd be a good candidate for hypnosis. Trances can be very useful clinically. Remember how Milton Erickson used a technique called confusion? He said things on the surface which seemed logically contradictory, conveyed an ingenious creative truth. I'll get one of the –'

'I've studied and practised hypnosis for two years, Max. Can I do it?' Anna knew she was speaking too fast, but she desperately wanted to help Kieran and if her hypnosis helped her become independent of her parents she'd get a higher assessment rating. They would both benefit.

She waited as Max studied her face for some time before answering. 'Do you think you can really help her?'

There was something in Max's expression that stopped her from saying *yes* confidently. 'I don't know, but I'll try my best,' she said simply.

'What supervisor could ask for more? You can start hypnosis next week.'

Anna's face flushed with pleasure. 'That's the best news I've had today. Thanks, Max.'

'How many psychologists does it take to change a light bulb?' Max said seriously.

Anna stared at him in confusion. Was this some sort of test?

'It's a joke,' Max said, smiling at her.

Anna felt relief flood through her. 'I don't know.'

'Only one, but the bulb must really want to be changed,' Max

17

said. 'Remember that when you see Kieran.'

Alexandra brought their sandwiches and smiled at Max. 'I tell Luigi what you say about blood pressure, Dr.'

'And what did he say?'

'He shout and shout, so he don't hear. Then I shout and shout, then he listen and stop shouting. A miracle, I tell him.' Alexandra made the sign of the cross before walking off.

From the kitchen they heard Luigi singing.

'You should charge them, Max. They'd have killed each other months ago if it wasn't for you.'

'I don't think so,' he answered tersely.

Anna glanced at him quickly. He was frowning. She realised that Max didn't need compliments from a trainee. He'd published a vast collection of books and articles on Clinical Psychology and was an authority on Personality Disorders. What an incredible stroke of luck for her that he'd moved from New York to London all those years ago. But perhaps she'd aimed too high asking for his supervision. What if he gave her a poor grade for her thesis?

'So, how's the thesis progressing?' Max asked, as if reading her thoughts.

Knowing that Max was going to grade her thesis had forced Anna to focus on her research and writing, but it also gave her a great deal of pressure. She was determined not to reveal how much she still had to write. Max had helped her find a topic that had been under-researched. She was writing her thesis on *The Effectiveness of Cognitive Behavioural Therapy in Treating Gender-Related Depression*. She found it fascinating researching the differences between the male and female triggers for jealousy: the males feeling more jealous over sexual infidelity, while females being more threatened by emotional infidelity.

She looked at him confidently. 'Okay. I'm concentrating on how past aggressive behaviour in relationships is an indicator of future aggression at the moment.' Max often saved her hours of research by pointing her in the direction of the right books and journals to check. She hoped he'd do so again.

'Have a look at the MacArthur Study of Mental Disorder and Violence conducted in the States by Monahan. There's an interesting section on aggressive clients. You'll find it useful.'

'Okay. I'll have a look tonight.' Anna tried to look as if she meant it. She'd never have time tonight. She was going to see *Romeo and Juliet* at the National with Tim and her parents. She smiled as she thought of Tim's recurring quotation in their bedroom:

"*For I never saw true beauty til this night.*" Then he'd undress her. Slowly. Anna was suddenly aware that Max was giving her a strange look. 'Sorry...where were we?'

'Your thesis. You know I need it on my desk before your placement ends.'

Anna felt her heart race. God – how on earth was she going to finish it in two months? 'No probs,' she said casually.

Max winced and Anna suddenly remembered Marie telling her how Max hated slang. He certainly wasn't a typical American.

'Sorry, I'll have it on your desk in six weeks. Without fail.'

Max gave her a small smile. 'A little better, if over-confident.' He took another bite out of his sandwich and ate it slowly before saying, 'I've got a potential new client for you. The last client of your placement.'

Anna always felt a frisson of excitement when Max mentioned a new client. It was a challenge to be able to discover what their real problem was, but he'd never used the word 'potential' before.

'Why potential?'

Max always gave Anna some background into a client's history before letting her see him or her, but this time he was reticent.

'He told me …'

Max frowned as he ate the last portion of his sandwich. Anna suddenly realised that it wasn't eating that had stopped him speaking, but something else. Something she hadn't seen on his face before…puzzlement.

'He told you what?' She asked, very curious.

'He told me he was depressed.'

'So why are you puzzled?'

'Because dear, direct Anna – everything about the man negates depression.'

'Has he filled in one of the questionnaires?' The clinic had many questionnaires but Anna knew that Max preferred the Hamilton Rating Scale; he believed it was more accurate in measuring the severity of a client's depressive state than Becks.

'No. He said he didn't like questionnaires. I warn you now – he's not going to be easy. His demeanour, body language and speech all negate depression.'

'I wonder why he said he was then.'

'That's what you've got to find out.'

'Is he going to be very difficult, do you think?'

'I think he'll be challenging.'

Anna thought fast. Max had never said a client was challenging before, but if he had suggested that she should treat him, he must have confidence in her abilities. But was she ready for such a challenge?

'Perhaps he needs your experience, Max.'

'He doesn't want my experience. There must be a reason for

that. Do you want to see him?'

'What's he like?' she asked him.

'Like? That's a very vague term. He's intelligent and plays word games. Do you want to take him on?'

'I need another client to complete my placement, don't I?'

Max nodded as he wiped his hands on a paper napkin. 'Yes, I've just said that, but it doesn't have to be him.'

'Would you offer me a permanent job if I do?' Anna said, without thinking.

Max looked stunned by her request and Anna realised how crass the question must have sounded. She clenched her hands under the table in embarrassment. Why would he want to work with a woman who spoke before her brain was engaged? He liked dispassionate thinking.

'I don't do deals with trainees. Come on. Back to work.'

Max moved over to Alexandra to say goodbye before Anna could apologize. She stood up slowly, feeling a bit shaky. She'd blown her chances.

'Arrivederci.' Alexandra and Luigi called in unison. They stood in front of the kitchen holding hands. 'See you next Thursday.'

Anna glanced at Max who was holding the door open for her. She couldn't tell from his face whether there would be any more Thursdays.

'Lunch was great,' Anna said as they walked out into the street.

She glanced at Max as they turned into Wigmore Street. He was staring ahead with an inscrutable expression on his face. She'd obviously annoyed him. If only I could retract time, she thought.

'Your new client says he's a painter,' Max suddenly said.

21

'Says?'

'Well, I could say I'm a brain surgeon, but I'm not. Be prepared for invention, that's what I'm saying,' Max answered as they walked past the Wigmore Hall.

'Why don't you say he lies?' She'd done it again. Questioned him as if she knew as much as him.

'Because I don't know if he does, that's why. Just be prepared.'

'Like a boy scout?' Anna asked him, making a mock scout salute as they crossed the road together. Max suddenly smiled before grabbing her arm to stop her from colliding with a slow-moving car.

'Carry on like that Anna Nash and you won't be meeting any clients ever again.' Max guided her onto the pavement. 'Didn't your parents ever teach you about the green cross code?'

'The what?' Anna asked.

'It was a UK government programme devised in the 70s to make children stop, look and listen before they crossed a road. I read about it in the States.'

'I was born in 1988, Max.'

'All right, so you don't read history. Now stop making me feel old.'

She grinned at him. 'But you are,' she said instinctively. It was the sort of thing she said to her parents all the time, but Max wasn't a parent. He was her boss. She glanced at him nervously, waiting for him to frown, but all he did was smile. Max must be the most secure person I know, Anna thought with relief; he obviously didn't care he was middle-aged. Anna hoped she felt the same when she was older.

'So, any more details about the new client?' she asked hopefully.

'I told you, I haven't got any. It's your job to discover what's wrong with him.'

'Okay,' Anna said, determined to prove to Max that she was worth employing. A sudden thought occurred to her. 'Is he on medication?'

Max frowned as they sauntered towards the clinic. 'He says he's not, but-'

'Be prepared for invention?'

They smiled at each other as they walked into the clinic.

Marie was sitting in her usual, relaxed position at reception. 'I sent the new client up to Anna's office, Max. Was that all right?'

'That's fine, Marie. Can you give Anna his file?' He turned to Anna. 'Not that there's much information in it.'

Anna took the thin file off Marie and sprinted up the stairs. 'See you later, Max.'

'Come to see me after you've seen him.' Max called to her.

'Okay!' Anna shouted back.

If only she had known who was waiting for her in her office, she'd never have left the café; never have sprinted up the stairs with so much youthful enthusiasm, but she didn't. She hurried along the carpeted corridor, humming quietly to herself, blissfully unaware that she was about to meet a man who was going to ravage her life.

Chapter 2
STEFAN

I've almost finished the painting. It evokes your shadow, but not your substance. I can't capture that. And the sea was almost as difficult to orchestrate as you. I couldn't sculpt the waves or harmonize the shades of greens and blues and whites exactly. It must be exactly as it was. As I remember. It was a warm spring morning. Not usual for May. Was it May? No, it was a mild spring April morning and we were walking along the beach together. There was a light breeze. Then why weren't the waves flickering? The air was still.

'The sea tired, Stefan,' you said.

It was moving so slowly that day. Only the hint of ripples over the sea-shore. Our bare feet left yellow footprints: two big, two small.

You said 'my feet small.' I said 'They are perfect.'

And they were. *You* were perfect. *Are* perfect.

You pointed to the cliffs – your hand a dimpled starfish - and said 'How so high, Stefan?' And I said 'A giant made them high so he'd have something to jump over.'

And you laughed and the sun shone on your witchery of copper hair and I loved you more at that moment than I'd ever done before.

The painting is reflected hundreds of times in the mirrors. Hundreds of us walking along the sands forever; hundreds of you laughing up at me. Memories move like bright wings and fly around inside my head. In the distance, the limestone cliffs of your childhood slumber. A wedge of swans fly over our heads, shadowing your hair with hints of old gold and you shout out

24

with excitement.

'Look Stefan! Look! Look!' But I don't look up. I look at the joy on your face and know it must be reflected in mine.

A lone horsewoman gallops across the sands in the distance, but you don't see her because you suddenly notice a profusion of shells littering the sand. We collected hundreds that day and took them home to Bach Têg, our beautiful white house.

Do you remember? We made a collage of shells in your bedroom. Large blue mussels, yellow and orange cockle shells and fan-like scallops. We made a picture of our house, standing on top of the cliff with the sea-gulls wheeling below us and the sky spinning above us. And beside the house, you put our cardboard father.

'Where's mother?' I asked you.

'She inside house, playing piano, silly,' you said, smiling at me.

And my heart sang.

Chapter 3
MAX

Max closed the door as John Wilson walked out, relaxed back in his office chair and stretched. It had been a long afternoon treating four clients without a break. John suffered from claustrophobia so Max had to keep the door open during his therapy. He and his wife were living with his wife's parents until they could afford to buy a house. Their bedroom was small, he'd told Max, which created great problems for his marriage. His wife wouldn't make love with him if the bedroom door was open because her parents might walk past, and he wouldn't make love if it was closed. That night when Max looked into his bathroom mirror, a solution came to him. Buy two large mirrors, he'd told John during the next therapy session, put them on opposite walls and see what happens. Max smiled, remembering how delighted John had been when he came today. He and his wife had made love for the first time with the door closed because the room looked enormous in the mirrors. Then he told Max the reason for his claustrophobia: his father used to lock him in a small room whenever he'd been naughty. By admitting what had caused his problem, John had taken the first step towards recovery. Max sighed. Why could he transform other people's lives, but not his own? Perhaps he'd made a big mistake moving away from the States after Sadie's death.

He rubbed his eyes, trying to rub away his tiredness. He had Anna's assessment report to read. He hadn't been able to read it properly in the café with her looking at him. It unnerved him. He knew he should tell her to get a new supervisor, but he couldn't. He was pathetic. She was only twenty four and what was he? A middle-aged jaundiced man who could solve everyone's problems, except his own.

"Diagnostic Manual of Mental Disorders, Fourth Edition" *defines delusions as false beliefs based on incorrect inference about external reality that persist despite the evidence to the contrary.*

But what use was the ability to remember tracts from clinical psychology books if he allowed himself to suffer the same condition as many of his clients and didn't want to do anything about it? It had begun four months ago, when Anna had walked into his office on a cold, dark, November morning when he'd felt depressed. Not as depressed as most of his clients, but depressed. Dark mornings always depressed him since Sadie's death. But he wouldn't allow himself to dwell on the past. That's what Cognitive Behavioural Therapy had taught him. What he taught his students. Don't let clients dwell on their past problems. Make them focus on changing their behaviour in the present, so they don't repeat the problems of the past. Of course he knew why he wasn't applying this knowledge to himself; it was because of the way she walked as if buoyed with optimism; the way she breathed vitality; the way she smiled at him: she was intoxicating, effervescent Champagne.

He had allowed Anna to detach him from being analytical because he was enjoying the experience. The knowledge stunned him. He knew he should stop meeting her outside his office. Years of professionalism had disappeared in four short months. Meeting one of his students each week in a café to supposedly discuss her thesis! He couldn't believe the cliché he'd become. He'd been supervising students for over twenty years and had never, ever felt this way before. What had all his years of analytical training been for if he couldn't control his own behaviour? If he had to keep meeting her outside the clinic to imagine that they were a couple having a lunch together? That's why he'd chosen Luigi's. No-one would go there for a romantic lunch. It was too noisy. That was his strategy to alleviate any worries Anna might have about having weekly lunches with her supervisor. He wondered if she asked other students if they ever had lunch with their supervisors.

He loved how the intermittent light changed the colour of her hair as she sat opposite him in the café. How her expression mutated from vulnerability to confidence in a second. It was bewitching. The eagerness on her face as she asked him for a job. At Anna's age, he'd never have had the confidence to ask his supervisor for a job. But, of course, she had the assurance of love in her life. That hadn't come to him until he was much older and had lasted for such a short time. And had it really been love? He stood up, moving swiftly away from the perilous past and began pacing round the room. Something he hadn't done for years. The pain of knowing he could never offer Anna a job made his chest constrict. She must never know how much he'd wanted to shout to her in the café:

'Yes, I want you to work with me! I want you to be near me for the rest of my life!'

She must never know what it had cost him to be clinical because she was married to a colleague who referred clients to him. What an invidious position: to have the power to give happiness to the woman you love and not be able to use it or explain why. He both welcomed and dreaded the end of Anna's placement. There would be no excuse to sit opposite her in the café. No excuse to touch her arm as she crossed the street.

Max slumped back down in his chair and looked at the window. Instead of the horizon of bland houses outside the window, he saw only his reflection where each year of his life was

28

etched in every line on his face. He realised that of rigorous academic training, which gave him increase the psychological well-being of his clients, reduced to this moment of waiting; waiting like a love-teenager for a buoyant knock on the door. He looked at the clock. In five minutes, she would be here. He felt the tiredness leave his body. That's what's been lacking from my life, he thought. Energy. That's the gift she's given back to me. The energy to feel.

Chapter 4
ANNA

...r of her office, and saw a tall man with ...staring out of the window. He was totally ...ow tree that canopied over the back garden until he ... lick of the door. He turned to look at her and she experienced something she had never experienced before. Panic. He had the sort of face that adorned bill-boards – a face that hinted at exotic assignations; the sort of face that made male models a lot of money. He was wearing jeans and a roll-neck sweater, but no coat, although it was a cold day. Anna forced herself to observe these details rationally to stop the panic that was threatening to overwhelm her.

'Hello,' he said in a deep voice with the merest whisper of a foreign accent. 'I've been waiting for you a long time.'

Anna glanced at her watch. 'Your appointment was for 2 o'clock, wasn't it?' It was only 2.02. How could he have been waiting for a long time?

'Shall we sit down?' His confidence was unnerving; almost as if she was the client and he the therapist. He sat in her seat near the window as she said -

'That's my –' How could she finish the sentence? It would sound petulant to ask him to move. She sat down opposite him and studied his file. All he had written on the assessment form was Stefan Michel Peterson. Date of Birth. 10th April, 1977. Vienna. There was also a photo of a hotel overlooking a cliff with spectacular views. How had that got in his file? There was no other information there at all. She looked up at him.

'I don't like filling in forms, do you?' he asked, smiling at her.

His smile made her want to agree with him, but, of course, she couldn't.

'Then it would be helpful if you would answer some questions.'

'All right,' he said. 'As long as they are the right ones.'

Anna blinked. What did he mean? What *were* the right ones?

'In the past year, have you had two consecutive weeks or more during which you felt depressed, or when you lost interest in things that you usually enjoy?'

'Yes,' Stefan said.

'Have you had two years or more in your life when you felt depressed most days?' Anna continued.

'Yes,' Stefan answered.

'Have you felt depressed much of the time in the past year?'

'Yes.'

'How much time in the past week did you feel depressed?' Anna looked up from filling in the questionnaire to gauge his reaction. His face was impassive. 'Less than two days?'

'No, more like six days,' Stefan said, smiling at her, 'but not today.'

Why would a depressed client smile after saying he felt depressed six days a week? Anna thought; then remembered what Max had said about him: he liked playing games.

'Do you find it difficult getting to sleep?' She asked.

'Sometimes, but then everyone does sometimes, don't they?' Anna took a deep breath. Usually, she didn't ask her next question until much further into a client's treatment, but felt instinctively that he would rate her more highly if she did. 'Have you ever thought about committing suicide?'

Stefan studied her for some time before answering. 'Yes, numerous times.'

31

'Why?' She asked him gently.

'What do you think you've discovered about me so far?' Stefan tilted his head to one side as if assessing her; it was disconcerting. 'Do you think questionnaires carry any validity?'

'Yes, if someone answers truthfully,' Anna answered.

Stefan gave her a wry smile; as if he knew that she knew he was playing with her. 'I'd like to ask you some questions now…if I may.' Stefan was still smiling, but now the smile was relaxed; as if he was trying to put her at ease.

'Okay,' Anna said, trying to sound casual. She had never been questioned like this in her therapy sessions before. Clients ranged from the silent ones like Kieran, through to the garrulous ones who simply wanted to tell her all their problems so she could miraculously solve them in one session.

'Tell me exactly how Cognitive Behavioural Therapy works,' he said, as if he was her supervisor, not Max.

Anna placed his file on the table and looked at him. She was determined that this man wasn't going to faze her. 'CBT can help you change how you think and behave. But instead of focussing on the causes of your distress or symptoms in the past, it looks for ways to improve your state of mind now.'

'Does it, really?' he queried, making a steeple of his long, slender fingers. 'Go on.'

It was like having a viva to assess her competence to treat him, Anna thought. She felt an unaccustomed anger welling up inside her and forced herself to adopt a neutral tone. 'We use CBT to find out what a client's core beliefs are. What he feels about himself, his friends and family. The world in general. CBT works by identifying how your thoughts, ideas, attitudes and behaviour affect your day-to-day life.'

All the time she was talking, he kept nodding as if she was a child to be placated. Then Anna realised that he wasn't really listening to her, but simply staring at her face and hair. She resisted the urge to run her fingers through her hair in case it was dishevelled.

'Then we ask clients to agree to a treatment plan,' she continued 'and try to work on some goals that you can -'

'Goals are important, aren't they?' He leaned forward to look directly into her eyes and her heart jolted; she saw her eyes reflected in his. 'So how long have you been training?'

Anna shifted uncomfortably in her chair. This session wasn't like any other session she had ever had with a client.

'Clients should know about their therapists, don't you think?' He smiled again as if to reassure her.

'Well, first I studied a three year Psychology Degree and since then, I've been training in Clinical Psychology for two years so -'

'This is your final year,' Stefan stated, putting his hands star-like on the desk.

'Yes. Do you always interrupt people?'

There was a long silence.

Stefan turned in his chair to look out of the window and Anna groaned under her breath. Direct confrontation. How could she have been so stupid? Never allow yourself to show irritation with a client, Max had warned her, almost on her first day. Thank God, he hadn't asked for the session to be videoed.

'Could I ask you some more questions now?' Anna said, trying to sound calm and efficient.

He didn't answer for some time; then spoke without looking at her. 'That depends on what you ask.'

'How do you think CBT can help you?'

Stefan kept staring out of the window as if she wasn't there.

The contrast to his previous assertive behaviour was considerable, but Anna felt more in control of the situation with him not staring at her.

The minutes ticked by as Anna waited for his answer. Silence no longer unsettled her after treating Kieran. She looked out of the window and studied the Willow Tree Stefan was staring at so intently. It reminded her of a large 18th century lady lifting a long overfull skirt. She preferred the horse-chestnut trees in her parents' garden. They looked beautiful now – covered in clusters of white and pink flowers, waiting to be pollinated.

'Did you know that the willow is the tree of enchantment?' He suddenly said. 'In Celtic mythology it's associated with the myth of two scarlet sea-serpent eggs which contained the Sun and the Earth. These eggs were hidden in the boughs of the Willow tree until they hatched and brought forth earthly life. I love myths, don't you?'

Why was he talking about myths when she'd asked him why he had come? Why wasn't she concentrating? She always concentrated during her sessions with clients.

'How do you think CBT can help you?' Anna repeated, determined not to let her thoughts wander again.

Stefan turned from the window when he heard the determination in her voice. 'I'm depressed,' he said, smiling at her.

His smile disconcerted her. Max was right; everything about this man contradicted his simple statement.

'What do you think is making you depressed?' Anna asked, hoping her voice conveyed the correct mixture of interest and clinical detachment.

'Isn't it your job to tell me that?' Stefan answered.

Anna took a long deep breath; thankful that she practised

yoga. She would not let him provoke her.

'I want to help you, but I can't if you don't give me any information,' Anna said, dispassionately. 'Why do you think you're depressed?' She was amazed at how calm she felt.

Stefan studied his hands as if seeing them for the first time.

'My wife left me,' he said at last.

'That must have been a shock for you.' Anna suppressed a small smile of triumph. He had taken, what Max called 'the first step.'

'Oh, I knew she'd leave. I just didn't know when.'

'How did you know?'

'I'm clairvoyant,' he said seriously.

'You can see into the future?' Anna stared at him in surprise.

Stefan smiled at her and she knew he was playing with her again. Why would someone do that when they needed help?

'Mr. Peterson, I really would like to help you. Will you let me?' Anna asked.

Stefan's eyes creased with pain. 'Don't call me Mr. Peterson. I'm Stefan. I haven't changed my name like you.'

'I haven't changed my name,' Anna said in amazement.

Stefan sighed. A long sigh as if he knew she'd deny it. 'Semantics,' he answered. 'Someone did.'

'Mr. Peterson – Stefan. We don't seem to be getting anywhere. Do you want to stop the session?' Anna felt defeated, but what was the point in continuing with such a man.

Stefan suddenly looked panic-stricken. 'No, I don't want to stop. Do you want to know what's making me depressed?'

'Yes.' Anna wondered if this was another game he was playing.

'You,' he replied.

Anna was stunned. 'Me! But we've only just met! How can I

make you feel depressed?'

Stefan sighed even more loudly. 'Do I really have to go back to the beginning?'

'Of what?' Anna asked, totally confused.

'Your life,' Stefan answered.

***

Five minutes later, Anna was pacing up and down Max's office, almost in tears.

'I'm completely out of my depth, Max. He's the cat – I'm the mouse. He played with me the whole session.'

'Sit down, Anna. Let's analyse the situation calmly.'

Anna slumped into a chair, feeling totally despondent.

'He's resisting you by playing these games. He's transferring his problems onto you, so his problems become yours. But you're also allowing counter-transference to creep into the session too, aren't you?'

Anna was just about to deny this, when she realised that Max was right. She had allowed her emotions to transfer themselves to Stefan. He was reacting to her, just as she was reacting to him.

'Do you want to continue his therapy?' Max asked her.

Anna stared down at the dark blue carpet. Did she want to continue? Part of her did; part of her wanted to show Max what a good psychologist she could become; the other part was apprehensive. How would she cope with a client as difficult as Stefan?

'Do you think I'll cope?' she asked him, dreading the answer.

There was a slight pause; then Max said, 'yes, I think you'll cope.'

That's all she needed to know. Max had faith in her.

Chapter 5
MAX

It was 8 o'clock before Max left the office. He had written all his reports and left his office in its usual pristine state. As he crawled through the heavy traffic towards his Victorian town house in Kensington, he wondered, as he always did, when stuck in heavy traffic, why he was still living in London. Big cities reminded him too much of Sadie. He should have taken the job he was offered in Cornwall four months ago. He was going to and then Anna had walked into his life. He had turned down the 'opportunity of a life-time' he'd been told because he'd fallen in love with a married woman who was young enough to be his daughter.

He glanced in his rear view mirror and saw how bloodshot his eyes were. He knew he shouldn't work so hard. He should go out more, socialise with people so that he wasn't alone with his thoughts so much. He had women friends, but he hardly saw them. He was always so busy with his work; forging ahead with his career. He'd never really had time for socializing. Never really had time for Sadie. He overtook a car that was double-parked and turned into Royal Crescent. His headlights swept across the elegant curve of white stucco-fronted houses and he smiled. The sight always gave him pleasure; but, of course, like many other houses in the crescent, his was now divided into apartments. He lived on the ground floor, but it was large enough for his bachelor needs.

All the lights in the apartments were lit, except his. He should get a timer switch, he thought. The darkness was an invitation to burglars, but he never seemed to get round to buying one.

He parked his car some distance from his flat and got out.

The night air was what his mother would have called 'bracing'. Max pulled his coat tighter, shielding himself from the wind that tried to whisk inside it. As he walked along the crescent he looked into rooms occupied by his neighbours. He always found it strange that people allowed strangers to feast their eyes upon their private possessions, or even themselves in unguarded moments. Max never liked the thought of people staring at him without his knowledge. His curtains were always drawn against unseen eyes. He knew he was a contradiction; he liked looking into people's private lives, but hated others doing so to his. That, of course, was why he was a psychologist. He was fascinated by people and their strange foibles.

One of his neighbours had a collection of Samurai swords hanging over his fireplace. Strange how owning such lethal weapons could be legal, Max thought. He walked past the Samurai-sworded house and instinctively looked into the now familiar room. There was his neighbour standing in front of the fireplace talking to his tense-looking wife. Perhaps she was worried that one day her stock-broker husband would take a sword off the wall and hack her to pieces. Max smiled at the absurdity of the idea; then remembered a story he had read in *The Times*. A mild-mannered man had strangled his wife one afternoon because she stirred her cup of tea fifteen times before drinking it and she drank a lot of tea. She'd been doing this every day for 35 years he told the Judge and it irritated him beyond belief. 'Why, then, did you not tell her?' The Judge asked him incredulously. 'I didn't like to,' the mild-mannered man had answered. Oh, the terrible courtesy of the British, Max thought as he walked up to the steps to his flat.

He opened the door and inhaled the reassuring smell of lemon. His cleaner, Mrs. Jenkins, always used lemon-scented polish. He closed the door and walked into his large, but sparsely furnished lounge which contained a white leather settee, a battered old armchair, an equally battered drinks cabinet and a television. Sadie had bought the white settee; it had been one of her usual disastrous purchases; everything stained it. Max never used it now. He poured himself his nightly glass of whiskey; it was something he looked forward to, and deserved, he told himself. He switched on the television and relaxed into his old armchair. A bit like me, he thought as the chair sagged under his weight. Everything moving south. The television news immediately assaulted him with images of war, murder and vandalism: the nightly fodder of the 21st century. He turned it off. He didn't want any more images searing his brain when he was trying to sleep.

He sagged back into the chair again, thinking how young and vulnerable Anna had looked in his office. He'd wanted to put his arms around her; to stroke her hair and tell her he'd look after her. That everything would be all right and she mustn't worry about anything, ever again. Of course, he couldn't. He had to be detached and analytical. Talk about transference and counter-transference. Tell her to be detached. The hypocrisy of the situation demoralised him. He was telling a trainee to acquire qualities that he could no longer apply to himself. He drained his glass. He couldn't believe how negative he was becoming and yet, every day he showed clients how to change their lives by changing their thoughts.

He stood up and did some neck exercises. His neck always felt stiff after a busy day. He must tense his body when listening to clients, but he wasn't aware of tension; his concentration was totally focused on his clients' problems.

He frowned, thinking what he had said to Anna. 'Yes, you

can cope.' Could she? He was worried she couldn't, but how could he tell her that when she wanted his reassurance so much. His judgement was being eroded by a girl who could have stepped out of a pre-Raphaelite painting. And he seemed unable to stop the erosion.

Chapter 6
STEFAN

We always walked up the cliff hand in hand. Do you remember how I had to carry you up the last part because you got so tired? We didn't tell Mother I took you on the cliff path. She thought the cliffs were dangerous, but I was always there to look after you.

'You must never allow your sister to go outside the gardens alone,' she said. And I never did. I always locked the gate. I was in charge of the key.

In my memory we are always walking towards the house. The white house on top of the cliffs. Standing for hundreds of years against winds and storms. Waiting for us to return. I imagine everything just as we left it: Mother playing her Steinway piano by the window and looking out at the wide expanse of sky; the old Viennese clock in the corner, slowly ticking our lives away; my books scattered on the floor in front of me; you lying at my side, drawing pictures with a fat crayon. And in your pink and white bedroom, your butterfly mobile still moves in the breeze over your bed. The house has been empty for twenty one years.

Do you remember how mother played the piano for us? How her long, slender fingers flew over the keys. How beautifully she played. How we used to lie near her feet as she sang:

> *'Kommt ein Vogel geflogen,*
> *Setzt sich nieder auf mein' Fuß*
> *Hat ein Zettel im Schnabel,*
> *Von der Mutter Liebsten ein' Gruß.'*

How your eyes shone as you sang. The song was too childish for me, but I always joined in so you would know that our mother's music would join us together forever.

Do you remember the waves crashing against the cliffs outside my bedroom window? One night you crept into my bedroom and opened the window and we listened to the sea.

And I said to you. 'Do you know what happiness is?' And you shook your head and I said: 'it is the sound of the sea at night; your breath on my cheek; your shadow on the sands.' But you frowned at me, not understanding and asked -

'But why the sea angry, Stefan?' And I told you the sea was angry with the moon for making it crash against the rocks. And you frowned at me again and said. 'Silly Stefan.' Then you went to sleep in my arms.

I cannot return to the white house without you, Anna.

Today was a bad day. You played games with me. You were nervous. How could you be nervous of me? Telling me to fill in a form as if you didn't know the answers. As if you'd never met me before. I tried to help you by asking about your work, but you were so abrupt – asking me if I always interrupted people! So hurtful, Anna. I had to defend myself. Become more opaque. Then you wanted to stop the session! How could you even contemplate such a separation when all I want is to have you back in my life again?

You mustn't fight me, Anna. You must remember!

Chapter 7
CELIA

The Olivier Theatre was only half full; *The National* had taken a big gamble by using two unknown actors, Adisa Diagne and Charlotte Wheatcliff, to play Romeo and Juliet; there had been mixed reviews in the newspapers.

Celia was not impressed. The actor's diction wasn't clear enough. She glanced at Anna's face, glowing in the soft light from the stage and felt the familiar surge of pride. Anna was obviously entranced by the production. Perhaps I'm too old to enjoy avant-garde productions, Celia thought. Anna turned to smile at her; she smiled back. Tim suddenly yawned. Obviously, he didn't share her daughter's enjoyment.

The actors took their bow and the audience clapped; some with great enthusiasm; others with hardly a sound. The lights came on and Anna leaned forward.

'So what did you think?' Anna asked.

Paul frowned. 'I'm still trying to come to terms with it.'

Celia wasn't surprised. Her husband was a traditionalist; he liked Shakespearean plays to be Elizabethan.

They always went to the restaurant at *The National* because everyone, apart from Anna, was ravenous after a performance and didn't want to wait to eat. They gave their order to the waiter quickly before the rest of the audience came in.

Anna looked at her father. Celia knew that she wanted his verdict on the production.

'Come on, Dad. Spill the beans.'

'Where does she get such odd expressions from, Celia?' Paul asked his wife.

43

Anna squeezed her mother's hand and they smiled at each other.

'Why did Romeo have to leap around so much?' Celia said.

'Made me shattered watching him,' Tim answered. 'Obviously needed some valium before the performance. I'd have given him some if I'd known.'

They laughed as the waiter poured them some Margaux. He spilt some on the white table-cloth, distracted by Anna's smile; the wine spread out across the table-cloth like a small red relief map. The waiter apologized before rushing off to serve the other customers.

'I loved the way Romeo leapt around the stage during the fight scenes,' Anna said. 'It was like no other production I've ever seen.'

'There's a reason for that, darling,' Tim said.

They laughed again and touched glasses as they toasted each other.

'Dad – say something.'

They all looked at Paul. 'All right. I thought the diction in parts of the play was appalling. Beautiful Shakespearean words were swallowed up in a frenzy of overwrought activity. There was no sense of real passion between the two teenagers. Juliet was too excitable. Some of the props, like the chairs and tables in the café scene, seemed a mere deus ex machina device – so the actors could throw them around, and lastly, the drinking of tequila slammers and the machete-carrying mumbling thugs jarred on a traditional scholar who actually likes to hear the words the bard wrote.'

People from other tables had stopped talking to listen to Paul's speech. A woman cried 'Hear! Hear!' Several people applauded.

Paul smiled at them. 'Sorry, I got carried away.'

'That was a lecture, Dad. Not an opinion,' Anna said.

'Habits die hard,' Paul answered.

The waiter brought them their food. Anna and Tim had ordered steak. Paul and Celia had given up steak after the beef scare in 1996. They'd ordered chicken and rocket salad. Paul eyed his salad suspiciously.

'When did lettuce leaves become so exotic?' Paul asked no one in particular.

Celia smiled, remembering the wholesome English food of her childhood in Tunbridge Wells; the walks in Dunloran Park to feed the ducks in the lake; tobogganing down Sand Hill Lane in the winter; the wonderful concerts in the Assembly Hall with her parents. How can I remember the golden days so clearly and the dark ones hardly at all? She thought. She'd had a good career as a History Lecturer; not a long one as she'd wanted to be at home with Anna when she was small, but she loved her job. Now she was part-time, she had time to write all the articles and books she'd been too busy to write when she was working at University College London full-time. She was only sixty after all; there were still many things she wanted to do. And, of course, there were all her photo albums to fill; a constant joy of memories. Naturally, there were gaps. But everyone had gaps in their lives they would prefer to forget.

Celia realised that they were all staring at her. Had she been away for that long?

'Where were you this time, Mum?' Anna asked playfully. 'Lost in the past again?'

Celia smiled at Anna. She was so lucky to have such a lovely daughter. 'I'm just waiting for your father's lengthy review of the play, darling. He's writing it in his head as I speak.'

'I'm still writing it,' Paul replied, taking out a small note book and jotting down some comments.

'Well, I'm sure you'll tell us your final verdict,' Celia said dryly as she looked across the restaurant. On the far wall, she suddenly saw a painting of a seascape and a wonderful image flashed in her mind; a copper-haired little girl was making sandcastles with her father on a beautiful strip of yellow sand, her face crinkling with concentration.

'Do you remember us taking you to Plymouth when you were four?' She asked Anna.

'We took her to Bournemouth,' Paul stated emphatically, replacing his pen in his jacket pocket.

'Don't be ridiculous. We've never been to Bournemouth,' Celia argued, equally emphatic.

'Here they go,' Anna said to Tim.

'He's going senile since he retired,' Celia continued. 'Can't remember a thing.'

'Oh, can't I? Then what sonnet is this from? *"Be wise as thou art cruel: do not press my tongue-tied patience with too much disdain, lest sorrow lend me words, and words express the manner of my pity-wanting pain."*'

'Oh, don't be ridiculous, Paul. I teach History, not English. I can't remember all Shakespeare's sonnets.'

'It's 140,' Anna said.

Paul beamed at her. 'Aha! – some-one in this family has a brain!' He winced as Celia dug him hard in the ribs. 'Ahh! I've married Attila the Hun!'

'I wonder if I'll be attacking you when we've been married thirty years,' Anna said to Tim.

'I expect so. With a machete, I should think,' he answered.

They laughed and Celia remembered the first dinner she and

Paul had had after they were married. She'd asked him if he thought they'd be speaking to each other in thirty years' time. Thirty years. How was it possible for such a long space of time to disappear so quickly? She smiled at Paul, wondering if he remembered.

'Quite an achievement,' Paul suddenly said.

'What is?' she asked.

'That we're still married.'

Celia leaned over and kissed him. Yes, it was quite an achievement. Especially after all that pain. She never thought she'd recover after the miscarriages she'd endured. Paul had been her rock.

'What *is* this?' Anna said.

'The young haven't got a monopoly on romance, you know,' Paul answered.

'Oh, I forgot to tell you - I've got a new partner,' Tim said.

'What's the connection between romance and your new partner?' Anna poked him in the ribs in mock indignation.

'Good grief! She's started hitting me already and we've only been married a year!' Tim said and they all laughed again.

What a wonderful evening it was, Celia thought.

'What's he like?' Paul asked.

'He's a she. And she's very competent. Same age as me.'

'Old, you mean,' Anna said, grinning at him.

'Yeah, all of 36. It's surprising she can walk really. She's returned to work after having kids.'

'How old are her children?' Celia's face clouded. No mother should leave a young child to go out to work.

'Five and three. She brought them to the surgery once. They're lovely kids.'

They were suddenly silent. Celia knew how much Tim

47

wanted to start a family, but Anna had her training to complete. She was too young to have children Anna kept telling them and Celia agreed. It would be much better for her to get her certification and a couple of year's clinical practice under her belt before starting a family. She had been 36 before Anna came into their lives.

'They're very young,' Celia said, disapprovingly.

'Oh, come on, Mum. Women have a right to a career as well as men. Why should they be penalised because they have children? You worked when I was a kid.'

'You were nearly ten before I went back to the University. I had an awful time getting a job then.'

'That's why women don't want to leave their careers for so long. It's not fair that working–'

'Stop, you two,' Paul said, turning to Tim. 'These two have been arguing about working mothers for years. Very exhausting women in this family.'

Tim smiled. 'I know.' He looked at Anna and his smile faded. 'Clare's a great asset to the practice, but I'm glad she's working with us for another reason too.'

'Which is?' Anna asked.

'Her arrival gives us a great opportunity.'

'What opportunity?' Anna looked wary.

'I can take some time off and we can have a holiday.'

Anna stared at Tim in alarm. 'I can't go away until I've finished my placement and Max gave me a new client today. And there's my thesis. I've only got six weeks left to write it.'

'You could go after Anna has finished her placement, surely, Tim.' Celia was concerned by the sudden pressure Tim was putting on her daughter.

'I'm sure Max won't object if I asked him,' Tim said to Anna, ignoring Celia. 'He knows I haven't had a holiday for over a year. He'll extend your placement.'

Anna was silent.

'Come on! Two weeks away. Any where in the world. You choose.'

'I can't, Tim,' Anna said quietly. 'I have to finish my thesis.'

A look of annoyance flashed across Tim's face.

'Can't you wait two months so that Anna can finish her work then you can both have a wonderful holiday?' Paul asked him reasonably.

'I need a break now, Paul. Not in two months. Anna knows how much pressure I've been under for months at the practice without a partner. Now I've just got a really good one and I need a break!'

Celia was amazed at how quickly the evening had turned sour: from relaxed banter to charged tension in the space of five minutes.

They finished their food in silence and Celia suddenly wondered if she'd made a big mistake in thinking her son-in-law was the best thing that could have happened to her daughter.

Chapter 8
ANNA

Anna lay in bed, full of tension. She could feel Tim's anger from the bathroom; every turn of a tap, every click of a light conveyed it. She was stunned by Tim's sudden reversal of mood. He was acting like a petulant child who couldn't get his own way - like one of my clients, Anna thought with a flickering of fear.

The bathroom light snapped off. Anna rolled up in a ball and closed her eyes as Tim entered the bedroom.

'I know you're not asleep,' he said as he lay down beside her.

Anna wasn't sure whether to acknowledge this fact or not. She didn't know if she had the energy to argue about having a holiday she didn't want. She wanted to finish her placement and thesis. They both lay in bed, separated by different goals.

Tim's mobile rang; he'd forgotten to switch it off. He swore as he got out of bed to answer it.

'Hello,' he said in a curt voice. 'Can't it wait until the morning? I'm in bed.' He listened for a few minutes. 'It's not urgent. We'll talk in the morning.' He switched his mobile off and got back into bed. 'That was my new partner. Worrying about a patient.'

He lay down stiffly beside her and Anna concentrated on keeping completely still. Suddenly, she felt Tim's arm creep around her shoulders; his head nuzzling into her neck.

'Sorry, my sweet. I've been a shit tonight, haven't I?'

She rolled towards him and they hugged each other.

'Definitely out of character, Dr. Nash.'

'I'm tired, that's why. I really need a break, Anna. Will you change your mind?'

She pulled away to look into his hazel eyes. He did look very tired. Guilt surged through her; the deadly quality that could sabotage people's lives, she'd learned from her training; forcing people to do things they didn't want to do. How many times had guilt made her say yes to her parents when she had wanted to say no? How many times had she apologized to Tim after an argument that hadn't been her fault?

'Couldn't you just take time off and stay at home?' She countered. 'You can relax here.'

'You know I won't relax at home.' Tim stroked her hair, seducing her with his touch. 'I'll start working on some project or other and go back to work as tired as when I left. Please, Anna. How about just one week? That's all I'm asking and you can choose where we go.'

How could she refuse such a simple request? 'All right,' she said.

Overjoyed, Tim started kissing her all over her body. Normally, she responded instantly, but this time, instead of being submerged in sex, she was distanced by worry: how would Max react? How would she finish her thesis in time? How would she enjoy a holiday with this much stress? What about her career? Her life?

Hours later, after they'd both collapsed into sleep; Tim lay motionless, but Anna tossed and turned in a turbulent dream:

A woman is lying in a small, single bed, fast asleep. A yellow candle lights the room. A beautiful glass butterfly hangs over her head. Suddenly, a slight breeze moves across it. The sound of glass music. The woman wakes up and stares at the butterfly, entranced.

The door opens silently. A dark figure stands there, watching her. The woman suddenly becomes aware of him and gasps. Wind whips through the room and the glass butterfly flies over the ceiling making splinters of music.

The figure moves towards the bed, into the light of the candle. Stefan. The woman screams.

Anna jolted upright in bed, her palms sweating, her heart pounding. What did the dream mean? She swung her legs out of bed, trying to remember what she learned in her training about dreams, but she was too tired to think clearly.

She went into the bathroom and washed her hands and face, looking at herself in the mirror. Her eyes looked startled; her hair was windblown. How could that be? Nausea suddenly overwhelmed her as she realised that the dream was somehow prophetic. A huge black hole was opening in her life and there was nothing to fill it with.

Chapter 9
STEFAN

You won't remember where I was born, Anna. It was in our apartment in Gärtnergasse, Vienna. Mother had a long Viennese mirror near the front door. I used to stare into it and wonder who the person was staring back at me. How can an image define who we are? And yet, I still look in mirrors, hoping that one day the face staring back at me will reveal the truth; that there will be a moment of epiphany when everything will be explained.

I remember the smell of Mother's old photograph albums so clearly; the musty smell of old leather which hit my nostrils the moment I opened the albums. I used to sit by the window as the last rays of the dying sun flickered over aunts and uncles before resting on the angular, asymmetrical face of a thirty five year old man. His black eyes used to question me each week. 'And what courage have you ever shown?' he'd ask me. 'I'm only eleven,' I used to tell him. 'I *will* show courage, one day, when I'm older.' I think I have now, but the memory is incomplete without you.

Every day until I was eleven, I walked the streets of Freud and Mahler; Schiele and Klimt; Mozart and Beethoven. Vienna was populated with people who marked the future with ideas and music and painting. Young Adolf Hitler lived in my city as one of the faceless poor, sleeping in a squalid homeless shelter. He wanted to be a painter, but wasn't good enough for the Academy of Fine Arts in Vienna. Imagine, Anna, if the Academy had accepted him, we might never have had World War II; our parents would never have met and we would not exist. Can you see how important small incidents are to the whole of life? I must make you see that we have to create our own destiny and not be influenced by others.

I was there, Anna. How could you not know? Sitting so close. The empty seat behind you was waiting for me. I looked at your face as you looked at the stage. You were engrossed in the play and I was engrossed in you.

"Alas, that love, whose view is muffled still, should, without eyes, see pathways to his will!" How did Shakespeare know the human heart so well? How do you know it so little? Do you know that a word is the skin of thought?

You leaned towards the older man, seeking his approval. Why not seek mine? Are your eyes so blind? We are two suns set in different spaces but you cannot see.

Your face became shadowed in the restaurant. What did he say to make you look like that? His face closed like a clam when you spoke to him. What did you say? I wanted to attack him for upsetting you, but I can't. Not yet.

Chapter 10
ANNA

It was nearly 4 o'clock before Anna finally slid into a deep, dreamless sleep after her disturbing dream. At 7 o'clock their radio alarm clock pierced the silence with agitated ringing. But this morning she didn't move. Eventually Tim stirred, leaned over Anna and silenced it. She was sleeping peacefully; her beautiful russet hair spread out on the pillow. He kissed her gently before getting out of bed to have a shower.

Five minutes later, Anna was startled by John Humphries haranguing David Cameron on the *Today Programme*. The radio was their back-up, in case the alarm didn't slice into their sleep.

She staggered out of bed and switched the radio off. She couldn't cope with confrontation at this hour.

Tim walked into the bedroom and dressed quickly, looking at the clock. 'Christ, I'm late. I'll skip breakfast. See you tonight, darling. Tell Max not to work you too hard.'

Just as he was at the door, he turned. 'Oh, I've invited him and your parents for drinks on Wednesday night. Is that okay?'

He was out of the door before she could say it would be good to ask me first.

She walked over to their large bedroom mirror and yawned. How could she work when she looked that tired? She had no idea how she was going to cope with Stefan Peterson when her energy levels were so low. He had booked his second session for 2 o'clock.

***

Anna was already sitting in her office at the clinic by 1.30

p.m. She'd told Marie to phone her the moment Stefan arrived. Max had asked her to video the session; not because he didn't trust her judgement, he'd said, but to help her assess why Stefan had come for therapy. The video camera was angled towards the desk so it could record his dialogue and body language.

She stood up and did some deep breathing exercises to fight the tiredness that was threatening to overwhelm her. The phone suddenly rang. She jumped.

'He's arrived, Anna. Shall I send him up to you?' Marie asked on the phone.

'Yes, please, Marie.' Anna put the phone down and carried on with her deep breathing. Oxygen flooded into her brain, making her focus: Stefan Peterson was a troubled man and she was there to help him.

She sat down, feeling more relaxed. A small knock on the door. That was quick, Anna thought.

'Just a moment,' she shouted, moving over to the video camera. She switched it on; then suddenly saw yellow catkins on the willow tree outside the window. She smiled, wondering how long they had been there.

'Come in,' she shouted, sitting down with her back to the window.

Stefan opened the door and walked in. Anna was disconcerted by the haggard look on his face; his eyes were shadowed with exhaustion. He leaned a large portfolio against the table leg as he sat down.

His evident exhaustion made Anna feel in control of the situation. 'Hello, Stefan. You look tired. Didn't you sleep well?'

Stefan hunched down in the chair and stared at her. 'I was walking most of the night. You look tired too. Didn't you sleep well, either?'

'I'm fine.' Anna was determined to show Max how competent she was. She glanced down at Stefan's notes.

'Is that on?' Stefan said, pointing to the video camera.

'Yes, do you mind?'

He shook his head. 'Not if you don't mind someone assessing your performance later.'

Anna shifted awkwardly in her seat. Assessing me? She thought. We're assessing you! She breathed deeply before saying 'Stefan's an unusual name.'

Once again, Stefan's eyes filled with pain.

'Not if your mother's Austrian,' he said quietly.

Why should he look hurt? Anna wondered.

'Your father obviously wasn't with a surname like Peterson.'

Stefan put his head in his hands and said 'Somewhere there was once a flower, a stone, a crystal, a Queen, a King, a Palace, a lover and his beloved, and this was long ago, on an Island somewhere in the ocean 5,000 years ago.'

Why was he playing games with her? She desperately wanted to know, but she wasn't going to be deflected.

'So where were you walking?' she asked.

'You're very lucky,' he said, looking out of the window.

She couldn't help herself asking 'How?'

'Having a view like that is very good for the soul. Have you noticed the catkins on the violet willow? It's very late for catkins. They usually come out in February.'

A small jolt went through Anna. It was as if he knew she'd been looking at them before he entered the office. She studied his notes again and tried to forget the unforgiving eye in the corner of the room, watching them.

'The last time we spoke you told me you were depressed because your wife had left you.'

'No, I told you my wife had left me *and* I was depressed,' Stefan stated.

'You don't think there's any link between the two?'

'No.'

Anna looked at his exhausted face. It seemed as if his wife was a stranger to him. 'So why do you think she left, Stefan?'

Anna forced herself to sit back in her chair, wanting to look the perfect picture of relaxed efficiency when she and Max watched the video together later. Stefan stared out of the window. She waited, patiently.

At last, he spoke: 'She wanted what I couldn't give her.'

'And what was that?'

Stefan looked from the window to her. 'Myself.'

Anna experienced a jolt of …what? She couldn't identify the feeling.

'You mean physically?' she asked casually.

'No, I mean mentally. She always felt I was somewhere else.'

'And were you?'

'Of course I was.'

'Where?' Anna was intrigued.

'In the past. Trying to recall my life with you.' He leaned forward in his chair as if to emphasize what he was saying. 'Memories are only kept alive by retrieving them, Anna.'

Anna desperately wanted to look at the video camera as if Max was already watching and could help. But the only person watching her at that moment was Stefan. She was alone with a very disturbing man.

'So if you knew your wife would leave you and you didn't do anything to stop her, why did you feel so vulnerable?' Anna asked the question she thought Max would have asked.

'Because of the crushing weight of loneliness. You must have felt like that when you were taken away.'

For a second, Anna thought she'd misheard him. Taken away? What on earth did he mean? Of course, he was playing more games with her; she was not going to be intimated.

'Cognitive Behavioural Therapy concentrates on the present, Stefan. How negative thoughts create a negative state of mind which in turn create negative actions. If we -'

'But we are formed by what happens to us in the past,' Stefan interjected. 'Not the present.'

'I agree,' Anna said, 'but if we constantly go back to situations in which we believe we're a failure, we never overcome our negativity. As your therapist I have to find out what's making you depressed now so you can become the person you were meant to be.'

Stefan smiled at her and Anna suddenly identified the emotion she felt - elation! What was happening to her usual ability to detach herself from emotional involvement with a client?

'The person I am meant to be,' Stefan said. 'I like that. But I never take actions without considering the consequences. I've always been like that, even as a child. Don't you remember?'

'I'm trying to help you, Stefan. Let me ask the questions.'

'Of course,' he answered as if he'd do anything she asked.

Anna stopped herself from glancing at the video camera before she asked a question. She hoped he'd answer honestly.

'If you could change one thing about your life, what would it be?'

'It's all right, Anna. You don't need to set me goals. I'm already very focused, so you can rule out Borderline Personality Disorder. People suffering from BPD never think ahead.'

Anna tried to keep her expression neutral, disguising her

surprise at his remark. 'So what are you focused on?'

'Achieving what I want.'

'And what's that?' Anna asked.

Stefan smiled at her and shook his head. 'You want me to do all the work.'

Anna couldn't help glancing at the video camera. What would Max say about his reaction?

'Shall I tell you about a typical day in my life?' he asked as if he knew she wanted to create a good impression on Max.

'If you'd like to,' Anna answered with relief.

'I get up at six and have two slices of toast and two cups of coffee. How many do you have?'

'Then what do you do?' Anna countered, hoping that he'd reveal something important.

'Start work.'

'What work?'

'You should know. I'm sure Dr. Paris told you what I did.'

Why had she thought, for a moment, it would be easy?

'I paint and I write,' he said at last, looking at his fingers. Anna suddenly saw small specks on paint on them. She was annoyed that she hadn't noticed them earlier. She was trained to be observant.

'What are you painting at the moment?' she asked.

Instead of answering, Stefan picked up his portfolio and opened it. Inside was a large poster of Klimt's *The Kiss*.

'You need stimulation, Anna. The walls are too bare. May I?'

Before she knew what he was asking, he had pinned the poster to the wall. He was right. The walls *were* too bare. The golds and reds and blacks in the poster were picked up by the sun and reflected around the room.

'Do you like Klimt?' he asked her as they both stared at the seductive poster.

'Yes,' Anna answered, thinking how easily he manipulated conversation. She was startled by a sudden thought: he could become a better therapist than her.

'Are you all right?' He studied her face. Did she look as startled as she felt? 'My great, great grandfather knew him.' Stefan said.

'Who?'

'Gustav Klimt.' He spoke gently as if she was a child. 'They were both members of the Vienna Secession. Perhaps you didn't know that?'

Anna was just about to change the conversation when she was suddenly mesmerized. Stefan was trailing the tips of his fingers over the undulating woman's body in the poster. She had never seen such a seductive gesture before.

Then he spoke:

Wrapped in a timeless dimension
The lovers gleam from a golden halo,
silently isolated in space.
Reality has no part to play
in their richly ornamented lives.

A bell of gold
defines them
in ornate contrasts,

The phallic man,
strong rectangles
of black and gold,
turns towards her,
bull-like in his desire

to kiss a universe of love
across her canvas.

The passive woman caresses
curves of floral colour,
dissolving into his paradoxical abstraction.
She kneels before him
on symbolic meadow flowers
accepting his transformation.

They rise out of gold
to unite in the eternity of one kiss:
petrified in the non-consummation of their love.

There was a long silence as Anna and Stefan stared at each other.

***

Anna sat in Max's office tense with expectation. Max had watched the whole video without saying a word. Something he had never done before. She glanced at him occasionally expecting him to stop the recording to discuss her questions, but his face was tense; his only strong reaction was to clench his hands when Stefan recited the poem. His face conveyed nothing.

She was startled when he suddenly jumped up, switched the recording off and began pacing up and down the room.

'Was I that bad?' she asked him nervously.

'I'm taking over his treatment,' Max said abruptly.

'Why?' Anna suddenly knew that she didn't want Max treating him.

'You know why, Anna. Look at the video.'

'I can cope with it, Max.'

Max carried on pacing around the room and didn't answer.

Anna was surprised by an overwhelming certainty: she could help Stefan and no one else could. But she had to convince Max.

'If I can't cope with him, I shouldn't be a psychologist, should I?'

'I don't think you can help him, Anna. It's my fault. I thought you were ready for a difficult client.'

'How can you be certain I'm not if you don't let me try? Please. Let me try.'

Max looked at her for a long time. She couldn't read his body language, but knew that if he didn't let her continue Stefan's treatment she might never have the confidence to treat a difficult client again.

'What do you think his symptoms reveal?' Max asked abruptly.

'I think he's suffering from a schizotypal disorder. He questions my questions all the time.'

'So do many personality disorders. Think again.'

Anna was confused. Max seemed to be annoyed with her, but she couldn't understand why.

'Tell me what did I do wrong in the session?'

'You know what you did wrong - you weren't detached - you allowed him to dominate the conversation – you allowed him to manipulate you.' Each phrase was spoken in staccato as if Max was stabbing her with words.

'I won't allow that to happen again.' Anna took a deep breath. 'I need to prove I can do this, Max.'

Max stopped pacing and stared at her, but didn't speak.

'Please let me.'

Max closed his eyes, then opened them and said. 'What did your body language reveal, Anna?'

Anna stared at Max. She had been studying Stefan's. Occasionally she used mirroring to relax a client; to show them that she respected their opinions; to show them she was open to them. But when she was with Stefan, she had been completely unaware of her body language. On the video she suddenly saw herself smiling when he smiled at her; moving when he moved; steepling her fingers when he did: her every movement had been a mirror image of his and she'd had no awareness of the fact at the time. She was stunned. Her body had betrayed her; she was attracted to him.

But she was happily married. It didn't mean anything. 'I want to prove to you that I can do this, Max. Please let me continue?' She asked him quietly.

Max slumped into his chair and stared at his desk, so deep in thought that Anna wondered if he had heard her. At last he spoke.

'If I agree, you must, *must* remain detached, Anna. Tell me you can do that.'

How could she have possibly known when she woke this morning, from yet another disturbed sleep, that her future would be weighed down with doubts?

'Yes, I can,' she answered, digging her nails deep into the palms of her hands.

Chapter 11
STEFAN

I often walk at night to escape rooms; rooms that stop me thinking. Last night I went to Kensington Park. I've been going there for years, Anna. I know how to disable the lock on the gate. The tranquillity of being the only person in the Kyoto Japanese gardens is like a palliative: I stood listening to the soothing waterfall; the rustlings of small animals in the bushes; watching how the distant street lights created pools of illuminated mosaics. I walked over the giant stones in front of the waterfall and sat down and closed my eyes. I listened to secret words tumbling in front of my feet for a long time.

But even the tranquillity of the park couldn't still my excitement at seeing you again. I walked for hours until it was 3.a.m and I was at the River Thames. I remembered how much you loved water. All of London was sleeping or so it seemed. The only sounds I heard were my footsteps on the paving stones as I walked towards the Millennium Bridge. The lights from numerous buildings created black pools of shadows around the base of the bridge, surrounding it with sprayed fingers of coloured lights in the water. I wished I had my drawing pad with me so I could recreate the scene. Above me, the stars flashed like stilettos. If only you could have been there to share such beauty with me. What were you doing when I was looking at spectrums of light, Anna? Dreaming of the past? Dreaming of our beautiful Welsh house?

I carried on walking until I reached a street full of drunken teenage girls with skirts like pelmets. What are their parents thinking of - allowing them to get into such a vulnerable state?

Over-painted peahens gyrated their hips at me as if I'd be interested in such lewd behaviour, then one vomited at my feet.

Beauty is disappearing, Anna. The world is collapsing and no one seems to care.

You looked as tired as I felt today and yet I ran up the stairs to see you. Eager to breathe in your beauty. It hurt me when you asked about my name. As if you didn't know it was Austrian. Don't hurt me like that again, Anna.

But you liked Klimt's poem. I could tell. The way your sapphire eyes shone when they looked into mine. I must be patient, but it is so hard.

You don't want me dwell on the past and that's all I want to do. All I want *you* to do. You agreed – we are formed by our past and yet you try to block me every time I try to move you backwards. Trying to set me goals in the present.

I have my goal, Anna. She was sitting opposite me today.

Chapter 12
MAX

Max was sitting in Anna and Tim's lounge which was full of art-nouveaux furniture and paintings. He had been sitting there for a number of hours in an out-of-body experience; watching himself going through the motions of polite social chit-chat with Anna's parents and Tim. He stared at the leaves and flowers and vines trailing across the wall opposite him, wondering why Anna liked sinuous shapes so much; they were starting to make him feel nauseous. He glanced across at the others; it was like watching an old black and white film in which all the characters were smiling and charming and incredibly insubstantial.

He found that his glass had been miraculously topped up again. When had that happened? The evening held no interest for him because the one person he wanted to share it with had gone to bed early. She was exhausted; she hoped they'd understand. Of course, everyone said in surprised unison. Anna never went to bed early.

Perhaps it was the pressure of treating someone like Stefan, Max thought. He should never have let her treat him. He knew he wouldn't have let the other trainees deal with someone so formidable, but he really thought Anna would cope with him. But would he have thought like that if he didn't love her? He asked himself. 'You weren't detached,' he'd admonished her. *Nor are you, Max Paris. Not anymore.* He looked in surprise at another full glass of whiskey in his hand. How many had he had? Well, Anna's parents were driving him home, so what the hell.

'Would that be all right with you, Max?'

Tim was staring at him expectantly.

'Would what be all right?' Max hoped he wasn't slurring.

'Anna and I want to go on holiday in a couple of weeks. I really need a break at the moment. You know how stressed I've been in the practice. Now that I've got a new partner, I can take some time off. I told Anna I'd ask you to extend her placement. I hope I haven't overstepped the boundaries of friendship.'

Max felt submerged anger surge through him. Tim wasn't a friend – he was a colleague. *Anna didn't tell me she wanted some time off!* He wanted to shout. He'd never extended anyone's placement. Why should he? He was doing them a favour by having them in his clinic.

'Stress is what brings most of the clients to my clinic. I don't want to see you there, Tim. But Anna has to finish her thesis in six weeks. That's the dead-line. As long as she gives me her thesis at the right time, I'll extend her placement.'

Tim looked relieved. Max realised that he thought he'd object. I could, Max surmised drunkenly. I could tell him to piss off. Who the fuck does he think he is? Asking me if his trainee wife can swan off on holiday and leave me alone?

'That's very good of you, Max,' Celia said, smiling at him. 'Anna told us how inspirational you've been in her training.'

Inspirational! Max inwardly screamed. I don't want to be inspirational. I want to fuck your daughter and the only thing stopping me is the fact that I'm her supervisor!

Max smiled back at Celia with what, he hoped, looked like warmth.

'So where are you two going?' Paul asked.

'I fancy the Caribbean,' Tim said, 'but Anna has the final say. Somewhere exotic and hot, I hope.'

I hope wherever you go is freezing cold and full of cockroaches, Max thought, then suddenly laughed, imagining a poster advertising this holiday. *Come to freezing Bongo Bongo Land and feast on cockroaches with cream and anchovies!*

Max looked around the room; everyone was staring at him.

'Sorry, did I say something?' Words were becoming difficult to form.

'I think we ought to be going home,' Celia said. 'Max and Tim don't have the luxury of being able to sleep late like Paul and me.'

Paul stood up immediately and Max wondered if he had been as bored as he'd been after Anna had gone to bed. He tried standing; it was surprisingly difficult. Suddenly Paul and Tim were on either side of him, their hands under his arms, hauling him to his feet. He smiled at them. The last time he'd felt so drunk was after his graduation ceremony; he'd celebrated in every pub in Oxford.

'Night, Tim,' Paul and Celia chorused as they pushed Max gently onto the back seat of their Audi.

Celia was a good driver; the journey was smooth, but Max still felt the whiskey swilling nauseously around his stomach. He wanted to ask them to stop, but didn't have the energy. They were whispering about him, but he couldn't make any sense of their words. Anyway, what did it matter? He was pissed off with always having to be the perfect professional; the man who sorts out everyone's problems; who's always caring and considerate.

Max slumped over on the back seat, remembering his last drive with Sadie. Their row about his best friend; the friend he thought she was fucking. She'd told him she'd been having an affair with Harry for years because he was a selfish, uncaring bastard and she was pregnant. *You're even more delusional than your clients, Max Paris - caring and considerate! Remember driving like a demon? Remember killing Sadie!*

He suddenly passed out.

Chapter 13
CELIA

Celia drove away from Max's house, feeling completely exhausted. It had taken them over half an hour to get Max up the stairs and into his bed. Paul should have called Tim to help him, but Tim had been drinking too and Paul didn't want him to drive.

She glanced at Paul beside her, half asleep. She knew she was still able to surprise him; perhaps that was why they were still happily married.

'I'm not asleep', he said suddenly. 'It takes more than one drunken psychologist to wear me out.'

Celia suddenly felt very happy. 'I hope Anna and Tim are as happy as we are.'

Paul looked at her in surprise. 'That's a compliment.'

'I know,' she answered.

'You don't do compliments.'

'I don't normally help my husband half carry eminent psychologists up the stairs either.'

'It's worrying that he's Anna's supervisor,' Paul said.

'Well, we've only known him for four months. I'm sure it was a one off.' Celia yawned loudly as she slowed down at some traffic lights.

'I just hope he's as good as his reputation. He certainly didn't inspire confidence tonight,' Paul said tersely.

'He wouldn't be able to do his work if he drank like that often. Anyway, it was partly Tim's fault for giving him so much to drink.'

Celia stretched her shoulders up and down. It had been a

long evening.

'Are you all right?' Paul asked.

'I just feel as if every muscle had been torn from my body.'

'Max is no light weight, is he? ' Paul said. 'I wonder why Tim kept topping up his glass so often.'

Celia accelerated as the lights changed. She'd wondered that too. Tim usually forgot about his guests after serving them the first drink. In fact, Tim had acted strangely all night; as if he was nervous about something. However, she wasn't going to worry Paul any more than he was.

'He must have been softening Max up so that he'd agree to extend Anna's placement,' Celia answered.

'That's a bit irresponsible. He knows Max has to work tomorrow.'

'So has Tim,' Celia countered.

'But he didn't have so much to drink. Max will have a terrible hangover in the morning.'

'I wonder why he's not married,' Celia said. 'He doesn't seem happy, does he? His house was very bleak.'

'Don't suppose he spends much time there. Anyway, whether he's happy or not has nothing to do with us. I don't care whether he's a transvestite, gay or anything else. As long as he gives our Anna a good report.'

Celia smiled. She loved him calling their daughter 'our' Anna. He started calling her that the moment they'd brought her home.

'He doesn't listen much,' Paul said.

'Who?' Celia asked. He really was getting very difficult to follow these days.

'Max, of course. Who else are we talking about? Why don't you listen?'

71

Celia was just about to argue with him when a red Passat hurtled around a corner, narrowly missing them and speeding off into the distance. They both shot forward as she slammed on the brakes.

'Bloody idiot!' Paul shouted at the car's retreating headlights. 'Are you all right, love?' He turned to Celia with concern.

Celia sat for a moment before answering. The incident had shaken her; tiredness had made her reaction time much slower than normal.

'That boy racer could have killed us.'

'No boy racer owns a car like that,' Paul answered. 'Do you want me to drive?' He touched her arm. 'You're as white as a ghost.'

'No, I'm fine. Anyway, you can't drive. You've over the limit,' Celia said as she started the car.

They drove the rest of the way in silence; both subdued by their brush with death. Celia was relieved when she turned the car into their road and saw their solid 1930s detached house standing at the end of it, lit subtly to deceive burglars. It was far too big for them now, but neither of them wanted to move: there were too many memories of Anna inside it. She turned into their driveway and stopped the car; exhaustion spreading through her body as she relaxed into the security of home.

'You know something odd,' Celia said as she got out of the Audi. 'That car looked just like Tim and Anna's.'

'What car?' Paul asked.

'The red Passat that nearly killed us,' Celia said as they walked up their garden path.

'There are hundreds of red Passats in London.'

'But I recognised part of the registration number.' Celia turned to look at him to emphasise her statement.

'How could you see the number plate when the driver was travelling at high speed?' Paul asked as he opened the front door.

'Because I've got excellent recall, that's why.' Celia went into the kitchen. 'I'm having a cup of tea. Do you want one? I bet you can't even remember what their registration number is.' She poured water in the kettle, waiting for him to answer.

Paul sank into a chair. 'That's because I don't care what their registration number is, Celia. That's why.'

'You see – I was right!' She gloated. 'It's HU08 SEY. I always remember things like that. I remember seeing SEY on that car.'

'I'm too tired to argue, but that's rubbish,' Paul said, yawning.

But later, as she climbed the stairs, she suddenly visualised the red Passat as it sped away; the letters SEY were clear. She pushed the image away. Paul was right. It was ridiculous. It couldn't have been Tim's car. He was fast asleep beside their daughter.

Chapter 14
ANNA

Anna was lying in bed, exhausted, listening to the muffled sound of voices drifting up the stairs. She got up to look for some ear plugs; she had to get a good night's sleep. Tomorrow was her third session with Stefan. She knew that Max wouldn't allow her any more sessions with him if it didn't go well and she might not have the courage to continue her training. She did some deep breathing to relax her body, but her thoughts were chaotic: could dreams be prophetic? What did the dream about a butterfly hanging over her mean? Why had she agreed to go on holiday? Why did she feel distanced from Tim? How would she cope with Stefan? She found some ear plugs and put them in, then slid under the duvet and fell into an uneasy sleep.

A woman is high on a cliff looking down on the curved, yellow expanse of beach. It's deserted except for the woman wearing a green dress. The woman trails her toes in the water. Anna can't see the woman's face.

Suddenly, in the distance, a man walks towards her. The woman turns to look at the crashing waves and sees him. Her body tenses. The woman strides up the beach away from him, her feet making deep imprints in the sand. He strides after her. She starts to run. He runs after her. Her loud, ragged breathing echoes round the bay as she runs faster and faster and faster.

Anna jerked upright in the bed, her heavy breathing slicing the air; her hair soaked with sweat. She turned to Tim, but he wasn't there. The clock read 1.30. She got out of bed, listening for noises from downstairs. Nothing.

'Tim!' She shouted into the silence. Where on earth was he? Anna went to the bathroom and saw how pale she looked in the over-bright light over the mirror. Her nights and days were now dotted with strange dreams and a disturbing man. Why was the woman running away from the man? Why was she dreaming about the sea? Questions circled round and round her head as she washed her face. She opened the bathroom cabinet, looking for some sleeping tablets; she had to get some sleep. Then she saw her mini-pills, half hidden at the back of the cabinet and felt a sudden thump in her chest. She couldn't remember when she had last taken one. How could she have forgotten when it was so important? She hung onto the basin, feeling suddenly dizzy. Psychosomatic, she told herself. Remember what Max said: control your emotions; don't allow them to control you. She took the pills out of the cabinet and looked at the dates. She hadn't taken one for three days! That was impossible! She was meticulous about taking them because Tim had told her that although they were safer than the oestrogen and progestogen pill, they were less effective. She was just about to take one when a gruesome thought stopped her. What did the pill do to a foetus? She suddenly recalled small spells of dizziness which she'd put down to tiredness, but hadn't Tim told her that pregnancy changed women's sleeping patterns? She held on the basin tighter, chanting the words: *I am not pregnant. I am not pregnant.* She was too young to be pregnant; she had to finish her training. Of course, Tim would be delighted if she was; he'd been researching into both family histories for months. He'd discovered that they came from prodigious stock. Their child could be the next Einstein or Leonardo da Vinci, he kept telling her. His obsession with genetics worried Anna. What did it

75

matter if their child was brilliant or not, as long as he was loved? But she didn't want a child yet. When she was older, she would be like her mother and devote herself wholly to her child. But not now. Not yet. Please God.

Anna went back into the bedroom and crawled back into bed. *I am not pregnant*, she kept chanting to herself as she drifted off to sleep. *I am not pregnant.*

Hours later, she stirred as Tim slid into bed beside her, but didn't wake for she was deep in another dream.

A three year old girl lies in her bed. A teenage boy sits beside her and winds up a music box. A man and a woman shout at each other in another room. Soon their words are muffled by the strains of Mozart's lullaby lulling the little girl. A tiny ballerina turns on top of the music box. The shouting gets louder and louder. The little girl covers her ears, trying to block out the sound. The boy sings to her. The little girl sucks her thumb and watches the ballerina turning, turning, turning.

Suddenly, the door crashes open and a drunken man falls into the room and bangs into the bed. The children jump. The man gets up and walks towards them. The children's eyes widen with fear.

Anna jerked upright for the second time that night, terrified for the children in the dream; her heart pounding against her rib cage. Who were they? She reached out in the darkness for Tim. He was there. He stirred in his sleep at her touch. She felt a fluttering in her stomach and silently groaned, remembering her blackout over dates. She would have to get the morning-after pill from the chemist.

She put on her bedside light and looked at the clock. It was 4.30. Six hours before her meeting with Stefan. She felt sick with apprehension.

Chapter 15
STEFAN

I've finished the painting, Anna. At last, I've caught the glints of gold and copper and auburn in your hair; the verdant colours of the Welsh coast; the panoramic sweeping curve of golden sands; the purple frieze of heather on the cliffs; the three limestone cliffs creating giant shadows across the sand; the moody tones of the Atlantic sea. I used eleven colours to paint the mercurial sea: from Idanthrene Blue, Prussian Blue, Ultramarine, Cerulean Blue Deep, Cerulian Blue, Cobal Turquoise, Cobolt Teal, Phtalo Blue Red and Phtalo Turquoise, Green Gold and Phtalo Green Blue. Perhaps you won't care that I used so many colours, but the sea has to be much darker near the horizon and the waves have to reflect both the shadow of the cliffs and the blue luminosity of sky. I painted the spine of the waves in varying shades of turquoise. [Yes, turquoise has shades too.] Then I flicked small sprays of Old Ivory onto the canvas to create flying foam. I have created the sea for you, Anna.

Picasso once said that there are painters who transform the sun into a yellow spot, but there are others who can transform a yellow spot into the sun. I have transformed a transient moment into infinity.

The painting traps us in time. We are forever walking along the yellow curve of sands and staring up at the wedge of white swans flying high above us. The cliffs will always tower in the distance and the woman will always gallop across the sands on her black horse. I have trapped time, Anna. I want to live in the painting forever. With you.

I must sleep a little now. Soon, I will be sitting near you again and my heart sings.

Chapter 16
ANNA

Anna was sitting in the kitchen, eating breakfast with Tim, thinking about where she could get the morning after pill. Perhaps the local chemist had some. She didn't want to go to her G.P. There was patient confidentiality, but her doctor knew Tim. She wouldn't take the risk. She looked at Tim guiltily. He'd be so angry if he found out she was thinking of 'aborting' their baby. She knew his views on the morning-after pill only too well. One of his patients kept asking for it and it really angered him.

Keep the conversation neutral, she thought. 'So what time did everyone leave?'

'What?' Tim stared at her as if he didn't know what she was talking about.

'My parents and Max came, remember?' She couldn't look at bad as Tim could she? He had dark circles under his eyes.

'Oh, last night. Max really hit the bottle. Your father and I almost had to carry him to the car.'

'Max!' Anna was amazed. She had never seen Max drink much. 'So that's where you must have been when I called out for you.'

'What?' Tim gave her an odd look.

'I woke up and you weren't there.' He must have hit the bottle too, Anna thought. He was usually lively in the morning.

'When?'

'How much did you drink last night? You can't seem to remember anything.'

'It took us a long time to get Max into the car,' Tim said, not looking at her.

Anna yawned loudly and Tim looked up.

'Are you okay? You still look shattered.'

'I am. Didn't sleep well…I can't imagine Max getting drunk.'

Tim finished his muesli and got up. 'Well he did. I've got to go. Clare has to take her boys to school so I said I'd open the surgery.'

Anna wanted to ask him about the morning-after pill. Should she take it? Was it safe? Would he forgive her if she did? But, of course, she couldn't.

He bent over to kiss her. 'I'll be home by 6. Don't forget to choose our holiday. Have a look on the web. Bye.'

He was out of the door before she could answer.

Anna drank far more coffee than she usually did to caffeine her into alertness. She rang Marie to say she'd be a little late for work as she was working on her thesis. She hoped Max wouldn't mind; then remembered what Tim had said about his drinking. If he'd drunk as much as Tim said, he'd have a really heavy hangover this morning.

She walked to the chemist, hoping no one else would be there when she asked for the morning-after pill. Of course, there were four other people waiting for prescriptions. Eventually Anna had to go up to the young girl behind the counter.

'Could I have the morning-after pill please?' she whispered.

'The what?' The girl asked in a loud voice.

Anna couldn't believe that she didn't know what she was talking about. Was she deliberately trying to embarrass her? 'Could I speak to the pharmacist, please?'

Anna could feel everyone staring at her; judging her. A young woman without any morality who just wanted sex without any consequences.

A middle-aged man with thinning hair and round glasses came out of the pharmacy and looked at her. He's judging me too, Anna thought.

'Can I help you?' He asked.

The girl must have told him what I want, Anna thought. Why is he asking me?

'I need the morning-after pill, please?'

The man looked at her disapprovingly. 'People normally get them from their doctor.'

'I haven't got time to go to the doctor,' Anna said. 'Could you just give me the pills please?'

Anna felt her face burning. Was everyone still looking at her? Did they all know that she wanted to destroy a foetus?

'It's only effective if you've had unprotected sex up recently.' The pharmacist spoke as if he was giving a lecture in a large hall. 'It has a 95% success rate within 24 hours, but this falls to 58% between 49 and 72 hours. There hasn't been any research about whether this affects an unborn baby. Do you still want it?'

***

The tube was full of the living dead, strap-hanging and pretending they were somewhere else. She squeezed herself out at Oxford Street; the used, hot air hitting her nostrils as the train screeched off. The strap-hangers shuffled onto the escalator and stared unseeingly at the out-of-date adverts on the way to the surface. Anna decided to walk up; desperate to get past people to breathe in fresh air.

It was drizzling with rain when Anna finally managed to get out onto a bustling Bond Street, but she hardly registered the fact; she was still walking out of the chemist with five pairs of eyes trained on her. She turned left into Marylebone Lane and crossed the busy road as if the cars weren't there; a taxi screeched to a halt as she walked in front of it. The driver stuck his head out of the open window and screamed abuse at her; she smiled apologetically before running across the road towards Wigmore Street.

Marie was on the phone when Anna walked into reception. She waved to her as she walked past, but Marie gestured to her to wait. She finished the phone call and looked at Anna. There was no Mono-Lisa smile on her face this morning.

'Better warn you. Max isn't in a good mood. He looks…' Marie looked around in case anyone was listening. 'He looks as if he's had a heavy night, if you know what I mean.'

'Yes, I do,' Anna said. 'Thanks. Have you got my files?'

Marie leaned towards Anna confidentially. 'Your client's already here,' she said, giving her three files.

Anna's throat suddenly felt tight. 'What client? '

'The gorgeous one,' Marie whispered. 'I can't even remember what Brad Pitt looks like any more. Is he married?'

Anna ignored the question. 'Where is he?'   Anna said, looking around.

'He asked if he could wait in your office. He likes the view, apparently. I told him he could wait here. I would have liked the view then, but he didn't want to,' Marie said, smiling at her.

Anna picked up the files and forced herself to stroll up the stairs towards a man who was trying to hijack her life.

***

The sun was slanting across the room, highlighting Stefan's hair with hints of copper when Anna opened the door. He was looking out of the window, but turned a radiant face towards her.

81

'Anna – how lovely to see you.'

He gestured towards a chair like a Prince trying to make a subject feel at ease and Anna felt like a small child. He sank into her chair by the window and stared at her.

'You look wonderful, but tired. What have you been doing?'

Anna concentrated on adjusting the angle of the video before switching it on and turning a neutral face towards him.

'So how do you feel today, Stefan?'

'Good. Especially now I've seen you.'

Anna could hardly see him; the sun was directly in her eyes. She walked across the room towards the window; intensely aware of his closeness as she pulled down the blinds. The room was immediately full of filtered light. She walked past him and sat in the chair opposite him. His eyes travelled over her face; she felt as if she was burning.

'You're very interested in the past, aren't you?' she asked him, determined to control the session.

'Aren't you?' He replied. 'It makes us who we are.'

'All right, so tell me about your past,' Anna said, breathing in slow pockets of air.

Stefan immediately stared down at the desk as if afraid to look at her.

He always wants to talk about the past and yet it terrifies him, Anna thought. She had never dealt with a client so complex before. She knew that Max would want her to concentrate on the present, but the past was consuming Stefan.

'Tell me what your parents were like?' She said gently, not knowing she was guiding him towards the edge of an abyss.

Suddenly he stared at her intently. 'Mother sang to us in German before we went to sleep every night.'

'That's a lovely memory. You said 'we'. Who else did your

mother sing to?'

Stefan shook his head, looking at her with disbelief. Why? Anna thought.

'And what about your father?' She continued. 'Was he musical too?'

'No,' Stefan answered curtly.

'Did you have a good relationship with him?'

'I don't want to talk about him.' Stefan was now whispering.

The father is the key, Anna thought; the knowledge relaxed her. 'Okay, then tell me about your childhood. Was it happy?'

'It depends what you mean by a happy childhood,' Stefan answered, looking at her with the same hurt expression she had seen the last time they had met.

Why did he always look so hurt when she mentioned his past? As if she was somehow responsible. 'Most people would say a happy childhood was one that was full of love,' Anna said simply.

The moment she mentioned the word 'love', Stefan's expression changed. Anna was forced to look away from the intense pain that seared his face. Should she stop? What would Max do? Of course he'd guide him away from the past. Max would move him forward in time, but just as she was about to do so, he spoke, in a voice so soft, she could hardly hear him. 'I was happy... mostly... until I was fourteen.'

She looked at the video apologetically, but how could she not ask? 'What happened then, Stefan?'

She jumped nervously as he leapt out of the chair, pulled the blind up and stared out of the window; his face like granite. She almost groaned out loud; this was the worst session she'd ever had with a client.

'Did you know that most people spend six years of their lives dreaming?' Stefan said in an authoritative voice as if he was giving her a tutorial. 'That's over 2,000 days spent in another world. Do you dream a lot?'

Every nerve in Anna's body tingled. How did he know?

'What happened when you were fourteen, Stefan?' She had to discover the truth but dreaded hearing what Max would say when he watched the video.

'Do you dream a lot?' He repeated, still staring out of the window. 'It's important. Please tell me, Anna.'

She knew he wouldn't let the question go. 'No,' she said.

He turned then and looked at her as if he knew she was lying. 'You look like a dreamer. Carl Jung wrote that the dream is the small hidden door into the deepest and most intimate sanctum of the soul. Robert Louis Stevenson was able to recall his dreams so clearly that he wrote them into stories. He dreamt serially. Do you know what that means?'

Anna shook her head; she knew she should take control again, but she couldn't.

'He had control over his dreams. It's called lucid dreaming. You can control your dreams to meet another person if you want to. It's like a true meeting of souls on another plane. Have you ever experienced anything like that?'

Anna found it difficult to speak; he was staring at her intently.

'Shall I tell you about one of my dreams?' he asked her when she didn't answer.

He waited patiently for her to answer.

'If you want to,' she whispered at last.

'I'm walking along the curved shoreline of a beautiful beach with my sister who's wearing a green dress. She's only three so I hold her hand tightly in case she falls. Suddenly she looks up and

84

sees swans flying over head and runs after them. I have to run after her, frightened she'll fall into the sea.'

'And did she fall?' Anna asked.

No,' Stefan answered. 'I caught you.'

Anna's heart thumped hard against her ribs as she whispered. 'I wasn't there, Stefan.'

'Yes, you were. You just can't remember.' He looked at her with great sadness. 'You know what the past is for many people? A jigsaw puzzle with lost pieces. I'm trying to help you find the pieces, Anna.'

She closed her eyes, suddenly feeling faint and Stefan was kneeling beside her, whispering close to her.

'Es tut mir leid, mein Liebling. Ich habe das alles falsch gemacht. Vergib mir.'

She listened to the unknown words and opened her eyes - she had never seen such love in a man's face before. It took her breath away.

'Sit down... please,' she said, shakily. 'I just felt a little faint, that's all.'

Stefan rushed to open the window. 'You need more air. Come breathe here.'

He guided her towards the window as if she was an invalid and Anna was shocked to discover that she liked the feeling of dependency she was experiencing – she, who always liked being in control; who always hated her parents telling her what to do or think when she was a child! She was enjoying being dependant on a delusional stranger! She breathed deeply and the world stopped its slow spin.

'Are you feeling better?' He looked at her with gentle concern. Did Tim ever look at her like that?

'Yes, I'm feeling better.'

'Do you want to continue?' he asked her.

'Do you?' she asked him.

'Of course I do. I want you to remember.'

Anna sat down in her seat by the window. This session was surreal, but she had to continue. 'Sit down, Stefan.'

He sat down and smiled at her; happiness etched on every section of his face.

'You said that the past is like a jigsaw puzzle. Do you mean you can't remember parts of yours?' Anna asked him.

'No, I mean many people have missing memories like you. I want you to remember our past.'

'Stefan – we haven't got a past. I've lived in London all my life.' Anna tried to slow down her breathing to stop her heart from racing.

'We spent three long summers in Wales before you were taken away.'

'I wasn't taken anywhere, Stefan. That's a false memory.'

'You can't remember because you were so young, Anna. Every summer we went to our white house in Wales, full of beautiful Viennese furniture. Your bedroom was pink and white and there was a butterfly mobile over your bed. I bought it for you when you were a baby. You loved it.'

Anna felt the nausea rise again. How could he know about her dream? 'I've never had a butterfly mobile. My parents have kept all my toys.' Why was she telling him that? Max had told her never to reveal personal information to clients. She never had before.

Stefan leaned across the desk towards her. 'They didn't have you as a baby, Anna. You were adopted when you were three and a half. I have been looking for you for twenty one years. I am your brother.'

86

At that moment Anna knew that she should never have pleaded with Max to continue this man's treatment.

'You haven't inherited my memory. I can remember being in my pram, Anna – as Piaget could. He remembered a man trying to kidnap him when he was a baby.'

'His nurse gave him that memory. She wrote about it years later.' Anna had studied false memory syndrome in her training and Piaget was one of the examples they used.

Stefan looked at her incredulously. 'And why would she do that?'

'Because Piaget's parents thought the nurse had saved their son from being kidnapped and gave her a reward. She later confessed that she'd lied because she wanted the money. The parents told Piaget about this imagined incident and he subsequently remembered something that never happened. We often remember things that people plant in our minds. I can look at old photos and my parents tell me stories about them and from that I think I can remember the event.'

Stefan was shaking his head violently from side to side. Why on earth had she argued with him?

'They're not your parents!' You must believe me!' He was shouting at her.

Anna shrank back in her chair.

He looked at her with deep sorrow. 'I'm sorry. I'm sorry. I didn't mean to shout at you. It's just so hard trying to convince you of the truth.' He sighed softly. 'I must be more patient.' He suddenly smiled. 'You know what my earliest memories are? The smell of my mother's milk; her perfume; the caress of her touch. I wish you could remember these things too.'

Anna got up from her chair. She had to get out of the room. 'We have to finish now.' She walked carefully towards the door.

'Have you seen your birth certificate?' he asked, just as she was about to open the door.

Anna had never thought about her birth certificate before.

'You haven't, have you?'

Anna opened the door. 'I'm sorry, Stefan, but your session is finished for today. I'll see you next week if you make an appointment with the receptionist.'

He stood up, staring at her intently. 'Log onto your computer and type in Family Records. You'll see an adoption section. You can order a certificate in your real name: Anna Renate Peterson. Renate is our mother's name. Come to my house and you'll see the proof.'

Chapter 17
MAX

Max couldn't remember feeling this hung-over since he was a student. In spite of the numerous pain-killers he'd taken, it still felt as if someone was trying to drill numerous holes into his head and there was a cement mixer churning in his stomach. The previous night was a blur of alcohol. Something he had always hated since Sadie's death – being out of control. That's why he'd only drunk in moderation for the last twenty years. He couldn't remember how many whiskies he'd had; he couldn't remember how he'd got home or into bed. Tim must have driven him home. Thank God Anna had gone to bed before he got drunk. Even so, his professional prestige must have taken a nose-dive. Tim would have undoubtedly told Anna all about his debauched behaviour. Was it debauched? He vaguely remembered Anna's parents being there and groaned loudly. God, how embarrassing. Getting paralytic in front of a trainee's parents. He propped his hands onto his desk to support his head, trying to cope with the awful abuse his body had sustained.

He was supposed to be dealing with the paper work which mounted daily on his desk, but the drilling in his head was making the tortuous work even more tortuous. He knocked back the Alka-Seltzer fizzing on his desk and shuddered. It tasted foul or was that the lingering bitterness of booze? He got up and went into the small toilet next to his office and washed his face for the third time, carefully avoiding looking in the mirror. He knew what he looked like; he'd seen the shock on Marie's face when he walked past her this morning.

Thursdays were dedicated to administrative work; he hated

this part of his job, especially when he came to Anna. Was he being objective enough with her assessments? He leafed through them and found his assessment of her last clinical viva.

Anna Nash. Clinical Viva on Case Study 4.

General Presentation:

The student's presentation followed a clear logical structure with material being presented fluently with very good use of presentation aids. The presentation also kept well to time boundaries.

Clarity and coherence of background information about referral issues and service context:

There was clear coverage of background information relevant to the case presentation such as referral details, the service context and any issues concerning multidisciplinary working. There was also a clear demonstration of taking a substantial role in the assessment.

Assessment:

There was clear description of the assessment method chosen, the rationale for this & the results of the assessment with links to appropriate theoretical models & relevant empirical evidence. This was demonstrated by reference to and evidence of understanding of at least two key models and three key papers/authors.

Clarity and coherence of formulation and reformulation:

Formulation took account of relevant theoretical models and incorporated information from the case under consideration. Efforts were made to reformulate and to consider the situation from more than one perspective.

Evidence of awareness of and reflection on clinical / ethical / process issues:

A very good critique was offered of both the process and results

90

of this work. Attention was paid to ethical and other professional issues.

<u>Response to questions from the assessors:</u>

Questions were responded to in a confident and thoughtful manner.

Max looked at Anna's other assessments; they were all equally positive. He fetched his other trainees' files from his book shelves and waded through them to ascertain if they were as good. After leafing through four, he realised they weren't. Perhaps that was because the students weren't as good as Anna, he reasoned. He couldn't have allowed his judgement to be so impaired after so many years' experience. Could he?

There was a knock on his door. The sound was hard-wired into his brain. Anna. He froze. Not today. Not when he looked like this. The knock was repeated. Max looked at his diary. Anna. 11.30. Thesis Progress Report. Jesus Christ! When he was feeling like this! When he looked like this!

He staggered across the room and opened the door. There she stood, looking as young as Alice in Wonderland; he felt as old as Methuselah.

'Come in, Anna. I'd forgotten all about our meeting.'

Anna crept in, very unlike her usual self, Max thought, but he didn't have the capacity for caring today.

'Sit down and tell me what wordage you've reached?'

Anna sat down and stared at him nervously.

What was the matter with her? Couldn't she understand English? 'How many words have you written so far?'

'Oh... I can't remember, off hand.' Anna looked at him apologetically.

Normally, this would have melted him, but today holes were

being drilled in his head.

'You've only got four weeks to finish your thesis. It has to be roughly 20,000 words exclusive of appendices, footnotes, and tables.'

'Yes, I know… Max, can I -'

'What?' he asked abruptly.

Anna's mouth tightened. He saw her breathing deeply. 'I've finished the literature and reflective reviews,' she said at last.

'You haven't forgotten a methodological critique, have you?' Max wanted to lie down in a dark room, not talk about a thesis on depression. 'Don't forget to include detailed information for future research and the clinical and ethical implications arising from your thesis.' Max was on auto-pilot. He suddenly realised she wasn't listening to him, but staring out of the window. There was nothing to see out of his window except uninspiring houses. He'd chosen this office precisely because he didn't want distractions when he was working.

'What are you staring at bricks for?'

Anna looked startled. He knew he was being harsh. It wasn't her fault his head was pounding with pain. It wasn't her fault he was in love with her.

'Sorry… I'm not feeling too good.' Max almost smiled at his absurd understatement.

'I'll come back another time,' Anna whispered.

And suddenly, she was gone and all the light left the room.

Chapter 18
STEFAN

If only you could remember Mother's singing, Anna, the past would flood back inside you; you would remember the house; you would remember the sea.

You looked shocked when I told you. They did not tell you about your adoption, did they? How could they do that? Stretching out long years of lies. Did you know that a lie tightens its grip on the user's throat each time it is used? Those people's throats must be squeezed dry now. Love should be founded on truth, not lies.

I wish I didn't have such powers of recall then I wouldn't remember the moment you were taken away from me so clearly; the pain so clearly. You were wearing the dress mother made for you; the green dress which shone when you danced, my little firefly. That day, I had taken you for a walk, away from the orphanage in which we were so unhappy.

We walked past the old lady's garden, full of red and purple wallflowers, blue forget-me-nots, sweet violets, yellow primroses, brilliant pink shamrock and rosemary. I remember colours, Anna. You leaned over to smell the rosemary and said 'Where's home, Stefan? We go back soon?' You remembered the beauty of mother's garden; full of radiant colours and heady aromas. I couldn't tell you that we couldn't go there anymore. They wouldn't let us.

We hid in a world of browns and purples, greys and soft greens. One day you will remember the wood, Anna; the bracken which glowed a phosphorescent burnt-sienna in the damp air. I held you up to a silver birch so you could pick a purple haze of twigs. I loved the tall beech trees most, towering up against the sky; the pencilled beauty of their branches etched against the grey of the clouds. Then the sound of the chiff-chaff; the perfect counterpart to the sharp beauty of the branches. So much wonder inside the woods, Anna; so much ugliness outside. They found us there at dusk, asleep on a carpet of leaves. They held me fast when I fought them; when you screamed my name over and over again. And I was helpless to protect you as they carried you away from me.

They left me alone in an empty room with only searing images for company. My body was like a floating weed with severed roots for years. I have been starved by centuries of loneliness, Anna, but now I have found you again.

I have written you a letter today that you will receive on your birthday. Then we will be together forever.

If only I could paint the intense joy I feel.

Chapter 19
ANNA

Anna ran out of Max's office and down the stairs and out of the clinic. She didn't see Marie's amazed face as she ran past her. She was dazed by Stefan's words and incredibly hurt by Max's harshness. She had wanted help from Max, not severity.

She had to see her parents; to have their reassurance that everything in her life was exactly as it should be. Stefan was a highly delusional man, that's why he was so convincing, Anna told herself. That's why she knew she shouldn't question her past. Her perfectly secure past. She knew exactly who she was: the much loved only child of Celia and Paul Baker; the much loved wife of Timothy Nash.

Stefan was trying to tear down the secure structure of her life because he didn't have any himself! *How dare he ask me to his house! Does he think I'm that gullible?*

Anna walked up the path towards her parents' house and saw her mother in the greenhouse. She was surprised; she thought she'd be at UCL, but her presence immediately made her feel calmer. She had watched her mother gardening since she was a small child. Stefan was a million miles away.

She opened the greenhouse door and Celia turned to her in surprise.

'Hello, darling. What's the matter?' Celia said.

Anna had always been amazed that her mother knew how she was feeling from a single glance. She gave her mother an unexpectedly long hug, loving the smell of damp earth which clung onto her; the smell of her childhood.

'Nothing. I was just passing.'

They walked up the garden arm-in-arm, past Anna's old swing and her tree house high in the tree.

'Remember the day Dad caught me in the tree house with that boy? Can't remember his name,' Anna said.

Anna and Celia laughed. Her father had found her kissing him on the tree house floor.

'How could I forget? Your father talked of nothing else for months. He almost nailed the house up to stop any other boy seducing his little girl.'

'I was 16, Mum.'

'I know, darling.'

They smiled at each other as they walked into the kitchen.

'I'll make us some coffee and you can tell me what the problem is.'

'There's no problem, Mum.'

Celia glanced at her and Anna knew she'd have to tell her.

'I had a very difficult client this morning. He upset me,' Anna whispered in a flat voice.

'What did he do, darling?' Celia said as she put the coffee machine on.

'I'm not supposed to discuss my clients, Mum.'

'You're not, darling. You're talking to your mother. What could be more confidential than that?'

They smiled at each other again.

'Where's Dad?' Anna asked.

'In his dark room as usual.'

Her father had always been interested in photography; the kitchen was proof of it: photos of family holidays adorned every wall. But since retiring, he had time to develop them himself. Anna looked at the numerous photos of her with her mother or father; they always seemed to be laughing.

Everything here was normal; everything was just as it should be. The familiarity soothed Anna like a sedative.

'It's not what he does so much as what he says,' Anna said.

The coffee machine performed its usual belching sounds as Celia took the china mugs out of the cupboard.

'So what does he say?'

Anna thought about this. 'It's so weird. There's something familiar about him. As if I've met him before.'

'Perhaps you have. You go to lots of lectures. Perhaps he was at one and you saw him. Is he the same age as you?'

'No, about eleven years older. He's a painter. He wouldn't go to psychology lectures.' Then Anna suddenly thought: how do you know?

'Well, we all get that déjà vu feeling, sometimes, don't we?'

'I suppose so, but this is going to sound even more weird. You know what he told me? He said I had a butterfly mobile when I was a baby. How on earth would he know what I had as a baby?' Anna looked at her mother incredulously. 'I didn't have one, did I?'

'Of course not, darling. What a strange thing for him to say. What do you think is wrong with him?'

The door suddenly opened and her father stood there, beaming at them both.

'What's this? A gathering of the sisterhood?' Paul said, before kissing Anna.

Celia poured some coffee for them.

'What are you doing here, sweetheart?' he asked Anna.

'Just passing.'

Celia gave him a coffee; spilling some in the saucer.

'Steady, Celia,' Paul said, then sipped it appreciatively.

97

'Umm, that's so good. On the last leg of the thesis yet?' Paul smiled at his daughter.

'Not quite, Dad. It's a long haul,' Anna said quietly.

'Oh, don't we know it. Your mother and I worked flat out for six months on our theses. Did we tell you?'

'Only a hundred times, Paul,' Celia answered.

'Well, I'm proud of my thesis. "Shakespeare's Use of Dramatic Irony". Became my first published book.' Paul sipped more coffee.

'I know, Dad,' Anna said.

'When are you two going on holiday?' Paul asked.

Anna stared at him for a long time. The holiday! She'd forgotten all about it. How could she finish her thesis if she went on holiday? All the stress she'd felt when she'd arrived flooded back.

'You've been working too hard, darling. You need a holiday,' Celia said. 'It'll take your mind off that client.'

'What client?' Paul asked.

'I've got to finish my thesis, Mum.'

'Can't you take your lap-top and do a bit of work on it when you're there?'

'Doesn't anyone listen to me in this family?' Paul said.

'That's a great idea, Mum.'

'Obviously not,' Paul said in a peeved voice.

'We do, Dad,' Anna said, leaning over to kiss his cheek. She knew she'd have an argument with Tim about taking work on holiday, but she wanted this qualification more than she'd wanted anything else.

'Where are you thinking of going?' Celia asked.

A sudden image flashed into Anna's mind. 'The Welsh coast,' she said with absolute certainty.

Chapter 20
MAX

Max sat in his office after Anna had left, listening to the wind whistling angrily through small cracks in the window. He felt lousy; not from the drink, but because of the way he had treated her. He was appalled with himself. His shelves were packed with files; clients who wrote to him thanking him for turning their lives around; saying how much they valued his expert advice. He was trained to be considerate and sympathetic with people. The suppressed knowledge suddenly hit him: he was only considerate and sympathetic with people he didn't love. It had taken him thirty years to learn such a simple fact. *But it doesn't have to be like that, Max,* he told himself. *Heal yourself! Change the way you think!*

He should have helped her! She'd looked nervous and worried when she came to see him. He suddenly remembered why: she was seeing Stefan Peterson today. Damn!

He raced out of his office and into Anna's to look for the video tape of her last session. It was still in the video recorder. He was surprised; she was usually meticulous about labelling the tapes.

Max rewound it, staring out at the beautiful trees outside the window. He'd never work with a view like it. The tape clicked. Max pressed the start button and sat down. Soon he was lost in Anna's face as the sun shone on it. Why was she sitting directly facing the sun? Max thought. She can't see his face properly. As if she'd heard his thoughts, she suddenly stood up and walked to the window. Max watched the expression on Stefan's face change as she moved passed him; he wants to touch her! Max suddenly experienced a long forgotten emotion bubbling up inside him: hot, jealous rage; it was so overwhelming that he had to get up to stop the video. Jealousy. Something he hadn't felt since Sadie's death. Something he thought he had conquered. 'Jealousy is an emotion experienced when a person is threatened by the loss of an important relationship with another person.' [Parrott, 2001.] Recalling information had never been a problem for him, but he had no relationship with Anna apart from his role as her supervisor. Remember that, Max Paris, he told himself. Jealousy was a completely erroneous emotion in this situation.

Max restarted the tape, forcing himself to watch dispassionately; to ascertain how well Anna coped with a highly manipulative client.

She was asking Stefan about his fascination with the past; her voice, interested and professional. Good. Max was suddenly arrested by the incredulous look Stefan gave Anna when she asked him who else his mother sang to. The look was genuine: he thinks the other person is Anna, Max thought. He stopped the video and spoke into his Dictaphone:

'Memory disorders have been linked to certain psychotic symptoms including delusional thinking. However, memory deficits per se are clearly insufficient to cause delusional thoughts because otherwise most amnesiacs would suffer with delusions. Additional factors must therefore be important. One view of delusions is that the proneness to form false beliefs may, in part, reflect over-confidence in incorrect or implausible judgments.'

He stopped the Dictaphone and started the video-tape again. Anna was asking Stefan about his father. His face changed subtly; it was a difficult expression to interpret because of its subtlety, but Max was trained in subtlety; Stefan's expression hinted at a combination of fear and hatred; an expression that Anna missed by writing something in his notes. The father again, Max thought. What terrible problems parents can create. Suddenly, all the pain of that night drive hit him as he remembered Sadie telling him that she was pregnant. That child would be older than Anna if it had lived. He forced the painful past back into a small submerged part of his brain and concentrated on the video.

He suddenly saw Stefan jump up when Anna asked him what had happened when he was fourteen. *So some event when he was fourteen has created the thought patterns he has now*, Max thought. Again Stefan shaped the conversation: how did he know that people spend six years of their lives dreaming? Or that six years equates to 2,000 days? It was the kind of information an autistic person would remember and yet he wasn't autistic. Max found him fascinating, but he didn't like the way he was manipulating Anna. *Or is it the fact that she's allowing herself to be manipulated that you don't like,* he asked himself? Anna hadn't allowed the other clients to manipulate her like this, but, of course, the other clients weren't as charismatic or complex as Stefan.

Max was fascinated by Stefan's dream where he was walking beside the sea with a little girl; he could see that Anna was equally fascinated – no, she was mesmerized. But when Stefan said he was trying to find the lost pieces of her past, she looked confused. Anna was starting to believe him! Where was her clinical detachment?

Max jumped up - Stefan was helping her walk to the window. What was the matter with her? Why didn't she stop him? Max froze the frame; Anna was staring out of the window, but Stefan was looking at her; Max was completely disarmed by the look of love on his face.

Max started the tape again; Anna was talking about false

memories. Max smiled. That was more like it. She was gaining control. Then suddenly Stefan asked if she's seen her birth certificate. Oh, this man is clever, Max thought; planting small seeds of insecurity in his therapist.

He switched the video off and thought about what he had seen. He was annoyed with himself; he should have helped Anna when she came to see him. He'd known what a challenge Stefan would be. He couldn't blame booze. It was his responsibility. She was only a trainee. He should have recommended he go somewhere else. But his interest had been piqued: the man intrigued him; he'd wanted to see if Anna could cope. *No, I thought she would cope!* But how easily Stefan Peterson had undermined her confidence; how convincing he'd been in planting the idea that they had a common past.

But Anna would surely remember the psychological experiment he'd talked about in one of his lectures in which two hundred College students were asked to recall five events that had happened to them in their childhood. The researchers then spoke to the students' parents and asked them to tell their children about a false event, like an overnight hospitalization for a high fever or an ear infection, or a birthday party with a clown or a hot air balloon ride that supposedly happened at about the age of five. Each group of parents told their children the invented stories and the researchers subsequently interviewed the students three times. The researchers found that none of the participants recalled the false event during the first interview, but 20% said they remembered something about the false event in the second interview and by the third, 50% of the students were so convinced by the false memory that they were even embellishing it.

He picked up the phone and pressed for reception.

'Marie, do you know where Anna is?'

'She left here about half an hour ago, Max. She looked a bit upset actually.'

Max put the phone down. He had to find her.

Chapter 21
CELIA

Faintly, the chimes of the clock in the kitchen carried to the greenhouse; Celia was intent on planting something that would colour the future; pansies, hyacinth and narcissus brimmed with shades of yellow, blue, pink and mauve in the wicker basket. She'd always loved making things grow. Just as she finished putting compost around the flowers, the glass door opened and Anna stood there. Celia knew immediately something was wrong; her face had that fixed expression she always had when she was stressed and trying not to show it.

'Hello, darling. What's the matter?'

'Nothing. I was just passing.'

Celia took off her gardening gloves and hugged her. Just passing. Anna worked miles away. 'Come on, I'll make us some coffee.'

They walked arm-in-arm back into the house, past the profusion of rhododendrons, azaleas and vivid blue hydrangeas; past Anna's old wooden swing and her tree house high in the old oak tree where Anna and her friends had played for many happy hours and where Paul had discovered Anna with her first boyfriend.

Anna smiled as she looked up at the tree-house, the strain washing out of her face. It couldn't be very bad if she smiled so easily, could it? Celia hadn't seen that strain on Anna's face for many years.

They descended three moss-covered steps to the terrace at the back of the house. Celia opened the kitchen door and they walked into the ticking tranquillity of a large kitchen.

'Where's Dad?' Anna asked.

'He's in the dark room as usual.' Celia answered as she got the ground coffee from the cupboard; her mind conjuring up all sorts of scenarios: Death. Divorce. Disease. Why do we always indulge in idle chit-chat before saying something important? Celia thought.

'I've got some of your favourite coffee,' Celia said, putting some into the coffee machine, knowing she sounded too enthusiastic. 'Not fair trade, I'm afraid, but sometimes my conscience is overpowered by my taste buds.' Stop prattling! She glanced at Anna's tight face.

'Sit down while we wait for the coffee to percolate and you can tell me what the problem is.'

'There's no problem, Mum.' Anna answered as she sat down in her usual chair.

Celia glanced at her, knowing there was. She felt her stomach rumble with nervous tension. Either she's ill or she and Tim are divorcing and she doesn't want to tell me either scenario, Celia thought.

'I had a very difficult client this morning. He upset me,' Anna stated in a flat voice.

Relief washed over Celia in waves. She leaned back against a cupboard. Everything was all right. 'What did he do, darling?'

Celia knew she would say that she mustn't talk about a client to anyone, but she was her mother.

'It's so weird, Mum. There's something familiar about him. As if I've met him before.'

'Perhaps you have.' Celia said, her body suddenly turned cold. She was worried by the odd look on Anna's face. 'You go to lots of lectures. Perhaps he was in one of them and you saw him. Is he the same age as you?'

Celia couldn't remember what Anna replied, but she remembered what Anna said next.

'He told me I had a butterfly mobile when I was a baby. How on earth could he know anything about my childhood? I didn't have one, did I?'

The room seemed to be swaying; Celia leaned against a cupboard until it stopped moving.

'Of course not, darling. What a strange thing for him to say. What do you think is wrong with him?'

The door suddenly opened and relief swept over her again; she had never been more relieved to see Paul in her life.

'What's this? A gathering of the sisterhood?' Paul said, before kissing Anna.

Celia poured some coffee for him; her hand was shaking, but thankfully nobody noticed. She watched Anna and Paul talking and thought about the happy times they'd had together when Anna was growing up; about the stories she'd read her. She'd introduced her to Herodotus when she was ten. He claimed to have seen ants the size of dogs in India; people who lived in caves and chirped like bats in Libya and flying snakes in Egypt in his book 'The Histories'. Anna had been so fascinated that Celia had introduced her to more and more wonderful stories from history. How lucky she'd been, Celia thought. Why should she feel threatened by a man she'd never met? A man who was suffering from mental problems?

She suddenly shivered, remembering a quote she'd given her students the week before: 'Herodotus shows us the ruin that comes to those who overreach their natural boundaries, who fail to heed sensible warnings or act without understanding the web of reciprocity that connects all things.'

Was he right? She asked herself. Was everything connected? But even if it was, surely it was better to have a lie that heals than a wound that hurts?

Chapter 22
STEFAN

You looked so beautiful today. With the sun on your face and your hair a copper halo. Your face could always catch the last seconds of the sun, Anna. I was so worried when you felt faint. But it allowed me to touch you. You have no idea what that meant to me. I have been starved of your love for so long.

I've almost finished the family room. The photographs start in 1977 with my birth. You won't recognise me lying in an old Viennese pram. It was our mother's pram when she was a baby. It was yours too. I have many photographs of mother and me in Vienna; she used to take me to Art Galleries and concerts and read me books: she gave me my love of art and music and words. Before you were born, mother took me to the Secession building. It was nicknamed 'The Golden Cabbage' because of its colours and shape. Gustav Klimt was its first president and our great, great grandfather, Max Kurtweil had his paintings displayed with him. Imagine that, Anna - we are descended from a man who worked with Gustav Klimt!

I was eight when Renate first took me to the building. She told me to look up when we got to the entrance. There are words carved in stone: "To every age its art and to art its freedom". That is what art should do, Anna – make us free. Art makes me free.

One day I will take you to Vienna, Anna and we'll go to museums and I'll show you Gustav Klimt's paintings. People see his despoiled paintings on chocolate boxes and think him kitsch; they don't see how his paintings transform colour and manipulate light; how anatomy becomes ornament and ornament, anatomy.

I will take you to the Secession Building to see his Beethoven frieze. Here is a celebration; the unification of the arts: painting, sculpture, architecture and music. It decorates three walls and has six plaster panels decorated with gold and semi-precious stones. Schiller's "Ode to Joy" is my favourite panel; two naked lovers embrace in a kiss which could transform the world.

Love can transform us, Anna. But who listens to that message now?

I am waiting for you to come to me. I wait every day.

Chapter 23
ANNA

Anna put her keys down onto the hall table and listened. There was complete silence in the house. Then she heard the click of keys: Tim was on the computer. She walked down their narrow hall and opened his study door. He turned around in surprise.

'What are you doing home so early?'

She kissed the top of his head and stared at the screen. He was on the genealogy site again. He had discovered three hundred relatives they'd never known they'd had. Anna couldn't see the point in it. What did it matter if her great, great, great grandfather lived in Leeds or Liverpool? She felt no connection to a man she'd only heard about recently.

'You're early too,' she answered.

'Clare's doing the afternoon surgery. Her kids are with their father for a couple of days.'

'You didn't say she was divorced.'

'Well, it's hardly relevant. Look what I've just discovered.' He turned back to the screen excitedly. Anna sighed quietly. More distant ancestors. What was this obsession with the past? Anna thought. Why did everyone want their ancestry to go back to King Canute? The knowledge wouldn't change their lives. Since Tim had become obsessed with genealogy, she realised they'd stopped going out so much; he was either working, playing squash or on the computer. It was her mother's fault, of course. She worked in the past and had got Tim hooked on it now. It's the present that's important, Tim, she wanted to shout at him. Let's live now!

'I've discovered ten more cousins living in Australia. What

do you think about that?'

'Great. What do you want for dinner?'

He was typing furiously and didn't answer.

'What do you want for dinner?'

He suddenly sat back and smiled at her. 'You know something, my beautiful girl – if we had a child he could be a genius! Look at our family tree. It's full of lawyers, doctors, judges, a couple of architects and University Lecturers. Can't get much better pedigree than that!'

Anna was suddenly standing in the bathroom looking at her pills. Stefan had pushed all thoughts of pregnancy out of my mind. She held onto the back of Tim's chair.

'You okay? You look a bit pale?' Tim studied her. 'Can't be ill, we're going on holiday, remember?'

So it's not concern for me, she thought angrily, just concern about the holiday.

'I'm fine. Don't get too carried away with the genius theory. One of my great Uncles was a lowly clerk.' Anna said. She disliked Tim's obsession with genetics intensely.

Tim looked momentarily deflated and turned back to the screen. 'What was he called?'

'Samuel George Baker.'

Suddenly, his name disappeared from the screen as Tim deleted him.

'You can't do that!' Anna was shocked. 'A family tree isn't a Mensa Test, Tim. You can't choose your relatives!'

'I can. Sam's out. Now then, our holiday. What exotic place have you chosen?' He sat back in his chair, hands behind his head and smiled at her.

Anna's stomach tightened. She knew he wouldn't like her answer.

110

'The Welsh coast,' Anna said, quietly.

'Wales in April! Are you bloody mad! We'll either be soaked or blown off a bloody cliff! I'm not going to Wales. Look at these last minute deals I've found. We could go to the sun really cheaply.'

Anna walked out of the study as he trawled through all the websites he'd found.

A half an hour later, Anna was putting the finishing touches to her Spaghetti Bolognese and listening to Radio Four. She'd known Tim was self-centred when she married him, but she'd dismissed it; thinking that he had to have time for himself; he had to make so much time for his patient's complaints. It was ironic that they both listened to people with problems in different parts of their anatomy; he to their bodily complaints; she to their mental ones. He was right. They were both tired. They both needed a holiday. She sprinkled parmesan cheese over the sauce and was about to call him, when he was suddenly behind her, nuzzling into her neck.

'Okay, Mrs. Nash. You win. Wales it is - come gale-force winds and rain, pestilence and flying leeks.'

And suddenly they were hugging each other and everything was wonderful. Anna ignored the small insistent voice in her head which said: why haven't you told him?

The phone suddenly rang; Tim picked it up as Anna took a bottle of Chardonnay out of the fridge.

'Dr. Nash speaking.' There was a small pause; Tim made a comic face at Anna; she smiled at him. 'Hello, Max. You haven't forgotten that Anna's away next week, have you? You won't believe where we're going – Wales! Anna's choice. She's always been very odd.' Anna dug her fingers into his ribs. 'Hey – that

111

hurt! Sorry …talking to Anna…what?' He frowned as he listened. 'I spoke to you when you came here for drinks. You okayed it, remember? We've already booked the holiday …yes, okay. I'll tell her. Bye.' He put the phone down. 'I don't believe that guy! He said he couldn't remember a thing about us going on holiday.'

Anna groaned silently as she put the open wine bottle on the table. 'Did he sound very annoyed?'

'Yes, but God knows why. It's only a week for Christ's sake,' Tim said, pouring out two glasses.

'I won't have any wine tonight,' Anna said, pushing her glass towards Tim. It's for health reasons, she told herself. Nothing to do with pregnancy.

'Max said he wants to see you tomorrow at two,' Tim said.

Anna's stomach contracted. He's seen the video, she thought.

'Isn't tomorrow your day off from the clinic?' Tim asked her as they sat down.

'Yes.' Why does he want to see me? Anna thought. All sorts of scenarios entered her head. *I don't really think you're suited to clinical psychology,* she could hear Max saying.

'Could do with a bit more garlic,' Tim gestured towards the food. 'Wants to do a Spanish Inquisition on your thesis, apparently. Christ knows why you wanted him to be your supervisor.'

Anna suddenly lost her appetite. She hadn't written much recently. Stefan Peterson and strange dreams had prevented her.

'You know why. He's supposed to be one of the best psychologists in the country,' Anna said. She forced herself to eat a little. She needed food to help her concentrate.

'Well, let's hope he's more considerate towards his clients than his trainees. Doesn't give a centimetre, does he? Don't let him push you around, Anna. Do you know what he'd be if he was a dog? A Rottweiler.'

Anna knew she'd have to work for hours; she'd never get a good grade for her thesis if she didn't.

***

The next morning Anna was up at five, working on her lap-top in the sitting-room. She'd researched and written for four hours the previous night and had written over 4,000 words. She was now three-quarters of the way through her thesis. Tim had told her she was being obsessive, but it wasn't his career at stake. She went into the kitchen and poured herself another coffee and brought it back into the sitting room. She scrolled down the page of her latest chapter to read what she'd written.

The Effects of Intimate Partner Violence on General Mental Health

In attempting to address questions about cause and effect between abuse and depression, it is important to note that the difficulty in studying depression and abuse is that few studies have looked at depression as a specific entity.

The clock struck the quarter; Anna glanced up and gave a small scream. She had forty five minutes to get to the clinic. She picked up her lap-top and raced out of the room.

Chapter 24
STEFAN

I have many photographs of mother playing the piano, Anna; she wanted me to be a pianist like her, but I only wanted to paint and listen to her playing. I have a photograph of her sitting at the piano in Hayden's house in Haydengasse. She was allowed to play Hayden's piano at a concert! I was so proud of her. She told me that Hayden wrote music every day from eight until half-past twelve, then he took a walk or visited friends. He had lunch between two and three. Then he composed until eight in the evening. Only after eight in the evening did he vary his activities in any way. Mother wanted me to learn from him, I know. Hayden's father was a village craftsman. Imagine the courage and tenacity he must have had to become world famous!

When you were born, Anna, I was eleven years old. I don't know why mother waited so long for another child, but I loved you the moment I saw you. You had downy fair hair and looked so fragile I thought you might break if I touched you. I listened to your whisper breaths and realised that Mother was right: happiness is as elusive as a butterfly – if we pursue it, it vanishes, but listening to you breathe; watching you take your first step; waiting for your first word – 'Stefan' - I touched it.

Mother told me that it was my duty to protect you and I did; every day until that terrible day when they took you away. I was overwhelmed by an unbearable feeling of loneliness; as if I was on one side of a glass wall and everything else was on the other. When you were taken away the world became silent.

Now I can hear music.

Chapter 25
MAX

Max was reading Anna's thesis, trying to ignore her presence on the other side of his desk.

'Most studies have looked at depression as a component of topics like self-esteem and mental well-being. In one example, the variables of self-esteem and depression were studied in a group of lesbian and heterosexual abuse survivors (Tuel & Russell, 1998). Twenty-three lesbians and 17 heterosexual women completed the Beck Depression Inventory (Beck, 1967), the Rosenberg's Self-Esteem Scale (Rosenberg, 1965), and the Index of Spouse Abuse-Revised (Hudson & McIntosh, 1981).

Max forgot that Anna was in the room as he became immersed in her findings. They were well researched.

'Hypotheses stated that once demographic effects were controlled, emotional and physical abuse would correlate significantly with depression and self esteem. In addition, physical abuse would have a stronger relationship with depression and self-esteem when emotional abuse was controlled. Finally, the gender of the abuser would not correlate significantly with depression and self-esteem. Results indicated that physical abuse seemed to predict depression and emotional abuse seemed to predict low self-esteem. The gender of the abuser did not have a significant effect on either variable.'

Max closed her lap-top, knowing that he hadn't been wrong about Anna; she had all the hall-marks of an intelligent, insightful psychologist. He looked up and saw how tired she looked. She must have been working on this all night.

'This is good, Anna.'

'You really think so?' She radiated so much sudden vitality that Max felt his energy levels rising to match hers.

'I wouldn't have said so if I didn't think so,' he answered.

'No, of course you wouldn't,' she said, grinning at him.

Here was his Anna; the girl who wasn't in awe of him. She sat there; unaware of the intense feelings she created within him.

Max pushed her lap-top across the table towards her. 'If the rest of the thesis is as good as that, you'll get a decent grade.'

Anna opened her arms, looking as if she wanted to hug him and Max clenched his fists under the table before saying lightly.

'Even though I've been coerced into giving you a week off.'

'And who could coerce you, Max?' she answered.

You could, Anna Nash, but you don't know it, Max thought. 'Actually, I think it's a good idea you going away soon.'

Anna stared at him in surprise. 'Why?'

'Stefan Peterson. Remember what you said to him about Piaget? People can be coaxed into "remembering" entire events that never happened. He's a clever manipulator who's starting to undermine your confidence. You're becoming vulnerable.'

Anna immediately lowered her eyes to her laptop. 'I shouldn't have tried to persuade you to let me carry on treating him,' she said in a quiet voice.

'He might need to see a psychiatrist. I'll take over his treatment and assess him.' Max paused before adding. 'You know he's in love with you, don't you?'

'Yes, but that's part of his problem, isn't it?' Anna said.

'And you're starting to fall in love with him,' Max answered. 'That's part of your problem.'

116

Max watched Anna tense in her chair; knowing she desperately wanted to deny this possibility.

'But if he thinks he's my brother, how can he fall in love with me?'

'Delusional people, especially one as delusional as Stefan Peterson, think and act in bizarre ways,' Max said, reaching into his desk and pulling out a journal to give to Anna. 'Read the article on GSA by Dr Maurice Greenberg, a consultant psychiatrist.'

'What's GSA?'

'Genetic Sexual Attraction,' Max answered. 'It's increasingly acknowledged by post-adoption agencies to be a common feature of reunions between blood relatives who've been separated at a young age or who've never met before.'

'But we're not related.'

'But he thinks you are, Anna. The feeling is the same.'

He watched Anna thinking about what he'd just told her. It was a lot for her to assimilate.

'What will he do when he finds out I'm not?'

'I don't know,' Max answered truthfully. The knowledge disturbed him.

'But don't I need to complete his treatment to finish my placement?' Anna asked, looking worried.

'I'll have another client waiting for you when you return from your holiday.' Max wanted to beg her not to go. Not to leave him. 'Tim said you wanted to go to Wales. Why Wales?'

Anna took a brochure out of her pocket and gave it to Max. 'Look at that view. That's why.'

The landscape in front of Max was stunning; a sweeping panorama of impossibly yellow sand, blue sea and heady cliffs, topped by a white hotel in the distance.

'Rhossili Beach has been named one of the most beautiful in the UK by travel writers from all over the world. And that's the hotel we're staying in. Isn't the view incredible?'

'Yes,' Max answered, thinking if only he could share it with her. He looked up and saw her shift awkwardly in her chair. He waited; knowing she was mirroring what she felt.

'What are you going to tell Stefan?' She asked him at last.

'That you're on holiday and I'm taking over his treatment. Forget him, Anna. People like Stefan can create black holes for therapists. Remember who you are, not who Stefan thinks you are.'

'I feel sorry for him.'

'So do I, but I won't let compassion interfere in my treatment or assessment of him.'

Anna rubbed a hand across her forehead. 'I didn't do what you told me to, did I? I'm still not detached enough.'

She looked so vulnerable that Max wanted to throw his arms around her; to tell her that he didn't want her to be detached at all. He wanted her to remain exactly as she was. Perfect.

'No, you're not,' Max answered. 'Clinical detachment is vitally important if you are going to be able to assess your clients accurately.' Max hated the cloud that suddenly shadowed her face. He wanted her to be happy. The knowledge shook him. He'd never felt empathy for Sadie – just desire.

'Has your hypnosis helped your other client, Kieran?'

Anna's face immediately became radiant. 'Yes. She's becoming more confident and assertive each time I see her.'

'Then the hypnosis is obviously working.'

'She told me she wants to train to become a teacher. I'm so pleased for her, Max. She's standing up to her father for the first time in her life.'

118

Max smiled at Anna, delighted by her pleasure in her client's metamorphosis.

'If only I could do the same for-'

'Stop,' Max said. 'I told you to forget about him. Concentrate on finishing your thesis and come back here bursting with energy. Now let me get on with my work.'

Anna jumped up. 'Thanks, Max. I will. I'll have Kieran's report on your desk by the end of the day.'

Max pressed his hands on his desk as he got up, glad that it stood solidly between them. 'Tomorrow will be okay. Today is packed with meetings and clients. Go home and work on it. If I don't see you before you go, have a good time in Wales.'

'We will. I'll leave the brochure to make you envious. Bye, Max.'

She grinned at him before closing the door. The word 'we' rang in Max's ears. It's the wrong 'we', he thought as he walked over to the video recorder and switched it on. He wanted to refresh his memory of Stefan. He'd asked him to come in this afternoon and didn't want Anna to be there when he did.

***

There was a sharp knock on the door. Just as Max was about to shout come in, Stefan opened it and said. 'What do you want to see me about, Dr. Paris?'

'Come in and sit down, Mr. Peterson,' Max said in a relaxed voice.

Stefan came in, sat down opposite him and stared out of the window. 'Why have you chosen an office with such a sterile view?'

'I like houses,' Max said neutrally.

Stefan made a steeple of his fingers.   The same studied

119

gesture Max had seen him use in one of the videos Anna had recorded.

'So what do you want to see me about?' Stefan said again.

'I thought we'd talk about how you think you're progressing.' Max said.

'Where's Anna? I want to see her,' Stefan answered abruptly.

'I'm afraid you can't. She's gone on holiday.'

The colour drained from Stefan's face until it was almost white. Max got up from his chair and poured some water into a plastic cup from the water dispenser in the corner and gave it to him.

'Drink that.'

Stefan sipped the water slowly. 'Where has she gone? She didn't tell me she was going away.'

'I'll be treating you from now on.'

Stefan put the cup down and stared at him so intently that Max felt like a microbe being analysed under a microscope. It was a disturbing feeling.

'And why should I want to be treated by you. I want Anna.'

'Well, I'm afraid you can't have her.'

The men stared at each other like combatants until suddenly Stefan said: 'And what makes you believe that, Dr. Paris?'

Chapter 26
ANNA

It was a long time since Anna had been to Paddington station. The last time she'd been eight, going on holiday to Cornwall with her parents. Then she'd been overwhelmed by its size and the light that flooded down from the three glass roofs. Now she was surprised by the large number of shops that were there and how incredibly busy it was.

Anna and Tim stood in a long queue of disgruntled passengers waiting for a ticket.

'Shit!' Tim shouted, looking at the long snake of people in front of them. 'This is more fucking stressful than work! Our train leaves in six minutes and we won't be fucking on it!'

The woman in front of them turned to stare at Tim; it was obvious what she was thinking. Anna squeezed his hand, hoping his mood would lighten before they reached the hotel. She hadn't told him it was only three star; they'd stayed at five star hotels before and he'd complained about them. She prayed that this one would be as good as it looked; dreading finding it cold, damp and serving poor food. Tim wouldn't suffer inferior food in silence. Perhaps she was mad to have chosen to stay in a remote place in April; the days were still cold. She clutched her lap-top tight; the life-line to her thesis. She'd just started a new chapter and was anxious to finish it.

They eventually reached the head of the queue, got their tickets, raced down the platform and jumped on their train, just as the guard blew his whistle and the doors closed behind them. They stood by the doors, panting for breath as the train accelerated out of the station.

At last Tim managed to say, 'Got to play more squash!'

And suddenly they were smiling at each other and for the first time, Anna felt that the holiday could be good.

***

It was a long train journey but Anna didn't mind; she could concentrate on her thesis while Tim immersed himself in a book about the Gower Peninsula. She'd finished the section called *The Effects of Intimate Partner Violence on Mental Health*. There hadn't been many studies on depression in this area; most studies concentrated on self-esteem and mental well-being.

Tim suddenly looked up from his book and smiled at her. He already looked more relaxed, Anna thought.

'How's it going?' He asked.

'Did you know that once demographic effects are controlled, emotional and physical abuse correlate significantly with depression and self esteem?'

A pompous-looking man sitting opposite them looked up from his newspaper and stared at Anna in surprise. Men were often surprised that someone who looked like Anna could be intelligent. His expression annoyed her.

'The variables of self-esteem and depression were studied in a group of lesbian and heterosexual abuse survivors. Twenty-three lesbians and 17 heterosexual women -'

'It was just a general enquiry,' Tim said, smiling at her. 'Not a viva. On a scale from 1 to 10, how's it going?'

'It's about 7 at the moment, Tim. Thank you very much for asking,' Anna said with mock seriousness.

They glanced at the man, enjoying the look of bemusement on his face. They smiled at him. He immediately buried himself behind the newspaper.

'Did you know that sexually transmitted diseases have quadrupled in the last ten years, darling,' Tim said loudly. 'I think it would be best to jettison the lovers, don't you?'

The newspaper twitched violently as the man sprang up and scuttled off to find another seat. Anna and Tim leaned together and laughed. It was a good feeling, Anna thought. They didn't laugh as much as they did before they were married.

'This is going to be the best holiday we've ever had,' she said in a determined voice.

***

Tim didn't want to stay overnight in Swansea. If we're going to see the sea, let's see it immediately, he told Anna as they picked up their hired car.

It took them an hour and a half to reach the coast, even though they had Sat Nav; they'd got lost twice on the winding roads. They saw lights in the distance, but no hotel. The car juddered over a pot-holed path, into a bend. Suddenly, they saw the dim outline of the hotel.

'That's it!' Anna shouted excitedly.

Tim manoeuvred the car into a small road at the end of which was the forecourt of the hotel. He turned the engine off and sat staring into space.

'Fuck! How remote is this?' Tim eased himself out of the car and stretched. 'Just hope it's worth it.'

'Of course it is. Be positive.' Anna breathed in deeply as she got out. 'Can you smell that? It's the sea.'

'Bugger the sea,' Tim answered, getting their cases out of the boot. 'The only smell that interests me is food.'

Anna prayed that the hotel restaurant was still open as she opened the hotel door and they walked in. The hall was a large, tastefully decorated space.

'All right so far,' Tim said as he walked up to reception and rang a small bell.

They both jumped as a small, compact middle-aged woman appeared as if by magic. She wore a black dress and had the sombre look of someone in mourning.

'Good evening. You must be Dr. Nash.'

Anna could detect the remnants of another accent under her Welsh one, but she couldn't identify it. 'A bit later than expected.' The woman took in Tim's tight expression and added quickly. 'You must have had a long journey. Never mind, you're here now. '

The woman turned to Anna and drew in air through her teeth as she stared at her face and hair.

Anna glanced at Tim, wondering at the woman's odd reaction.

'You're still serving food, I hope,' Tim said. 'We're very hungry.'

The woman dragged her eyes from Anna's face and looked at her watch. It was 9 0'clock. 'Just a minute.' She disappeared behind a door, leaving Tim and Anna looking at each other.

'What a strange woman,' Tim whispered. 'Where's she gone?'

'She's asking the chef if he'll stay late because she has some difficult customers.'

'I'm not difficult. I'm hungry.' Tim looked around the place. 'Very quiet, isn't it? She seems very interested in you. Lesbos on the horizon, I think.'

He started as the woman appeared behind him, holding two menus.

'I asked Geraint to stay late, Dr. Nash. He's our chef.'

'Fantastic,' Tim said, beaming at her.

'But I would be grateful if you'd order your meal before going upstairs. He's had a long day, you see.' She smiled at them as she gave them both a menu.

'That's very kind of you, Mrs -'

'Owen. If you could just look at the menus, I'll give the order to Geraint straight away then you won't have to wait long.'

Anna glanced at Tim. She knew he didn't want to order food standing in a hallway, but Mrs. Owen was a quiet, but formidable force.

'We'll have Welsh lamb and vegetables, please,' Anna said quickly.

Tim glanced at her in surprise and was just about to disagree when Mrs. Owen took the menus off them and disappeared.

'How do you know I want lamb?'

'You love lamb. She's doing us a favour, Tim. We can't keep the poor chef up all night. At least you'll have some food.'

'Thank God for small mercies. That woman must be related to Houdini. I've never seen anyone move so fast.'

'Or so silently,' Anna added.

As if to prove them right, Mrs. Owen was suddenly, silently, beside them again. 'All ordered. I'll show you your room. It's one of the luxury ones, overlooking the sea. I thought you'd like that. It's beautiful in the morning.'

She walked lightly up the stairs and Anna ran up behind her. Tim grunted as he picked up the cases and plodded after them.

As Mrs. Owen opened the door of their sumptuously furnished bedroom, Anna was immediately drawn towards two large windows which Mrs Owen assured them over-looked the sea. It was a moonless night so Anna couldn't see out of the window.

'The food will be ready in twenty minutes. The dining room is on the right of the stairs. Breakfast is between 7 and 9. You'll see Worm's Head in the morning; it's a mile long serpent-like promontory jutting out into the ocean. I hope you have wonderful stay in Wales.' Mrs. Owen was staring once more at Anna. 'I'll leave you to refresh yourselves.'

And she was gone.

Anna and Tim looked at each other and burst out laughing.

Anna was enchanted by the small accessories Mrs Owen had placed in their room to make them welcome: not just the usual tea and coffee, but a variety of soaps and shampoos in the bathroom; Welsh oatcakes in the bedroom and a book on Dylan Thomas' poetry on a bedside table.

After their meal of wonderful Welsh lamb, they thanked the chef and collapsed into a deep, dreamless sleep.

The next morning, Anna was woken by the sun trying to slide into the room. She got out of bed, opened the curtains and gasped: in front of her was a wide expanse of indigo and blue and green; a silky sea glistened in the sunshine. And in the distance, the long worm-like promontory Mrs. Owen mentioned. They could walk there this morning. She held her breath in case it suddenly disappeared. How wonderful to wake up to such a magnificent view every morning, she thought. She stood there for a long time, knowing what she must do before Tim woke up. She released her breath slowly and crept over to her suitcase; lying at the bottom of it was the pregnancy testing kit she had brought with her. As she took it out, the case lid thumped shut and Tim stirred in his sleep. She tensed as he rolled over, throwing one arm across his face before sliding back into a deep sleep. She tiptoed towards the bathroom and closed the door.

She opened the kit and read: "The new Clearblue Digital Pregnancy Test with Conception Indicator is the world's first fully integrated digital early pregnancy test." Anna followed the instructions and looked at the liquid crystal display. A flashing egg-timer symbol appeared. In three minutes she would know whether she was going to be a mother or not. Three minutes. They seemed to stretch forever. How would she cope with a baby and studying? What would happen to her career? Would she ever be a clinical psychologist if she was pregnant? She stared at her tense face in the mirror, calculating the dates and suddenly groaned; if the result was positive, the baby would arrive slap-bang in the middle of her final exams. Her mother had told her that she'd never slept through the night until she was four years old. What if she had a baby like that? She'd have to give up her career. She closed her eyes, knowing that she was worrying about problems that might never happen; something she always tried to stop her clients doing. She took a deep breath and looked down at the LCD. The word **pregnant** leapt out at her. She hung onto the basin for support. Suddenly a number appeared underneath it – 5+. She was five weeks pregnant!

Anna crept back into the bedroom and got dressed; the implications of being pregnant swirling around and around her head.

They were having breakfast in the dining room; the spring sunlight dissecting numerous windows. They'd got up late and were the only people left in the room. Tim didn't notice how distracted she was; he was bowled over by the view. He looked relaxed and happy. Anna felt the usual pangs of guilt. Why wasn't she happy too? She was pregnant by the man she loved. She should be ecstatic.

'I've got something to tell you,' Anna said as Tim finished his cooked breakfast.

He looked at her, startled. 'That sounds ominous.'

'No, it's not. I'm pregnant.'

Tim dropped his knife and fork onto the plate. 'You can't be.'

It wasn't the reaction Anna had been expecting. She imagined he would throw his arms around her and hug her. He looked shocked.

'Why not?'

'You're meticulous about taking the pill. You told me you didn't want a baby until you'd qualified and had some clinical experience.'

Anna felt ridiculously upset by his reaction. Five minutes ago she hadn't wanted this child, now his reaction made her feel incredibly protective towards it.

'I thought you'd be ecstatic. You've wanted children for years.'

'Yes, but …' Tim paused and stared at his plate. 'Not now.'

Anna felt her heart race. 'What do you mean, not now? You mean you don't want children any more?

Tim stared out of the window. 'No, I mean I don't think now is the best time to have one.'

Anna felt breathless. 'Why? Because of the world population explosion or global warming or what?'

Tim looked at her. 'I'm sorry. I wasn't expecting anything like this. What test did you use?'

Anna's mouth crumpled. He was being clinical and she wanted euphoria and laughter. Her eyes filled with tears.

'I'm sorry. It's just a shock after …' His voice trailed away.

'A pleasant shock?' Anna was stunned by how lonely she felt; stunned by the sudden knowledge that if he didn't want their child, she didn't want him. She pushed back her chair and stood up. Was this pregnancy or paranoia?

Tim stood up and hugged her. 'Of course it's a pleasant shock. Just give me time to get used to it.'

Suddenly, Anna noticed Mrs Owen at the other side of the room, smiling at her as she cleared the tables. She smiled back, but her face felt stiff.

Back in their hotel room, they sat on the bed and Anna asked Tim all the questions she'd been wanting to ask him for weeks: how should she be feeling? When would the baby be likely to arrive? What should she do and not do? Tim answered every question with detached care. As if she was one of his patients, not his wife, Anna thought.

'However, no test is 100% perfect. This is about 99% accurate, so you still need to get another one done when we get home.'

'So I might not be pregnant?' Anna asked, suddenly feeling bereft. She couldn't understand her roller-coaster emotions. Was this what pregnancy was like? Full of erratic fluctuations?

'Most probably you are,' Tim said, 'but a second test will give us a more definite answer. A growing embryo produces a pregnancy hormone called Human Chorionic Gonadotrophin about a week after conception. Another test will definitely determine the presence of HCG in your body.'

There's no emotion in his voice, Anna thought; he sounds as if he's giving a lecture on pregnancy.

Chapter 27
STEFAN

Once upon a time there was a woodcutter who lived with his wife and two children deep in a forest. The children were sent out to play every day while the woodcutter cut his wood and his wife cleaned the house and cooked and sang songs. The children listened to her singing as they ran deeper and deeper into the forest. She told them never to go too far from the sound of her voice and they never did. They always stopped when her voice became too faint for them to hear. And so they played every day and were happy. The boy taught the little girl all about the forest: how to tell the blackbird's song from thrushes; how to find foxes and badgers; how to see spider's webs hanging in the trees like transparent dinner plates; which mushrooms and berries to pick for food and which to leave; how to make a small house out of branches and leaves when they were tired. He taught her everything she knew and she was beautiful and kind.

Then one day, their father had an accident with his axe and he couldn't cut up wood any more. He told the boy that he must cut up the wood for the family and sell it far and wide. And the boy did, but now he had no time to play with his little sister for he was always working. His father sat in the house and their mother didn't sing any more.

One day when the boy was cutting up the wood, his little sister wandered off into the forest. There was no song to guide her back home so she went deeper and deeper into the forest until it became so dark that she couldn't see her way home. They never saw her again.

Remember this story, Anna. Please.

Chapter 28
MAX

Max sat in his office wondering what to do. Should he call the police? And say what? A client made a veiled threat against one of the trainees. He could imagine the police's reaction. He didn't want to be the butt of their derisory jokes. He stood up and stared out of the window. Think logically. That's what you're trained to do. Okay. A client thinks he's Anna's brother. He obviously wants to protect her so logically he's not going to harm her... unless... he discovers he's not. What protection would she have then? But he's delusional? How could he find out? Max started pacing around the office until it came to him: a competent therapist could hypnotize him back to the moment of his trauma; then he'd discover that Anna couldn't possibly be his sister and she would be in danger. But he's not seeing a therapist, is he? Anna's gone away. Thank God, he thought. It gives me time to think of a solution.

He visualised her in his office before he'd seen Stefan. Her smile, lighting up the room. If only he could have gone with her, not Tim. He suddenly remembered she'd left him a brochure 'to make him envious.' She'd never know how prophetic her words were. He lifted up file after file onto his desk, looking for it. There was nothing there. He searched on the floor; on his shelves; everywhere. It had gone.

***

It took Max nearly five minutes to get a taxi to stop for him; he usually got one simply by lifting one hand. Think rationally he kept telling himself. A report instantly flashed into his mind: "*Evidence for delusional thinking comes from research*

131

documenting that simple memory intrusions are common in patients with schizophrenia." Jesus Christ! Max's body was suddenly covered in sweat. No, no, no, Stefan wasn't a schizophrenic; he didn't have hallucinations or disorganized speech or behaviour – he was just delusional. He suddenly hated the fact that he had a photographic memory. *Stop being melodramatic!* Tim was with her.

He paid the taxi-driver and stood outside Paul and Celia Baker's house. The last time he'd met them was an alcoholic blur; he hoped it was for them too.

The door opened as he walked up the path; Celia Baker must have been waiting for him.

'Hello, Dr. Paris. Nice to see you again.'

Max could tell from her eyes that she remembered the last time they'd met very clearly.

'Come in,' Celia moved out of the doorway to let him in.

'Thanks. I'm sorry to bother you.'

'It's no bother.'

He followed her down the hallway into a large slate-floored kitchen. Very lived in, Max thought, unlike his barren place.

'Would you like a coffee?'

Max didn't want any more coffee. His heart was already jumping with caffeine. 'Yes, thanks,' he said. He wanted time to assess what sort of woman she was. He could tell by her movements she was decisive; he could see, from the numerous photographs on the walls, how much the Bakers loved their daughter, and he knew by the direct way she looked at him that she wouldn't be easily fooled.

'I didn't quite understand what you meant on the phone,' Celia said.

132

Max wasn't surprised; he had been deliberately vague, wanting time to talk to Anna's parents; to see if they'd want to go down to Wales. But he couldn't tell them all his concerns.

The coffee machine belched loudly as it filtered the coffee.

'Got to buy a new machine, but we never seem to get round to it.' She smiled at him in exactly the same way as Anna did; Max was charmed.

'I'll call Paul. He's in his dark room. I almost have to drag him out of there to eat.'

As Celia walked out, Max looked at the whole of Anna's life mapped out in photographs: little Anna at the sea-side, on a horse, in a fun-fair; teenage Anna canoeing, cycling, dancing with boys; older Anna graduating, partying, marrying. A great sadness crushed Max; no one had ever loved him that much to map out his life like this.

'Hello, Dr. Paris.'

Max turned around to see Paul Baker staring at him, rather warily, he noticed. *What the hell did I do that night?*

'Please call me Max. I must apologize for the other evening. I don't normally drink much at all.'

'At least you weren't sick in the back of the car,' Celia said pragmatically.

Max was taken aback. 'Sorry, I thought Tim had taken me home. This is very embarrassing.'

'Nothing to be embarrassed about, Max,' Paul said. 'I told Celia that you weren't used to alcohol.'

Celia gave Paul a sharp look and Max realised she had obviously said that to him.

'No, I'm not,' Max replied.

'Sit down, please,' Celia said, handing him a coffee. 'And tell us how we can help.'

Max had worked out what to say in the taxi. 'I just need to explain something to Anna about her new client.'

'What happened to her other client? Ann told me he was difficult.'

Max stared at Celia and she put a hand over her mouth in sudden embarrassment. 'That's all she said. She never talks about her clients, does she, Paul?'

'No,' Paul said hastily. 'Never.'

Husband and wife glanced at each other quickly before smiling at Max.

Max suppressed a smile. Such stalwart support. 'I'm sure she doesn't. Her client doesn't want any more sessions at the clinic so I'm giving Anna a new one when she comes back.'

'I'm glad,' Celia said. 'I could tell that she was worried.'

So am I, Max brooded, sipping his coffee. 'Lovely coffee.'

'It's Javan,' Celia said. 'Anna's favourite. 'So how can we help you?'

So that's where Anna gets her directness from, Max thought.

'Have you got her address? There's also something I need to discuss with her about her thesis.'

Paul looked alarmed. 'Not a problem with it, I hope.'

'No, on the contrary, it's progressing well. I just wanted to give her some help with her research.'

Paul's face relaxed into a smile. 'That's very kind of you. Can't say my tutor gave me much help with mine. Did Anna tell you about my thesis?' Paul asked hopefully.

'Don't be ridiculous, Paul. Max doesn't want to hear about your thesis.'

Paul's face deflated.

'Another time, perhaps. If you could give me Anna's address?' Max needed to speak to Tim; he couldn't spend any more time in social chatter.

Celia looked at her husband. 'Did she give it to you, Paul?'

Paul shook his head. 'You know she always gives things like that to you.'

'Well, she didn't,' Celia answered. 'She was only going for a week. I don't suppose she thought it that important.' She stared at Max intently. 'It's not, is it?'

Max arranged his face so that it looked relaxed. 'No, not really. I just thought you might have it.'

'It's somewhere on the Welsh coast,' Paul said, trying to be helpful.

'Yes, I know,' Max answered, feeling a cold sea breeze blow over him. 'Well, it's not important.' He looked across at the photos. 'You could start a picture gallery.'

They smiled at Anna's glossy face smiling back at them.

'We've got hundreds more in photo albums,' Celia said.

'Far too many, I suppose,' Paul said, 'but we like them.'

Envy surged through Max's body; did these people know how fortunate they were?

As Celia held the door open for him, Max felt himself caught in the full force of a penetrating stare.

'Is there something we should know, Dr. Paris,' she asked him.

Years of treating clients had made Max a master of dissimulation. 'I'm afraid I'm a workaholic, Mrs. Baker.'

'It's Celia.'

'And unfortunately, I expect the same level of commitment from my trainees. Even if they're on holiday.' Max smiled at her and her face relaxed.

'I'll remind Anna when she gets home,' she said. 'Bye, Max. Try to relax more.' She shouted as he walked down the garden path.

Relax! - How could he relax when Stefan Peterson was looking for Anna?

Max gave Celia a relaxed wave before getting into his Peugeot and driving away at high speed, tight with tension.

Chapter 29
ANNA

The sun slanted across the bay casting shadows over moist clumps of seaweed near the shore line; two seagulls wheeled in the air making strangulated noises. It was low tide and in the distance, Anna and Tim saw the skeletal wreck of a Norwegian Barque caught in a massive storm in 1887 and driven onto the beach. Behind it, lay the promontory Anna had seen from her window, looking like the head of a gigantic sea-serpent rising out of the water.

They were walking along a long stretch of pale yellow sand, surrounded by sand-dunes, gull-limed grass and woods. They pulled their Gore-Tex jackets tighter for although it was sunny, it was also chilly. Anna loved it; she felt more alive than she'd felt for months as they paced over the sand; the blood surging through her body. Tim smiled at her and she almost forgot his lack of excitement about her pregnancy test. Almost.

'You look beautiful,' he said. 'Sea air suits you.'

They walked on a little further before he added. 'I'm sorry about yesterday. It's wonderful news about the baby.'

Anna looked at him. 'So you *do* think I'm pregnant? I thought you said I'd need to do another test.'

'I'm a doctor, remember. I've seen hundreds of women in the early trimester. They all have the same glow as you.'

'You really are glad?'

He stopped in front of her and held her hands. 'Of course I am. It's going to difficult with your training, but we'll think of something.'

All Anna's fears about her career suddenly surfaced again.

'What about your parents?' Tim asked.

'What about them?'

'Perhaps they could look after the baby while you finish your training.'

'It's a bit much to ask when Mum's lecturing at UCL.'

'Yeah and I suppose your Dad might not want a screaming baby to look after at his age.'

'Dad's not that old and our baby won't scream!'

A sudden gust of wind pulled her hair across her eyes. Tim pushed it back and smiled at her. 'So what are you going to feed him on – gin?'

Anna smiled and they carried on walking, hand in hand. 'I'll ask Mum and Dad when we get back.'

She suddenly stopped walking and watched the sun playing over the white tipped surf in the distance. Totally enchanted.

'Let's buy a holiday cottage here after the baby is born!' She turned to Tim in excitement.

'Don't be ridiculous! We've got a big mortgage. We can't possibly afford another place. Anyway, this place is okay for a week, but I wouldn't want to keep coming back here. There's nothing here but sand and sea.'

Anna was stunned by his reaction and stared at him in amazement. There was far more here than sand and sea; there was beauty and serenity and time to just *be*; qualities that were lacking from their lives in London.

'I love the buzz of London,' Tim said, as if reading her thoughts. 'I never want to leave it. And what would you do all day here?'

'Do? I'd look after our baby. Swim. Walk. Take up windsurfing. Masses of things.'

Tim was just about to argue with her when they heard the

sudden shout of a child and turned towards it; there in the distance a little girl was calling to her father to watch her. She was on top of a sand dune; the sun slanting across her excited face, banding her hair with yellow and brown. She jumped up high, her flimsy legs flailing in the air and landed in a heap at her father's feet. He clapped as she raised her face to his in an ecstasy of pure joy.

Why can't we retain that ability for intense joy when we're older? Anna wondered. She watched the father laugh as he picked his daughter up and put her on his shoulders. As they walked away, their elongated silhouette cast a long shadow along the sands. Anna suddenly smiled: that could be her child in the future. She turned to Tim, wondering if he was thinking the same, but he was frowning at the retreating figures.

'Penny for them,' Anna said.

Tim stopped frowning and smiled at her. 'Do you think I'd give away my brilliant thoughts for a mere penny?'

Anna hugged him before running with arms outstretched along the sand, towards the sun.

Two hours later they were eating sea bass at the hotel after their six mile walk across Rhossili Bay to Worm's Head and back again; Anna felt vibrant with sea-air and exercise. There were a number of other couples eating lunch too, but Anna didn't notice how often men's heads turned in her direction because she was absorbed in the panoramic view. But Tim did.

Mrs. Owen stepped over to their table and asked if everything was all right.

'It's better than all right. It's magical,' Anna said, smiling at her.

Mrs. Owen smiled back at her. 'That's because the Gower

Coast is a Welsh poem; full of prehistoric secrets, ancient woodlands and castles, and the most spectacular seascapes in Europe. It's a pity you're only here for the week, there's nineteen more miles of beauty to discover.'

'You ought to work for the tourist board, Mrs. Owen,' Tim said. 'You'd double the tourists.'

'Thank you, Dr. Nash,' She smiled at him briefly before turning back to Anna and staring at her in a way that made Anna feel that she ought to know her.

'You can't leave Wales before seeing the Dan-yr-Ogof Caves in the Brecon Beacons National Park. It's only an hour's drive from here. I'll give you directions.' Before they could ask her any questions she had disappeared out of the room.

'Do you think she's related to Merlin?' Tim whispered to Anna. They laughed and Anna felt as if nothing could spoil her happiness.

When they got to the Dan-yr-Ogof Caves, there were already a large group of people standing outside the entrance of the cave system, listening to an elderly Welsh Guide. Everyone was wearing hard hats.

The Guide turned to them and said 'Late comers, is it? Well, hurry up and pay and get some hard hats. I'll wait two minutes, no more.'

Anna and Tim glanced at each other; not knowing if he was serious. As Tim rushed to the kiosk to pay, Anna heard him saying.

'Good morning, ladies and gentlemen and welcome to Dan-yr-Ogof - the largest show cave complex in western Europe. Over 9 miles of passages.' The Guide looked around the group and added. 'That's 16 kilometres for those of you who don't understand Imperial measurements.'

The group looked suitably impressed by the vastness of the cave system.

'As you can see, the cave system is situated in a beautiful valley, flanked by mountain ranges of 2,300 and 2,600 feet set in wonderful scenery. And yes, I've been paid to say that.'

The group smiled at the Guide as Tim joined Anna and gave her a hard hat.

'You'll see water dripping from ancient stalactites which were around in the Stone Age, amazing cave and rock formations and streams roaring through narrow passageways. There are three spectacular caves in the complex: Dan-yr-Ogof Cave, Cathedral Cave and the Bone Cave where 42 human skeletons have been found. So don't wander off. I don't want you to add to the number.'

The group laughed.

'Now be careful when you enter the caves. Some passages are low and slippery. So no running, mind.'

The Guide wagged his finger at an elderly couple standing next to Anna and the group laughed again.

Tim leaned over and whispered to her. 'He was a comedian in an earlier existence.'

Anna smiled at him, thinking I'm really happy. This is what I should feel when I'm with my husband.

'Right, off we go then and keep your heads down mind, or you'll fracture your skulls.' The Guide winked at them before moving off into the cave entrance.

The group trouped after him. The tunnel they entered was narrow, low ceiled and partially lit. Anna was only 5ft 6 but she still found her hard hat occasionally banging on the cave ceiling. She heard the sound of constant *aows* as other people did the same.

As the group turned a bend they saw five stalagmites that looked like cowled nuns in white habits. 'Created over hundreds of thousands of years,' the Guide told them before moving off. Anna stared at them in wonder as people walked past her to stare at the multifarious colours on the walls and ceiling caused by minerals.

'This is amazing,' Anna said to Tim. 'Aren't you glad we came to Wales now? I've never seen anything like it.'

'It's quite interesting I suppose,' Tim said. Anna pinched his backside and he laughed.

They walked on up the tunnel bending lower and lower in an effort not to bang their heads when suddenly after passing a thick, pure white pillar, stretching between the floor and the ceiling, they entered an enormous high vaulted cave with a lake in front of them with a 40ft waterfall at the back of it. Everyone gasped as they stared around the vast cave. After the cramped tunnels it was exhilarating to feel space around them. The cave ceiling looked as high as St. Paul's with hundreds of stalactites hanging down from it.

What a magical place, Anna thought, noticing a small circular boat in the middle of the lake.
The Welsh Guide waited for everyone to gather around him, obviously savouring the moment.

'I think he wanted to be an actor, not a comedian,' Anna whispered to Tim, looking at the Guide's animated expression.

'This cave is made of carboniferous limestone, formed some 315 million years ago,' the Guide began. 'Because the rock has cracks and fissures, water has been able to flow through it, dissolving the limestone and carving out the cave we see today. In 1912 two brothers, Tommy and Jeff Morgan discovered Dan-yr-

Ogof using only candles and oil lamps. No luxury like lights for those lads. And you know how they crossed this lake?'

The Guide paused dramatically as he looked around at his audience.

'In a coracle.' He pointed to the boat. 'That's the small Welsh boat you can see in the middle of the lake. Now don't ask me how the lads got the coracle through the narrow tunnels because it's Welsh magic.'

Everyone smiled at him.

'And that's the very coracle the Morgan boys used. Built to last centuries Welsh coracles.'

He winked at the group before walking off. People wandered off into different parts of the cave, their voices echoing around the walls.

Anna was mesmerized by the underground lake with its fantastic waterfall cascading deep into its surface, creating wild spectrums of coloured lights at the far end of the lake. She didn't notice Tim wandering off with the others; she didn't notice anything until she heard the sound of an object being thrown into the lake; small concentric rings appeared on the lake's surface. She turned.

A man was standing behind her, his face in shadow under his hard hat. He stepped forward and Anna gasped.

'Hello, Anna,' was all he said but the effect on Anna was monumental; she froze. She could hear the echoes of people as if they were miles away and swayed. Stefan held her shoulders to steady her.

'I'm sorry I startled you, but I had to see you alone.'

'Anna!' Tim was calling her from the other side of the cave. 'Where are you?'

Stefan lowered his hands from her shoulders and took an

143

envelope out of one of his pockets.

'I wanted to give you something.' He held out the envelope and gave it to her before walking off. 'You'll understand when you see what's inside.'

Anna felt blood pounding in her ears and started shaking.

Tim was walking towards her, looking at her with concern.

'What's the matter? Are you feeling ill?'

When she nodded, he took her arm gently and guided her out of the cave in the opposite direction to Stefan.

Anna was lying on the hotel bed with Tim beside her. Her eyes were closed, but her brain was in overdrive. Stefan must have been stalking her for days. How did he find her? No one knew where she was going. She had shown Max the brochure, but he would never had told Stefan anything. If she told Tim he'd contact the police, then what would happen to Stefan? But if she didn't tell Tim, what would happen to her? Could she make the meeting sound like an accident? Don't be so stupid! Tim would never believe that! The bed moved as Tim sat up.

'We shouldn't have gone down there if you were feeling faint.'

Anna opened her eyes and saw him staring down at her, worried.

'I wasn't feeling faint before we went.' She'd have to tell him. 'One of my clients was on the tour. He told me a couple of weeks ago that he's my brother.'

Tim jumped off the bed in alarm. 'Jesus Christ! Why didn't you tell me a nutter was stalking you? - I'm calling the police!'

Tim reached for his mobile and suddenly Anna was out of the bed, her hand on his arm, stopping him.

'Don't. What proof have we got?' Why was she stopping him?

'Anna – a stalker has followed you from London. That's proof enough.'

'Max is treating him now. I'll talk to Max when we get back. He can decide what to do.'

Tim looked at her, annoyed. 'So Max knows more than me. The guy needs a psychiatrist – not a clinical psychologist.'

'Please Tim. If you contact the police, we'll have to go a police station and I'll be interviewed for hours. Then I'll have to write a statement. Imagine the stress. Let Max deal with it when we return. Please.'

Anna felt her mouth quiver. The shock of seeing Stefan in the cave was too much. She started to sob.

'Hush.' Tim put his arms around her. 'I won't contact them if you don't want me to. Hey - this isn't like you. We've been doing too much. Tomorrow we're resting, not walking. Shhh.' Tim was stroking her hair. She felt herself slowly relax.

Then he was kissing her hair, her face, her lips. His hands moved to her blouse. He started to undo the buttons.

'No,' Anna said, curling up in a ball on the bed.

'Sorry. Try to get some sleep. I'll go down and have a drink at the bar.'

She hadn't even opened the envelope Stefan had given her; she was too disturbed to touch it.

Her eyelids felt suddenly heavy.

She's swimming in the lake, trying to reach the coracle, but the green dress she's wearing is filling with water. She's fighting to get to the coracle. Someone is swimming behind her.

'Anna - wait!' She hears Stefan calling to her.

She tries to swim harder but the dress is pulling her down. Panic whirlpools through her.

Stefan touches her arm. She struggles, trying to push him away. Suddenly her mouth is full of water. She's under the water. She can't breathe.

Her dress billows around her. Stefan's face is near hers. He's reaching out for her. She tries to pushes him away but she can't. He's holding her, trying to drown her. Her head explodes with stars.

Anna shot up in bed, screaming 'Noooooooooooooooooo!'

The bedroom door opened and a shocked Tim looked into her contorted face and groaned.

Anna was sitting squashed against the train window, trying to forget the dream. It had taken Tim a long time to calm her. She was glad they were returning home; she wanted the security of home; her parents; she wanted Stefan to see Max; he would sort out his problems and stop him stalking her.

Tim was sitting beside her, looking at her with a worried face. 'Are you sure you're okay?'

'I'm fine. Don't worry. I overreacted.'

'No, you didn't. He must have been stalking us for days. If Max doesn't get him sectioned when we get back, I'm going to the police. Stress can affect unborn babies.'

Anna felt fear flicker around her body. 'How?'

Tim held her hand. 'Look, you're going to relax and not worry. You're married to a doctor, remember. When we get home you're going on a healthy diet and having a calmer life-style. By next week you'll be feeling so relaxed you'll be comatose most of the time.'

Anna smiled at him. It was a wonderful feeling knowing that Tim was looking after her. 'I'd better go to the loo before we get to Paddington.'

She was not going to be paranoid about Stefan. He was not on the train and he wasn't going to affect her or her unborn child. She wouldn't allow him to, she thought as she walked up the aisle of the swaying train.

There were two men waiting to go to the toilet before her and when she finally managed to get into it, she found the floor running with urine-coloured water and covered with scraps of toilet paper that people had pulled from an over-stuffed roll. She opened her bag to get some tissues and saw Stefan's unopened envelope; her stomach tightened. She hovered over the toilet seat, holding onto the rail against the movement of the train; she wasn't going to contaminate her body by sitting on something so fetid. She flushed the toilet and washed her hands looking around for something to dry them on. Nothing. There were more tissues in her bag, next to the envelope. She breathed deeply and took the envelope out; not realising that what she would find inside would transform her life completely. Inside, was a photograph: a woman and a boy about eleven were standing outside a large white house. The woman was carrying a baby. They both stared unsmilingly at the camera. Anna held the photograph up the light and moaned. The woman looked exactly like her.

Chapter 30
STEFAN

Here is one of the many memories I hold in my heart of Vienna for you, Anna, so you will know where Mother and I walked before you were born. Every day after I finished school and Mother had finished playing the piano we used to walk in our favourite park – the Stadtpark.

We used to penetrate the park's shady pathways and pretend that we weren't walking towards the lake. Then, at the last moment, we'd turn to each other anticipating the pleasure of seeing the Viennese sky reflected in the lake as we turned another bend. And there it was, waiting in all its luminance; waiting for us every day, full of reflections: the sky, the trees, the ducks, the people.

The park has many statues of composers who used to walk there; the golden figure of Strauss plays the violin everlastingly. Mother told me that Strauss played his first concert in the Kursalon; a chandeliered ballroom, at the edge of the park. The Viennese love to dance, Anna. I imagined their shadows dancing to Strauss' music in the Kursalon. Then we'd walk past the colourful flower clock which Mother loved towards the grey eyeless statue of Franz Schubert, endlessly thinking of another line of music for the manuscript on his lap as he stared, sightlessly into the distance. What is he staring at, Mother? I asked her once. He's staring into the future, she answered.

And in the distance, one day, we heard the laughter of copper bracelets and Mother smiled at me. I didn't know why.

There are moments so pure that they crystallize in the brain and remain a buried treasure; the first time I saw you nestled in

Mother's arms was such a moment; a clear bubble of happiness in which everything was perfectly formed and timeless.

I knew at that moment that our lives were joined by a silver thread and wherever you were, I was destined to be.

So now you know the truth. I didn't want to tell you; I didn't want to show you; I wanted you to remember, but you couldn't, so I had to give you the photograph so you could see Renate, our Mother. I know it is going to be traumatic for you and I can't spare you that pain, but it will be as nothing to the pain that I've endured for twenty one years without you.

The laughter of copper bracelets was yours, Anna. You are the future.

Chapter 31
CELIA

Celia and Paul were waiting at Paddington Station; both worried by Tim's phone call. Celia knew now that was why Max had come to see them while Anna and Tim were on holiday.

At least Anna was safe, Celia thought. Max would refer the man to a psychiatrist and they could all sleep peacefully at night. Oh, if only life was that simple; the beautiful tapestry she had woven around them was in danger of being unravelled. She must be positive; for Anna's sake and for Paul's.

She glanced at him. He seemed to have developed a few more lines on his face since hearing about the stalker, but perhaps it was her imagination.

The announcement of a train suddenly boomed in their ears from a nearby Tannoy. 'The train arriving on Platform 2 is the 17.25 from Swansea.'

'I don't know why they have to shout out information as if the whole world had gone suddenly deaf,' Paul grumbled as the train approached the station and slid slowly to a halt.

They'd talked about everything, apart from the stalker since Tim's phone call; both too worried to voice their feelings. 'I wonder what the good news is.'

Tim had told them that Anna had some good news that she wanted to tell them personally. Celia saw Anna and Tim emerge from the train and knew immediately that something was dreadfully wrong by her daughter's body language; she was walking in the compact way she always did when she was very upset; almost as if she was protecting herself by using as few muscles as she could.

'Hello, darling,' Celia said, when Anna was level with her.

Paul leaned over to kiss her, but Anna looked as if she had been embalmed; she was totally unresponsive to either of them.

'She's had a bit of a shock,' Tim said, trying to reassure them.

Celia had a terrible feeling of finality; as if she had been preparing for this moment for twenty one years.

'Let's get her home,' Paul said.

Tim looked at him. 'It's okay. I'll look after her.'

'She'll like the security of her old room, Tim, if she's had a shock.' Celia suddenly realised that they were all talking about Anna as if she wasn't there. Celia glanced at her; well, she wasn't really. She was looking around as if that awful client was watching her. Celia took Anna's arm and guided her out of the station.

'She's a married woman, not a child, Celia,' Tim snapped.

Celia heard the annoyance in his voice as he walked behind her with Paul, but she didn't care. He wasn't taking Anna to any house, but her home. She guided Anna through the seemingly hundreds of passengers who were going in the opposite direction.

'Her mother always knows how to comfort Anna best,' Paul said soothingly.

Celia felt a warm glow spread around her body at his words.

'I *am* here, you know,' Anna suddenly said, as if coming to life.

'Of course you are, darling.' Celia squeezed her arm. 'And Dad and I are going to look after you.'

Celia left Anna lying down in her old bedroom and bustled into the kitchen as if her life depended on it; perhaps it did. She told Paul and Tim to sit down and relax while she made a pot of tea.

Paul looked bemused as he stood indecisively in the middle of the room. He hated confusion and they were surrounded by it at the moment.

'So – here we are,' Celia said, wincing at her banality. Where are we? She asked herself. Not in the same place we were before that man switched their lives onto another track.

Suddenly the sky darkened outside, and the walls of the kitchen seemed to close in upon them. Clouds; gunmetal grey and black, hung outside the windows where the sun had once been. Celia switched the lights on and the clouds partially disappeared.

'What are we going to do?' Paul said, blinking like an owl in the sudden light. He stared at Celia as if her face held the answer.

'I've rung Max. He's going to find out more about the stalker's background so that he can assess him,' Tim said.

'But what can Max do if the stalker won't go to see him?' Celia asked as she poured out the tea with a less than steady hand.

'People can be sectioned under the Mental Health Act against their will, if necessary,' Tim answered.

'What does that mean exactly?' Paul asked him.

'He can be forced to go into a mental hospital.'

'My God, that sounds brutal,' Paul said.

'Not if it protects Anna. And it's only for 72 hours so that he can be assessed and treated.'

'So, after 72 hours he can start stalking her again,' Celia said in alarm. Things like this don't happen to ordinary people she thought.

Paul leaned over and squeezed her hand.

'If the psychiatrists believe he's a danger, he can detained for up to 28 days, Celia. What I'm more concerned about is Anna's state of mind at the moment.' Tim turned to look at them both in turn. 'She hasn't told you, has she?'

Celia and Paul looked at him fearfully.

'I don't think we could stomach any more bad news,' Paul whispered.

'It's not bad. It's good, but - '

'But what? For God's sake tell us, Tim,' Celia's voice was shrill.

Tim looked at her and said simply. 'Anna's pregnant.'

Celia and Paul stared at him as if they didn't know what the word *pregnant* meant. Then Paul suddenly gave a whoop of laughter, jumped up and threw his arms around Tim's surprised body.

'That's wonderful news, Tim. Especially after such a shock. Isn't it, love?' Paul beamed at Celia.

Celia sat in her chair thinking of Anna's career plans; knowing how important they were to her. Far more important than hers had ever been. What would happen to them?

Paul was staring at her, baffled by her lack of response. 'Celia?' He said in a troubled voice.

'Sorry.' She got up and kissed her son-in law. 'Took me by surprise, Tim. Congratulations. Of course, it's wonderful news.'

She studied Tim's expression trying to work out if he was pleased by the news or not; his face revealed nothing and yet he'd told them that he'd like at least two children, six months after being married to Anna.

'How does Anna feel about it?' Celia asked him.

'Very happy ... now. A bit upset at first, you know... about her career. She'd like to ask if you'd help out with looking after the baby.'

It all seemed too much to take in, Celia thought. First a

153

stalker and now a baby. She started to laugh. The men looked at her with concern. Perhaps she was becoming as unhinged as the stalker.

'Are you all right?' Paul's face crinkled with concern.

'I'm fine,' she answered. A baby in the house. Anna's baby. Tears poured down her face. 'I can't believe it, Paul,' she said. He gathered her in his arms and kissed her.

Celia took up a salad on a tray for Anna to eat. She suddenly realised what joy a new baby would bring. How wonderful to have new life in the family again. She tapped on Anna's door and walked in. Anna was curled up in a ball; her favourite position when she was troubled.

'Hello, darling. How are feeling now?' Celia put the tray down on Anna's bedside cabinet and sat down on her bed.

Anna turned sleep-blurred eyes towards her mother. 'What time is it?'

'9 o'clock. You've been asleep for a couple of hours. Tim's told us the news about the baby. It's wonderful, darling. We'll help out when you're working so don't worry about that.'

Anna lay flat on the bed, staring at the ceiling.

'Tim said you must relax and not worry about that strange client of yours. We've all got to think about the baby now. You don't want a lot of stress in your life with a baby coming.'

'What's it like giving birth?' Anna asked abruptly.

Celia's heart thumped. 'Well, it was a long time ago. And memory plays strange tricks, doesn't it? You forget the pain the moment you see your baby in your arms.'

'How long was your labour?' Anna's voice was cold; as if she was talking to someone she hardly knew.

Celia shivered. 'Oh, about six hours, I think.'

Anna stared at her. 'Six hours! I don't want to be in labour for six hours.'

'Well, we don't have any choice, darling. Nature decides for us. But at least you're living with a doctor. Tim will know exactly what to do. When's the baby due?'

Anna turned her head towards the wall. 'In seven months.'

Celia did some quick mental arithmetic. Anna would be sitting her final examinations in seven months. That's why she's unhappy, Celia told herself.

'I'm sure something can be arranged at the University so that you can take your Finals at a later date. Students are always asking me to sort out problems for them.'

'You've always been good at sorting out people's problems, haven't you?' Anna said in a cold voice.

Celia should have found pleasure in Anna's words; proof of her competency, but instead of feeling pleasure, she felt a sort of collapse; as if all the careful structure of their lives was smashing into smithereens.

Chapter 32
ANNA

Anna lay awake for most of the night, thinking about the implications of the photograph. The fact that it wasn't Stefan who had been lying to her, but her parents, made her feel as if she'd been in an appalling car crash, but no one could see her injuries. How could she ever have a normal relationship again with these people? People who had built her life and theirs upon layers of lies? Anna felt exhausted by monumental questions: if I'm not Celia and Paul Baker's daughter, then who am I? Where is my identity? Where is my knowledge of myself?

She pulled herself out of bed. Tim lay beside her; blissfully unaware of the turmoil she was going through. She didn't want to speak about it; didn't know how to; if she voiced her concerns they would then be real and she didn't want them to be real. She padded out of the room into the bathroom next door; a bathroom she had been entering since she was a little girl. She switched on the light, blinking in the sudden glare, and closed the door. Here was her past: here was the white bath in which her parents bathed her; here was the white sink where she'd taken a loose tooth out of her mouth when she was six and showed it proudly to her mother. Anna leaned against the door and placed her hands over her mouth. *Her mother.*

Two days ago, she knew exactly who her mother was; today, she had no idea. Her whole world had been built upon a fabrication. How could they do that? How could they lie to her for so many years? The people she'd called parents had nothing to do with her at all. Didn't they think of the psychological damage they could do to her?

All the small telling details of her past suddenly surfaced: she realised that they had always been evasive about her early life. Her mother always changed the subject subtly. Anna remembered the day the primary school teacher had asked everyone to bring in baby photos so that they could have an end of term game: 'Guess the Baby'. When she asked her parents for a photo, they gave her a photo of a tiny baby with wisps of downy hair, wearing a long white robe, lying in an old fashioned cot. She'd looked at it for a long time, not recognising that the baby had anything to do with her at all; she told them she couldn't take it in to school; it didn't look like her; no one would guess it was her. 'But that's part of the fun, isn't it, darling?' Her mother said. When she'd demanded another one, her mother told her that her other baby photographs had been accidently thrown away when they moved house. She'd always believed what they told her. Isn't that what parents were supposed to do? Tell the truth?

She looked at the stranger in the bathroom mirror. If she touched her face, would she see the movement reflected in the mirror? She walked out of the bathroom; too frightened to try and tiptoed down the stairs, past the old ticking clock she'd listened to every night since she was a child. It was 6 a.m. Everyone was asleep, except her.

She went into the dining room and opened her lap-top. After waiting a couple of seconds, she logged onto the Family Records site and clicked onto the adoption section. She ordered a birth certificate for Anna Renate Peterson.

There was hardly any traffic on the roads this early in the morning; she didn't care that it was so early; she had to know the truth.

It was the sort of anonymous street full of cramped terraced houses that could be found all over London, Anna thought, as she drove along it, looking for number 54. There it was. Although the whole street was lined with cars, there was a space outside number 54. That must be indicative of something, Anna thought, but she was too tired to know what. She stopped the car outside the house and sat, breathing deeply. She was terrified by what she might discover inside the house.

As she walked towards the front door, it opened magically before she reached it. Stefan stood there, smiling at her radiantly.

'At last,' he said as he moved back to let her in.

Chapter 33
MAX

'That's great, Sandy. Thanks a lot. I appreciate all your help.'

'You owe me a dinner,' she said, smiling at him. 'I'll be back in an hour.' She walked out of the office and left him sitting at a small desk.

Max should have gone through the proper channels to find out about Stefan's background, but that would have involved hours of paperwork and he needed to know now. He knew that Stefan's past would be traumatic; he carried all the emotional baggage of a person who had been taken into care at some point in his life. He'd asked Sandy, who was a social worker and one of his oldest women friends, if she could possibly find his file. He hadn't expected her to ring every social service office for him, but she had. Of course, Max knew why she'd spent so much time and energy in helping him; she wanted to be far more than a friend to him. Life was always so complicated. Max sighed heavily. He liked Sandy. They were often in meetings together and usually in agreement over the best course of action to minimize clients' problems, but he'd never wanted any more from their relationship than friendship; especially after meeting Anna.

He opened Stefan's file, feeling apprehensive; he'd never felt apprehensive opening other clients' files, but no other client was convinced he was the lost-long brother of the woman he loved. The file stated that Stefan Michel Patterson was born in Vienna on 17th April, 1977. Max looked at the calendar on the desk. His birthday was in seven days. His parents were called Renate and James Patterson. His mother was a pianist; his father a banker. Soon Max was immersed in the life of a young boy who lived in

Vienna until he was eleven. Why on earth was he taken into care with his background? Max was intrigued. His English father had taken a job in London when Stefan was eleven. Going to live in a large, anonymous city after living in a small, intimate city like Vienna must have been traumatic. Poor kid. Of course, with an English father he must have been able to speak English, but what a tremendous cultural shock for a boy starting secondary school; especially one as sensitive as Stefan. His sister was born on 26th September 1988 in London. Max's heart thumped hard. Anna's birthday was on 26th September. Just a coincidence, he told himself. He knew from long clinical experience that many of his clients believed the most bizarre things based purely on coincidence.

He carried on reading, utterly absorbed in discovering what had happened to put him into care. He found the answer on the third page of the file; his father had fallen from a cliff in a tragic accident and his mother had become too ill to look after the children. At fourteen and three years old the children were taken into care in South Wales. Why South Wales? Max wondered. They lived in London. What a terrible trajectory: from living in Vienna with a wealthy father and talented mother to being taken into care. Stefan was never adopted. Max could imagine how difficult he would have been at that age with that history. His sister had been adopted at three and a half, but there was nothing in the file about her whereabouts. And what happened to their mother? Why hadn't she looked after her children?

Max closed the file feeling desperately sorry for Stefan and desperately worried about Anna.

Sandy suddenly popped her head around the door. 'Helpful or not?'

'Yes, up to a point.' Max rubbed his eyes. They felt full of grit.

He might have to succumb to reading glasses soon.

'You look tired.'

'I am, but I must get as much information about this client as I can get. He's been stalking one of my trainees.'

Sandy's face immediately registered sympathy; that's why she was so good at her job, Max thought.

'Poor trainee. Might put her off clinical psychology for ever.'

'Not this trainee,' Max said, a little too firmly.

'Oh,' Sandy said, staring at him. 'Why not?'

Max certainly didn't want Sandy becoming interested in his relationship with Anna. 'I've got to assess whether this client poses a real danger or not. He's comes from a very traumatic background. Put into care at 14 with his much younger sister. She was adopted, he wasn't. He's been looking for her for twenty one years. Thinks she's the trainee.'

'Oh dear,' Sandy said. 'That sounds very obsessive.'

'The file mentioned that his father died in an accident in 1991. I'm trying to think of a way I could find out exactly what happened to him. Any ideas?'

Sandy pursed her lips as she thought about the problem. She was a rounded, good-looking woman, Max thought, the problem was – the chemistry wasn't there; he just didn't fancy her.

'You could log on line to newspaper archives and search for 1991. There might be an article about the accident in one of the newspapers, especially if the father was important.'

'He was a banker,' Max said.

'I bet they reported it then, especially if the accident was gruesome. You know what newspapers are like.'

Max winced, remembering all too clearly what they were like. They had reported Sadie's death in every gory detail. How she had smashed through the windscreen after Max had slammed on the brakes and skidded into a tree. How her body was a mangled bloody mess. Max had been cleared of dangerous driving by two factors: heavy rain the night of the accident and a brilliant defence attorney.

Sandy suddenly bit her lip. 'Sorry, Max. I didn't think.'

Max looked at her. 'It's okay. Long time ago. But I don't like on-line searches. They seem to take forever and you can't see the information properly.'

Sandy smiled at him. 'Didn't think you were a computer dinosaur.'

'I'm not,' Max said, thinking he must be. 'The last time I searched online I was still searching hours later and I still didn't find anything very useful.'

"What about the British Library?' She said. 'They've got a branch in Barnet where there are thousands of archived newspapers on microfiche. And the staff will help if you need it.'

She obviously thinks I'm a lost cause, Max thought as he stood up. 'Thanks, Sandy. You've been a guiding light.'

He saw her face fall as he moved towards the door. 'I'll call you next week. Promise.'

As he walked out, he thought about whether he should go to the police or not. He was reluctant to take that route after reading Stefan's file; the man needed help, not interrogation; he desperately hoped that the Newspaper Library would have some information that would allow him to help Stefan overcome his obsession with Anna.

Chapter 34
STEFAN

You came, Anna! You came!

The joy I felt when I saw you standing outside my house was the same intense joy I experienced when we were children, lying on the floor, listening to mother playing one of Mozart's beautiful sonatas. You used to lie on the carpet sometimes and stare up at the ceiling as she played, and your hands moved in time with the music. Or you would jump up and dance around the room as if nothing else existed, except music. And it didn't. Not when Mother was playing. I used to watch my little firefly dance and I knew that I was looking into the heart of the divine.

I felt your pain, Anna, when you looked at the photographs and saw your past; the past that was denied to you by those people who called themselves your parents. Now you can see why I knew you were my sister from the moment I saw you; you have become our mother; the same beauty; the same graceful gestures; the same fiery hair that changes with the light. It was dark copper on the dark morning you came to see me.

I will draw you later when I have slept. I have not slept for a long time; I hate these small slices of death, but I need rest now; I need strength to plan for our future.

Chapter 35
CELIA

'Celia! Paul!'

The sound slowly filtered in through Celia's sleep. Then a sharp knock on the door. She turned to see Paul lying dormant beside her.

'I need to speak with you.' Tim's voice sounded urgent outside their bedroom door.

Celia got out of bed, her legs feeling like lead as she shuffled towards the door. 'Just a minute,' she called, putting on her thick white dressing gown. It was only 7 am. There was a tight band across her chest restricting her breathing as she opened the door. Tim was standing on the landing looking dishevelled; the dark stubble prominent on his jaw.

'Anna's gone,' he stated baldly.

'What do you mean? Gone?' Celia couldn't think clearly. *Gone* sounded permanent.

'She's not in the house. I'm worried about her. She's been acting very strange, lately.'

'Well, she's being stalked. It would make anyone act strange, wouldn't it?' Celia was annoyed by Tim's comment. She had a sudden awful thought. What if the stalker was waiting outside for her? She put her hand on her heart as it gave a sudden leap.

'What's the matter?' Paul asked, sitting up.

'Anna's just gone out for a walk. Nothing to worry about. Go back to sleep,' Celia said.

Paul looked at the clock. 'A walk at this time of the morning?' He jerked out of bed as if he was a marionette. 'The stalker could be out there,' he whispered, his eyes full of fear.

'I'm sure he's still in Wales, Paul. We left very suddenly. He wouldn't have a clue where we'd gone.'

Paul relaxed a little. 'Thank God for that.' He looked at Tim, puzzled. 'Why the early call, then?'

Celia suddenly noticed that Tim was holding something in his hands.

'You'd better look at the photograph she left in the bedroom, Celia. I don't understand it.'

He gave Celia the photo that Anna had looked at in the train toilet; the one that had shattered her identity.

The men were stupefied by a low moan escaping from Celia's lips as she looked at the photo; at a woman who looked exactly like Anna.

Paul was suddenly beside her. 'My God - what is it?'

She gave him the photograph; his face turned a ghastly shade of grey. The photo fluttered to the floor.

Tim stared at them both in astonishment. 'What is it? Whose baby is Anna holding? Who's the boy? I don't understand.'

Celia fought back the dizziness that was threatening to overwhelm her; she would cope; she *would* cope. She had coped with trauma in the past. She would cope with this.

'Wait for us downstairs while we get dressed, Tim. If you put the kettle on I'll make us some breakfast and we'll wait for Anna to return. We have a lot to explain.'

Celia closed the door and Paul slumped onto the bed.

'Oh, my God. What must she think of us, Celia? Will she ever forgive us?'

He raised his grief-stricken face towards her as she stumbled into their bathroom and leaned against the door, heavy as stone.

Chapter 36
ANNA

It was nearly 12 'o clock when Anna returned to her parents' house. She entered the kitchen by the back door and saw Celia cutting up red peppers. It seemed unbelievable: the woman she thought was her mother was preparing food; such an incredibly ordinary thing to do on such an extraordinary day.

Celia turned around and stared at her. Anna saw a middle-aged woman with short brown hair who was supposed to be her mother; now she had no idea who she was.

'Anna,' Celia said in a strange undulating voice. 'We've been waiting for you. Your father and Tim are in the dark room.'

Anna sat in a chair; the same chair she had been sitting on for over twenty years and didn't know who these two strangers in the familiar kitchen were. It was a terrifying feeling.

'Why didn't you tell me?' Anna said in a whisper. 'How could you not tell me?'

She saw Celia shudder before speaking. 'You had nightmares for six months after you came to us. You didn't sleep through the night until you were four. Your father and I took turns to calm you down.'

'Why didn't you tell me?' Anna repeated.

'We decided it would be better if you forgot the past completely and just remember your life with us.'

'How old was I when you adopted me?'

Anna heard muffled sounds from another room as she waited for an answer to a question she would have thought impossible two days ago.

'Three and a half,' Celia whispered.

Anna stared at her incredulously. 'Three and a half! No wonder you only had one baby photo. Is that what they gave you in the orphanage?'

Celia gave a small nod.

'Did they tell you what happened to my real parents?'

Celia winced at her words. 'We were told they had died.'

'Are you telling the truth for once?' Anna asked her coldly.

Celia shrank back. 'That's what they told us, Anna. Honestly.'

'Honestly?' Anna snapped. 'That's ironic, coming from a woman who's been lying to me for twenty one years.'

Tears flooded Celia's eyes. 'Please, don't, Anna.'

'I have a brother called Stefan. Did you know that?'

Celia shook her head, unable to look at the bitterness on Anna's face.

'How did my parents die?'

'In a car accident,' Celia said almost inaudibly. 'We thought you might have been with them and could remember something. That's why we wanted you to forget.' Celia took a deep breath before continuing. 'I had three miscarriages before we adopted you. You can't imagine the depth of pain I endured. You were ours from the moment we saw you. It would be impossible for us to love you any more, Anna. We didn't tell you because we wanted to spare you any more pain.'

'But you didn't,' Anna said. 'You gave me more.'

Celia's face contorted with pain. 'Can you ever forgive us?'

'No,' Anna said. 'I can't.' Then she got up and walked out.

***

'What are you doing?' Tim looked at her in amazement.

Anna was tearing down her posters of *The Grateful Dead, Genesis, Guns N' Roses, U2*; she was tearing up numerous drawings of stick people; watching the disintegration of the

167

words MUMMY DADDY ANNA underneath them; drawings that represented a past she didn't have.

'Anna! Stop!' Calm down!'

But Anna didn't want to stop. She kept tearing down the evidence of an invented life; wanting to obliterate it until there was nothing left. Then she started on the wall-paper.

Tim held her wrists tight. 'If you continue like this, you'll damage the baby.'

At last Anna stopped. 'Are you worried about me or is it your perfect child you're worried about?'

Tim stared at her. 'You're not the Anna I know any more.'

'I'm not the Anna I know any more, either.' She sat on her old bed. 'You have no idea what I feel like, do you?'

'No,' Tim said. 'Not really. I know you must be angry that they didn't tell you.'

'No, I'm not angry. I feel disintegrated. As if the core of me has been removed. Can you imagine that?'

He shook his head and there was silence between them for a long time.

'They don't know anything about your birth parents, apparently.'

'So they've been talking to you, then,' Anna said in a tight voice.

'You've been out for four hours. Of course we talked.' There was more silence between them. Tim shuffled his feet. 'I can't believe you're related to that nutter who stalked us.'

Anna looked up at him, shocked. 'That nutter! He's my brother! What would you do if you found your sister and she wouldn't believe you were her brother. You'd stalk her!'

'No, I wouldn't, Anna. Normal people don't stalk anyone, whoever they are. That's what *abnormal* people do.'

'Well, perhaps my family *are* abnormal! Bang goes your blue-print for a perfect child!' Anna was shouting. Something she never did. Something Tim hated in a woman. 'So how to you feel about having a child with a bad family history?'

Tim stared at her as if he hadn't seen her before. 'Stop shouting. Stop talking like that.'

'Why? Isn't it true? Aren't you worried that I don't have a perfect genetic background? There could be mongoloids or degenerates or insanity in my family! What about that, hey! You even erased a lowly clerk! Will you do that to our child too?' Now Anna was screaming; as if her words could lessen her pain.

Tim stormed out of the room, leaving Anna staring at the ruins of her life all over the floor.

Chapter 37
MAX

Max was striding up the grey, traffic-infested street, watching ribbons of rubbish spin in a sudden gust of wind. He was glad to be out of the clinic, at least for a few hours; away from the demands of his clients. He crossed the road and saw a sign saying Colindale Avenue. At least he was in the right road. An elderly lady, wheeling a shopping basket, gave him perfect directions to the Newspaper Library and within minutes he was striding into the building and asking for help from the receptionist.

'You have to order the microfiche by dates, Sir. Which date in 1991 are you looking for?' The receptionist asked him.

When he told her he didn't know, she told him he'd need to work forward from 1st January, 1991. Max groaned – how could he possibly work through every day in 1991 in two hours. He explained that his research was urgent and he had to return to work soon. When he wrote his name on a registration form, there was a flicker of recognition on the receptionist's face.

'I've read your articles on Personality Disorders in one of our psychology magazines, Dr. Paris,' she said. 'Perhaps I could help you if you give me some more information.'

Within minutes, Max had a mass of microfiche beside him and an assistant. As they scrolled through September, 1991, Max tried to ignore a past which stopped him from discovering the truth about Anna's background: *F.W. de Klerk was sworn in as the State President of apartheid South Africa; Hurricane Hugo caused $7 billion worth of damage in South Carolina; an IRA bomb exploded at the Royal Marine School of Music in Deal, Kent.* Then suddenly, he saw the headline. Turning to his assistant, he told her he'd found what he was looking for. The young woman walked off as Max read:

BANKER DIES IN ACCIDENT ON WELSH COAST.

Two days ago the body of wealthy 54 year old banker John Peterson was found lying at the bottom of a cliff on the Gower Coast in South Wales. Mr. Peterson, who had been a senior executive at Merryl Lynch in London for three years, was staying with his family at their holiday home on the cliffs near Rhossilli Bay when the accident occurred. His wife Renate Peterson, (38) subsequently collapsed and was treated in hospital with severe shock. The couple have a 14 year son, Stefan and a 3 year old daughter, Anna. The son was too distraught to speak to the police after the accident. Both children have been taken into care until the mother recovers as no family members can be found to look after them. A police spokesman said that Mr. Peterson's death is being treated as a tragic accident.

Max took the microfiche out of the machine and sat thinking. So Stefan really did have a sister called Anna. If he had been looking for her for twenty one years, it was inevitable he was going to be obsessive. But his Anna couldn't be Stefan's sister. She wasn't adopted.

Max leaned back and stretched, knowing that he had to go to see Stefan; to help him overcome his father's death; to overcome the loss of his sister. But could he help him overcome the trauma of his mother leaving him in care for years and years?

Chapter 38
ANNA

Anna was staring out of her bedroom window when a shaft of sunlight pierced her. What she felt was grief; grief for a life that had been amputated. She had found a brother, but lost her past.

She knew, from the way Tim looked at her, that her words had rung true; he was worried about genetics. She hadn't told him that she had seen her early life in Stefan's house and it had looked wonderful. Photograph after photograph lined his study; of their mother and Stefan in Vienna, before she was born; of the three of them in Wales after she was born. She realised now that the memory of that time must have been locked deep within her; the memory of the sea; the cliffs; the white house. And the incredible painting he'd showed her; the painting of the two of them walking hand in hand along the Welsh shore with the three swans flying above them. It was the most beautiful painting she had ever seen and he had painted it for her.

She shook her head as she thought about what Stefan had told her about their parents. They hadn't been killed in a car accident. The woman she used to call mother was still lying to her. Stefan told her about their father's death; had told her that their mother was still alive!

The front door buzzed. She looked at the clock. It was exactly 2 p.m. The time when Max said he would come. Reliable Max. Anna went downstairs to open the door.

Max smiled at her, his face concerned. 'You look pale.'

She closed the door and they went into the sitting room.

'I'm sorry, Max. I know you're busy, but I need to talk to

someone. I feel as if I'm going mad.' She looked at him quickly. 'I know that's a very unscientific thing to say, but it's how I feel at the moment. Everything seems to be spinning out of …'

She started shaking; feeling as feeble as a rag doll and suddenly, Max was holding her tight; at that moment, she never wanted him to release her. Gradually she told him about her adoption; about her feelings of betrayal; about Stefan being her brother.

Max guided her towards the settee and they sat down side by side. He stared at her with amazement. 'Did Celia and Paul know about Stefan?'

'They said they didn't, but how can I believe them?' Anna answered in a flat voice. She rubbed her hand across her tear-streaked face.

'Are you sure that Stefan *is* your brother?' Max asked her gently. 'It could be a coincidence, Anna. You might just have been adopted at the same time as his sister.'

Anna looked at him, incredulously. 'And have the same name as Stefan's sister? I've got my birth certificate, Max. I'm Anna Renate Paterson and I was born on 26th September.

Max look at her sceptically. 'You've got the birth certificate of a child with the same Christian name as you, Anna. That doesn't prove Stefan's your brother.'

'Two three year old girls called Anna were adopted in the same year?' Anna said scathingly. What's the likelihood of that? Anyway, I've got something that will prove it, even to a sceptic like you.'

She brought out the photograph of the three of them standing outside the white house. She had studied the photo for a long time.

Max frowned as he looked at it. 'Whose baby are you

holding?'

'I'm not. That's my mother and the baby is me, Max. I look exactly like my real mother. That's why Stefan knew me the moment he saw me.'

Max was speechless for a few moments. 'Then why didn't he simply show you the photograph when he first saw you?'

'He wanted me to remember our time together. He can remember his early past vividly. He wanted me to remember our happiness.' Anna's mouth trembled. 'But I couldn't.'

'No more crying,' Max said. 'I can't understand why your parents -' He stopped when he saw her face. 'Your adopted parents didn't tell you about the adoption.'

'Apparently to protect me. I'd laugh if I could. They obviously know nothing about the psychological damage lies like that can cause.'

'No, they obviously don't. I'm so sorry, Anna. How do you feel now?'

'Cauterized,' she said.

'Have you told them how you feel?'

'No, I don't want to see them.'

'That's natural, but it will pass.'

Anna stared at him. How could the pain she was feeling be natural? How could anything based on lies be natural? How could Max possibly understand how she was feeling?

'You're experiencing feelings of great loss,' Max said. Not just the loss of your identity, but the loss of your birth parents.'

'And a brother,' Anna said. 'I've lost twenty one years with him, Max.'

'Yes and the loss will have been far greater for him. He knew about you.'

Anna put the palms of her hands in her eyes, trying to block out pain.

'Your parents -' Max stopped when Anna moved her hands to glare at him. '-were wrong not to have told you, but they're still the same people who brought you up, Anna. Who've loved and cared for you for twenty one years. The fact that they're not your biological parents doesn't alter that love.'

Anna watched a stream of sunlight dapple the wall opposite her and couldn't speak. She sensed Max staring at her, waiting for her response, but she couldn't forgive the people who'd taken away her identity.

'So when are you going to hand in your thesis?' Max spoke into the silence.

'What?' She turned to him in shock, not believing what he'd just said. 'You're talking about my thesis after what I've just told you!'

Max kept staring at her, his head a little on one side. 'I want it on my desk in three weeks.'

'Three weeks! I can't possibly -'

'Yes, you can. Start working and stop living in the past.'

Anna clenched her hands between her legs. She had never wanted to hit someone so much in her life.

Chapter 39
STEFAN

We had a party for you on your 3rd birthday. Just the three of us and Greta, the housekeeper, who was like a second mother to us.

Mother and Greta spent the morning making a picnic to take to the beach and I helped you draw. You used to love drawing then. Mother said you'd be an artist when you grew up and I'd be a pianist. But life never turns out the way people expect it to. I could never follow her brilliance at music, but I knew about colour instinctively. When I discovered tonality, I soared with musical paintings.

That morning I showed you how to mix colours together. You were enchanted to find that you could make green by mixing yellow and blue together. 'Magic, Stefan,' you said to me. And I said, 'yes, it's magic.' I showed you magic all morning.

After lunch, Mother and Greta carried the picnic hamper down the cliffs and I held your hand tightly in mine. I would never let you fall. There was no wind that day and magically, we had the beach all to ourselves. I'd brought fishing nets so I could show you all the creatures that lived in the rock pools. I took you to the pools near the sea as they had far many more creatures in them than the pools higher up the beach. These pools held many of the creatures that became stranded by the outgoing tide. You put your dimpled hands into the pool fearlessly and pulled out some serrated wrack-seaweed. You were always less fearful than me, even at three. When a crab bit your finger, you didn't cry, but looked at me so I could explain why he had done it. We found so many crabs that day; you were fascinated by their claws. We watched them walking sideways along the sand. 'Why they walk funny, Stefan?' You asked me. 'Because of the way their legs bend,' I told you. 'They squeeze into small holes so that fish with sharp teeth can't find them.' You wanted to know about the whole world and I wanted to tell you everything. That day we collected starfish and the most amazing coloured sea anemones. I told you that the anemone could only eat when its entire body was covered by water and you kept getting small buckets of water from other pools to pour over them in case the anemone was hungry. 'Look, Stefan,' you said, your nose almost on top of some green and strawberry form-anemones. 'They dancing.' And we laughed as the green and red tentacles swayed with each movement of water. Then mother called us to have our picnic and I washed the sand off your hands and you forgot the creatures in the pond in the delight of a birthday picnic.

We sat on a thick Viennese rug that Mother always used and had the most wonderful food in the world: roast hazelnut and muscovado torte with vanilla ice-cream and a Viennese nut meringue. We laughed as the sand got whipped into the meringue as we ate. Then we sang to you:

> *"Zum Geburtstag viel Glück!*
> *Zum Geburtstag viel Glück!*
> *Zum Geburtstag liebe Anna!*
> *Zum Geburtstag viel Glück!"*

And the sea-gulls screeched over our heads in a raucous accompaniment.

The happiness of that day will move in my mind until the day I die.

Chapter 40
CELIA

Celia woke up each morning expecting something awful to happen, yet wondering how it was possible to experience anything more awful than she already had. Paul hardly spoke to her now; they both grieved silently and it was slowly diminishing them. The loneliness was horrific.

And yet, she conducted lectures on *The Tudors*, amazed by her ability to smile at students and colleagues as if the bottom of her world hadn't dropped away, leaving her standing precariously over an abyss. She held herself together stiffly; clenching and unclenching her hands, hoping somehow that tension would hold her together.

She sat in the kitchen staring at Anna's glossy face, smiling at her from four walls; surrounding her with absence.

A sudden shout from the dark room.

'Celia! Come here!'

She hadn't heard any animation in Paul's voice since he had seen the photograph of baby Anna with her birth mother.

She hurried out of the room.

Paul was peering at a large photograph on his drying cabinet as Celia entered the twilight world of the dark room. The room was cluttered with development tanks, trays, measuring jugs, rails for hanging photos and an array of chemicals that reminded Celia of her chemistry lessons at school. She hardly ever went into the room as she hated the smell of the chemicals.

'Can I put the light on?' She asked. She knew from her past mistakes how important it was to ask this question.

'Yes, look at this.'

She switched the light on and Paul blinked at her.

Celia's body tightened as she saw an enlargement of a photo she never wanted to see again: Anna with her birth mother.

'Why are you showing me this again?' She said in a hurt voice.

'Look at the pixels!' Paul shouted with excitement.

'I have no idea what a pixel is,' Celia said.

'It's the smallest piece of information in an image. The more pixels in the photo, the better the image, but -'

Celia stared at him, confused by his excitement.

'The pixels on the woman's face don't match the other pixels in the photo. Look at the shadows under the nose and eyes. They should fall in the same direction. Can you see - they don't.' He looked like a small boy with a new bike.

Celia frowned at the photo; not understanding the significance of what he was saying.

'Now look closely around Anna's face,' Paul continued. 'Can you see minute tags around the edges? ' He turned to Celia triumphantly as if he'd discovered something momentous.

Paul might as well have been speaking another language. 'What are you talking about?' Celia was becoming worried. He was acting very oddly.

'The photo is a fake! – that's what I'm talking about, Celia.'

Celia stared at him for a long time, trying to understand what he meant. A fake? How could the photo be a fake? It was there, in front of her in all its awful beauty.

'Someone has superimposed Anna's face onto the woman's.'

Celia frowned as she stared at the photo. It didn't make any sense. 'Why would anyone do that?'

'To make us believe that the woman in the photo is Anna's mother. She must be Anna's mother because Anna looks exactly

179

like her. Now do you understand?'

Celia knew she wasn't a stupid woman but she still couldn't make sense of what Paul was saying.

'Anna's client is trying to convince her that she's related to him,' Paul said.

Celia stared at her husband in amazement. 'But why pretend Anna is his sister if she isn't?'

Paul frowned at her. 'That's what I can't work out.'

Celia's face crumpled in sudden trepidation. 'Oh my God,' she said.

Chapter 41
MAX

It was the first time that Max had ever visited a client's house, but the feeling that he must help Stefan overcome his traumatic past was too strong to resist. Or was it the fact that he wanted to help Anna discover the truth about her background? He didn't know the answer.

He got out of his Peugeot and knocked on the front door, noticing the peeling blue paint on the door and window sills. A large spider's web hung across the door; minute globes of water, suspended from its threads. He had pictured Stefan living in an artistic apartment in Canary Wharf, not in an anonymous suburb like Dollis Hill. He knocked again and a net curtain from a neighbouring house twitched. Max suddenly registered the significance of the spider's web. No one had been in or out of the house for days.

He walked over to the neighbour's house, trying to block out a feeling of foreboding. This door opened at the first knock. A large middle-aged woman stood looking at him.

'He's not been there for days,' she said before Max had opened his mouth. 'You a friend?' Her eyes travelled up and down his body and Max wished he was wearing a coat; her look was incredibly intrusive.

'I wonder if you could tell me when you last saw Mr. Peterson. It's rather important.' He smiled at the woman, trying to gain her confidence.

'You don't look like the filth. What you want him for?' She folded her arms across her vast bosom.

'It's personal,' Max answered, keeping his voice neutral. God, he'd hate a neighbour like her.

'He's bleedin' odd, he is. Goes out at night - walking. I mean, what sort of bloke goes out every night just to walk? It ain't natural.'

The urge to get in his car and drive off was so strong that Max had to put his car keys back in his pocket.

'It would be very helpful if you could tell me the last time you saw him?'

'Why?' She asked bluntly.

Max was glad that he'd had so much training; glad that he had learned how to control his emotions.

'His sister is ill. She wants to see him.'

He knew that he'd have to give this woman a good reason to tell him anything.

'What's wrong with her?'

Max suddenly remembered a proverb his father had told him when he had caught him lying as a boy. *You may go forward in the world with lies, but you can never go back.*

'Actually, it's a little personal.'

The woman's face lit up. 'Oh, women's problems, is it? I've had loads of them in my life. The things I could tell you.'

'Was it two days ago?' He interrupted her quickly.

'What?'

'Did you see Mr. Peterson two days ago?'

The woman squeezed her eyes together in an effort to recall anything as remote as two days ago. 'Don't think so. I had to go to see the doctor yesterday.'

Max arranged his interested, but detached expression as the woman told him in graphic detail about her visit to the doctor. He wondered why he was listening, but intuition told him that she might eventually tell him something useful.

'Oh, dear,' Max said. 'That does sound terrible, but Mr. Peterson's sister really needs to see him soon, so anything you could tell me about him would be very helpful. The areas he likes to walk in. The car he drives... that sort of thing.'

'Don't know where he walks. I'm not following a man at night, am I? Don't know what he's up to! He's got a white Vauxhall. Don't ask me the registration 'cos I don't know it, but he parks it over there and it's gone. That's all I can tell you.' She paused, looking suddenly suspicious. 'Hang on - why don't his sister know where he is?'

Max was just going to invent a reason when the woman suddenly banged the door in his face. Obviously he had the wrong sort of face to get information out of women on doorsteps.

He got back in his car and phoned Anna's number. There was no reply. He leaned back against the car seat, feeling suddenly drained; if only he could replay the moment when he was holding Anna over and over again like a video.

Ten minutes later he was driving through West Hampstead and saw a familiar figure standing on the doorstep of a large Victorian house. It took him a few seconds to register who it was. Tim. Must be a house call, he thought. Max drove towards some traffic lights near the house. An attractive dark-haired woman was standing near Tim, shouting and waving her arms in the air. Max stopped his car as the lights changed to red. Tim looked angry too; his face a mottled red. So he has problems with women on doorsteps too, Max smiled wryly; then thought about what would happen if he shouted at his clients. Very bad psychology to argue with patients, Max reasoned as Tim stormed off into the distance. He pressed the accelerator as the lights changed and then it hit him: Tim's practice was on the other side of London.

Chapter 42
ANNA

Anna had told Tim that she needed time alone to think about the future; she was staying in a vacant utilitarian room at the University until she had sorted out what she should do. She stared around and thought how depressing the furniture was: one battered desk, one narrow single bed, one retro desk-lamp; one white plastic paper bin. The room summed up the way she felt about life at the moment. But it was a good place to work on her thesis, and work she had for the last three days. She was going to show Max what she was capable of. In spite of his callousness, she was going to finish her thesis well before the deadline.

She sat down at the desk and looked at her last chapter on *The Hidden Existence of Emotional Abuse*. After reading an extensive American study, Anna was stunned to discover that only 29% of emotionally abused people saw themselves as abused, as opposed to the 67% of physically abused people who did. So that's why there was such a lack of documentation about psychological abuse, Anna thought; people weren't actually aware they were being abused!

She looked up from her lap-top, suddenly realising that Stefan was part of the 71% of people who were unaware. She knew, from the way he never spoke about their father, that he must have psychologically abused him and perhaps their mother for years. Poor Stefan. And then, to suffer further trauma by being taken into care and never being adopted into a loving family! It was amazing that he was as balanced as he was. She didn't think she would have been. With a sudden rush of insight, she realised she'd been the lucky one. She pushed the thought away; it was too raw.

She got up from the desk and did some deep breathing; she needed more oxygen and so did her baby. The baby. In seven and a half months she would be a mother. She placed her hands over her flat stomach and smiled. He was growing inside her in the darkness. It was utterly incredible. She was going to be a mother. Her career would have to go on hold; she would finish her thesis and placement with Max; then ask the University if she could complete her final year at a later date. She would look after the baby. He was hers. Her baby had now taken on a deeper significance; he was a link to her genetic background like Stefan. She hadn't decided what to do about Tim. His lack of empathy felt like a rejection; not only of her, but their baby. But she would cope. That's what her years of training had taught her: to live in the present and not allow negative thoughts to become automatic.

She'd decided that the only people she could rely on in the future were Stefan and herself. She didn't care what Tim thought about her family history; she had found a brother who loved her; who had been looking for her for twenty one years. Of course, he'd become obsessive in the process. Wouldn't anyone in the same circumstances? She hadn't told Stefan she was pregnant yet; she wasn't sure why. Perhaps she wanted time to get to know him better first.

He was taking her to see their mother this afternoon. Anna closed her lap-top, not sure whether to be terrified or ecstatic. How was it possible to see Renate and think of her as her mother? She'd always thought she had the best mother in the world when she was growing up. It was difficult to overcome that feeling. She stopped herself from thinking about the past and brushed her hair; she'd washed it that morning and it crackled with static vitality at each stroke. What would they talk about? What do you talk about to a mother you've never met? Anna felt full of nervous tension. Music. Renate loved music. Anna groaned. She knew nothing about classical music. Renate had been a concert pianist and her daughter knew nothing. But it wasn't her fault! If she'd been allowed to live with her real mother!

She stopped the negative thoughts.

Stefan had warned her about Renate's illness. She'd had a nervous breakdown after their father had died and she'd never fully recovered. But she was recovering now, Stefan said. Now that her daughter was coming to see her; now she had been returned to them.

The lift outside her room shuddered open. Anna waited for the secret signal. Four knocks. A pause. Then four more. Anna opened the door and there was Stefan, smiling at her as if she was the most beautiful woman in the world, and at the moment, she felt she was.

Chapter 43
MAX

Max showed his client Lawrence out and sighed deeply. He had been seeing him for a month to overcome his deep-seated jealousy towards his attractive wife; every man who looked at her became his rival. It had been an exhausting session because it had forced him to remember his own past. He'd been trying to make Lawrence accept that uncertainty was part of any relationship and accepting uncertainty didn't mean that his wife was being unfaithful. Lawrence told him he'd been trying to suppress his feelings of jealousy so Max explained that paradoxically, suppressing jealousy actually increased it. It had taken him months to learn about this paradox when Sadie had had business meetings in the evening. Jealousy had nearly destroyed Max. Lawrence needed to focus on his own personal goals, independently of his wife so that he could develop his own interests. Jealousy was a desperate dependency on another human being, Max told him. Lawrence thought about this; then suddenly said he was going to take up golf.

Max sat back in his chair and smiled wryly. Golf. Golf could produce a desperate dependency on golf and golfing clubs. He yawned as he looked at mountain of paper-work piled up on his desk; all accumulated since he'd been trying to help Stefan and Anna. He'd rung Anna again after seeing Tim with that woman whose body language was so revealing. Their affair was obviously running into rocks. Was that why Tim suddenly wanted to go on holiday? To get away from his mistress? He desperately wanted to protect Anna from any knowledge of the affair. It was unbelievable: why would Tim want another woman when he had

Anna?

The phone rang. Marie told him that Mr. and Mrs. Baker were waiting in reception for him. They'd asked if they could see him at the clinic. They obviously wanted to know how to cope with Anna's rejection of them.

'Give me five minutes, Marie. Then bring them up.'

Max poured himself a large cup of coffee. He needed the caffeine to stay alert. Good God – was there no end to work? He was shaken by a sudden thought: was work *his* desperate dependency? Well, if it was, it had succeeded; he no longer felt the emptiness he had after Sadie's accident. He sipped his coffee, thinking about the night that was etched on his brain. The windscreen wipers were redundant against the torrential rain. Max was driving and Sadie was screaming at him; *I'm sick to death of your paranoia. What I do or who I'm with has nothing to do with you!* He'd been driving them home after having dinner with friends and she'd spent the night talking to his best friend – her lover, ignoring him completely. He was shouting back at her, monumentally angry. *You're my wife! Of course it's got something to do with me! You're a fucking bitch!* She was undoing her safety belt, screaming at him to stop when a suicidal shape stepped off the pavement in front of the car. He swerved violently and Sadie had smashed right through the windscreen. She died before reaching hospital. He'd hit the bottle for months, riven with guilt. Until the night he'd found the courage to bag up all her possessions and discovered the letters. A great pile of them; letters from her lovers, all concealed behind boxes of shoes, at the back of her wardrobe. He'd felt as if someone had knifed him; she'd lied to him all through their marriage. But miraculously, overnight, all the crippling guilt he'd suffered disappeared and his heavy drinking stopped. *That's why I'm a good psychologist,* he thought. *I know what despair feels like.*

A knock of the door. Marie stood there with the Bakers; Paul was carrying a large folder in a heavily veined hand.

'Thanks, Marie. Come in and take a seat. Would you like a coffee?'

They shook their heads as they sat down; both looking as if all the vitality in their lives had been drained away. And, of course, it had, Max thought.

'We'd like you to look at this for us, Max and tell us what it means.'

Paul opened the file, took out Stefan's photograph and placed it on Max's desk, facing him.

Max frowned. He'd already seen the photo. 'I'm sorry, I don't understand.'

'Paul says the photo's a fake,' Celia said.

'It *is* a fake. I'm not just saying it's a fake.' Paul looked briefly annoyed as his knowledge of photography was called into question.

He launched into a technical discussion of how Stefan had doctored it, but Max was only half-listening. Dear God, if Stefan had gone to such lengths to prove to himself and Anna that he was her brother, he was far more mentally disturbed than he'd previously thought. Max drew his hand over his face, trying to disguise his alarm, but when he moved it, Celia Baker was staring at him intently; he knew she was as worried as he was.

'How dangerous is he, Max?' She asked him.

Could he lie convincingly to a woman who'd been lying to her daughter for twenty one years?

'He's suffered severe trauma in the past which he's suppressed; he's highly intelligent and manipulative, but he

189

believes Anna is his sister so he'll protect her.'

'But how can he believe that when he's superimposed Anna's face onto his mother's?' Celia said, frowning at him.

'Even if he has mental problems, if he's as intelligent as you say, there must be a part of him that knows he's invented their relationship,' Paul argued.

They both looked at Max, bemused and frightened by the situation.

'I don't think that's true. I've watched the tapes of Anna's sessions with him. He genuinely believes Anna is his sister and he's her protector.'

'So we don't have to worry about her safety?' Celia asked.

'We don't know where she is, you see,' Paul added.

'Tim will know, surely.'

Celia and Paul glanced at each other. 'We heard Anna shouting at him in her bedroom. Anna never shouts. That's what so disturbing. She's worried there might be genetic problems in her family background.'

'But there won't be, will there?' Paul suddenly looked delighted. 'She's not related to that man.'

'So the baby will be all right,' Celia said, looking at Max for reassurance.

Max went cold. 'What baby?'

'Oh,' Celia put her hand over her mouth in embarrassment. 'We thought she'd told you. She's pregnant.'

Max felt as if someone had punched him very hard in the stomach. Anna was having a baby. And it wasn't his.

He stood up and stared out of the window at the dying rays of the sun.

'You shouldn't have said anything about the baby, Celia.' Paul whispered to Celia. 'She'll still finish her thesis, Max. You know how determined Anna is.'

Max controlled the turbulence inside him and sat down again. 'Let's concentrate on the most likely places Anna could be.'

Celia and Paul glanced at each other. 'We don't know. You'll have to ask Tim. We don't know all their friends,' Celia said.

Tim was the last person Max wanted to speak with, but he knew he'd have to. 'You know you should have told Anna she was adopted when she was a child,' Max told them. 'It's incredibly difficult for an adult to cope with the shock of identity loss.'

Celia looked stunned. 'But she hasn't lost her identity. She's still our daughter. We're still the parents who nurtured her through every crisis.'

'Celia gave up her job at the University to look after Anna. She took her to school every day and collected her every afternoon,' Paul said.

'We read her stories every night and took her swimming every weekend,' Celia continued. 'We took her to plays whenever we could.'

'And the art classes, Celia. Don't forget those,' Paul added.

It went on and on. Max let them talk about the things they'd done for Anna because he knew about their awful weight of guilt; they were trying to justify their guilt to him. At last, they ran out of steam and sat in silence staring at him.

'Will she ever forgive us?' Celia asked in a small voice. 'If she doesn't, I don't know how we'll continue living.'

They sat opposite him, looking at him with such pain and vulnerability that Max wanted to hug them.

'You know that Anna has tremendous empathy with people. That's why she'll make a great psychologist one day, but now she's grieving for her lost past and you must allow her time to grieve. She must have time to find her new identity. All you can do, as loving parents, is to wait for that to happen.' Max paused before adding. 'It might take a long time.'

'How long?' Paul said, fearfully.

'I can't give you a time span, Paul. Each person grieves in different ways, but Anna is strong. When she's ready, she'll come to you. You just have to wait and be ready to receive her.'

Paul and Celia looked at each other; then held each other's hands.

Max had never felt so envious of love in his entire life.

'Could we have a look at Anna's office before we go, please?' Celia asked him.

After they'd gone, Max thought about Anna. He knew where she'd go. To the person who gave her some feeling of identity. Stefan. Max's hands felt clammy. He'd told Celia he wasn't dangerous, but he'd only watched on him on video; he'd never treated him. How did he know he wasn't dangerous?

He got up from his desk and started pacing. What was the name of the orphanage in his file? He couldn't remember; he hadn't thought the information important enough to store. He groaned, thinking what he'd have to do - ring up Sandy. She'd think he was ringing to invite her out to dinner. He picked up the phone and dialled her number. It was picked up immediately. Good God, she wasn't waiting for his call, was she?

'Max!'

He could hear the warmth in her voice. It made it far worse, but it had to be done.

'Sandy. I'm hoping you can help me again. I'm very worried about the trainee I told you about. The one who's being stalked. She's gone missing. I've got some new information about the stalker. It's not good.' He listened to the disappointment in her voice as she realised he wasn't asking her out. 'Could you give me the name and phone number of the orphanage Stefan Peterson was taken to? It might give me a lead.'

'Have you contacted the police?' She asked him.

Max's heart thumped. The police! 'No, not yet. I've only just found out she's missing.'

He waited while Sandy searched the file, visualising Anna lying in a ditch with her throat cut.

Sandy came on the line again: 'It's St. Mary's. 02920 734671.' There was a slight pause; then she said. 'You're never going ask me out for dinner, are you? I'd prefer the truth, Max.'

'You're far too good for me, Sandy. Find someone who can make you happy.'

He put the phone down, hoping that in a couple of months she'd thank him for the advice.

It was 6 o'clock. Would anyone be manning the phone in St. Mary's at this time of evening? Max lived in hope and dialled the number. The phone rang repeatedly; Max imagined cold, white corridors; small rooms where children were crying and the staff were over-worked. After the tenth ring, a young, exhausted voice said. 'St. Mary's.'

Max said he was searching for the records of two children called Stefan and Anna Peterson who were taken to the home in September 1991. It was a matter of life and death because one of them was missing and in terrible danger. Could she give him any information that would help the police find them? Max was amazed that the lies sprung so easily to his lips, but Anna might be in danger so any lie was worth it. Max held his breath as the girl said she would try to find the file.

The line was silent for so long that Max wondered if the girl had gone home and left him dangling on a line. Then suddenly, she was back, telling him that the little girl had died and the boy had disappeared from the home. Renate Peterson had been put into a mental institution after her husband's death.

The little girl had died! Max forced his brain to work logically and asked calmly if she could tell him the name of the Institute Renate Peterson was placed in. Sorry, she said, she didn't have that information. Max put the phone down. If Stefan's sister had died in the orphanage, who then was Anna?

And what had searching for a dead sister for twenty one years done to Stefan's mind?

Alarm bells rang repeatedly in Max's head.

Chapter 44
ANNA

Anna woke up as Stefan's tyres crunched over the long gravel path towards *Bryn Dail*; a Regency cream-coloured mansion with two Corinthian pillars on either side of a large door way.

It had been a long journey and Anna had been asleep for over an hour. Stefan hadn't told her that their mother lived in Wales.

She stared at the grandeur of the house in awe. Was this really where her mother lived? In a mansion?

Stefan stopped the Vauxhall near the entrance and turned to smile at Anna.

'Here we are. Don't be frightened of her, Anna. She lives in a musical world.'

'Why should I be frightened of her? You said she was getting better.' Anna immediately felt frightened. Why should he use that word?

Stefan put his hand gently over hers. 'I'm sure she will be after she's seen you. But...' He stopped and stared out at the sunshine filtering through the beech trees lining the drive. 'She's not always herself. Sometimes she forgets things. Sometimes she invents things, but she's still our mother.'

Anna moved her hand from under Stefan's. Why hadn't he told her this on the drive to *Bryn Dail*. Why tell her just before she was about to see Renate? She had no time to absorb the information; to make sense of it. She tightened her body to protect herself as she got out of the car.

Stefan put a protective arm around her shoulder as they walked up to the large Regency entrance. There were four steps leading up to the impressive double fronted door which was open.

'If she's playing Mozart, she'll be in a good mood. If she's really happy, she'll play one of his Sonatas. But Stravinsky's bad news. She only plays him if she's feeling stressed about something.'

How would she know what a Mozart Sonata sounded like? She knew nothing about music. She started her deep breathing exercises to try to slow her racing heart-rate.

Stefan turned to smile at her. 'There's nothing to be nervous about, Anna. I'm with you. You've got nothing to be nervous about ever again.'

They walked up the steps towards the inner door which had four large glass panels in it. *Nothing to be nervous about!* Anna felt sick. Was this nausea from pregnancy or fear? She held onto Stefan's arm as he pulled a large bell that hung at the side of the door. It echoed repeatedly inside the large building. Almost immediately, a slim, middle-aged woman was striding down the hallway towards them, wearing the same no-nonsense expression that Anna remembered on her Headmistress' face.

'That's Miss Haigh. She manages *Bryn Dail.*'

Miss Haigh opened the door and stared at Anna. 'Is this the cousin you told me about, Mr. Peterson?'

Anna looked at Stefan sharply. Why had he told the woman she was his cousin? Stefan glanced at her apologetically.

'Yes,' Stefan said, smiling at the woman. She didn't smile back.

Anna held out her hand and the woman gave it the briefest of shakes.

'How's mother today, Miss Haigh?' Stefan asked her as they walked into a large, white, clinical-smelling hall.

'We've had Mozart today. Bad day yesterday. Stravinsky all

day. Some of the residents are complaining, Mr. Peterson.'

'Oh dear,' Stefan said apologetically. 'But she plays Stravinsky well.'

'That's not the point. It's too loud. You need to tell her.'

Miss Haigh strode off, her sensible lace-up shoes echoing on the stone floor, and disappearing through a door.

'Why did you say I was your cousin?' Anna asked.

'I don't want her nosing into our family affairs, that's why. She's always asking me questions. I don't always give her the right answers.'

Anna was feeling dizzy; she'd been hyper-ventilating. She sat down a small hard chair lined against one of the walls. Stefan immediately crouched beside her, holding her hand.

'I told you, there's nothing to be frightened of, Anna. I'm here.'

'I feel a little faint. Give me a moment.'

Stefan stared at her with concern. 'I'll get you some water.' He ran down the corridor, towards the door through which Miss Haigh had disappeared.

Anna wished she knew something important about Mozart; all she could remember that he was a child prodigy. The sort of child Tim would like, she suddenly thought. The door opened. Stefan was carrying a glass of water towards her.

Her mother was in this house and she was terrified to meet her.

She sipped the water, trying to delay the moment.

'Are you ready?' Stefan stood up, waiting for her.

She placed the glass on the stone floor. It tinged into the silence. There was no sound of music.

Stefan guided her up the corridor, through three doors, until they reached another smaller corridor. Anna could hear the faint sounds of music in the distance. It was beautiful. Was that her mother playing? Anna turned to Stefan and he smiled at her.

'I told you how wonderfully she plays. This is a very good day, Anna. She's playing Mozart's Sonata in A major. It's one of her favourite pieces.'

Anna relaxed as she listened to the exquisite sounds coming from the room at the end of the corridor. How could anyone object to someone playing music that well? An immense feeling of pride suddenly surged through her. She was related to a woman who could make music sound magical. She beamed at Stefan.

'I didn't know. I didn't know,' Anna was crying.

'Shhh, Liebling. You mustn't cry. This is one of the happiest days of my life. The three of us are united.'

Stefan opened the door and the music flowed through Anna. Renate was sitting near the window, haloed in light from a small fringed lamp on the piano; her greying auburn hair piled on top of her head. Her back was perfectly straight. But it was her hands that mesmerized Anna; long slender fingers, so like Stefan's, sped with agile grace over the keys; she seemed melded to music. Stefan and Anna waited for the last cadence to die.

She closed the piano and turned. Anna's heart rate soared as her birth mother looked at them.

'What do you want?' Her voice was completely at odds with the beauty of the music; it was hoarse; as if words were not a medium she liked to use.

'It's Stefan, mother. I've brought Anna to see you.'

'I know who you are. I said what do you want?'

Anna wanted to run away and hide. This wasn't the greeting a child should have after twenty one years. Anna wanted her mother to run across the room and hug her; to tell her how much she loved her; how much she'd missed her. Her body tightened like a bow.

Stefan was holding her hand, guiding her towards a woman who didn't want to meet her, then suddenly Renate studied Anna and her face transformed. She reminded Anna of an older version of a woman in a Pre-Raphaelite painting; she looked beautiful.

'Come into the light,' Renate said.

Anna moved into the light and Renate gasped. 'Du hast ihr haar. Du hast ihr haar.' She turned to Stefan. 'Endlich hast du ihr gefunden.'

'What did she say?' Anna said.

'I said Stefan has found you – at last.' Renate opened her arms wide and said. 'Komm zu mir, meine Kind.'

Anna didn't need a translation. She stepped into her mother's embrace.

Chapter 45
CELIA

'I can't believe I let you talk me into this,' Paul said as he drove towards Dollis Hill.'

'We're only going to talk to him, Paul. I'm not going to attack him with an umbrella, am I?'

'I don't know. Have you brought an umbrella with you?' Paul said cryptically.

'I'm simply going to ask him where Anna is. She might even be with him. It's worth a visit, isn't it?'

'What's the number again?'

'54.'

Paul turned into Stefan's street, looking for numbers, but they couldn't see any in the dark.

'Just park the car and we'll walk,' Celia said.

There was a small space at the end of the street; Paul spent a long time trying to fit their large car into a small space with Celia sighing beside him.

'I'm doing my best!' Paul snapped.

They got out and walked along the street which was lit by windows with partially drawn curtains and the occasional street light. Celia was carrying a backpack.

'What on earth do you need that for?' Paul frowned at her, annoyed with her impatience at his parking performance.

'I wouldn't like to live here,' Celia said. 'It's depressing.'

'Well, fortunately, no one is asking you to,' Paul said.

'It's there,' Celia said, pointing to a dark house on the opposite side of the street.

They crossed over the road and stood outside Stefan's house.

Celia knocked on the door and waited. Stefan Peterson controlled all their future happiness, she thought.

'He's not here,' Paul said. 'Unless he likes living in the dark.'

Celia knocked again. There was still no response. 'Let's go around the back.'

Paul looked at her. 'Why? He's not here.'

'How do you know?' Celia said. 'Sometimes we don't answer the door at night. There must be a passage at the back of these houses. Come on.'

Celia strode up the street and suddenly saw a small alleyway between the houses; Paul plodded behind her. She disappeared down the alley before Paul could stop her.

The alley ran across the back of the terraced houses. Celia switched on a torch and counted the houses to Stefan's.

'You've brought a torch!' Paul said in amazement as he stumbled after her.

'Of course I brought a torch. How else are we going to see in a dark alleyway?'

'I didn't know we were going to be in a dark alleyway until this moment. You're not going to do something we're both going to regret, are you?' He looked at her. 'Celia?'

But Celia wasn't listening; she was trying to open the gate at the back of Stefan's house with a wire hook she had in her backpack; it wouldn't move.

'For God's sake, Celia – stop it. Let's go home,' Paul pleaded.

Celia suddenly thumped the gate and it opened. 'There we are,' she said walking into Stefan's small back garden.

'This is trespassing! We can't go into people's back gardens at night!' Paul hissed at her.

'Well, we are,' she said pragmatically. 'Hold the torch, will you?' They were standing outside Stefan's back door which had

201

four small-paned windows. Paul wouldn't like what she was going to do, but that wasn't going to stop her. She took out some gloves from her backpack and put them on. She gave another pair to Paul.

'What are you doing?' His eyes looked wild with fear in the torchlight.

'Put them on,' Celia said.

'What are you going to do?' Paul whispered in alarm.

Celia put a thick piece of cloth over the window pane near the door handle and thumped it hard. The glass smashed into small pieces and fell into the house.

Paul groaned loudly. 'Oh my God, we'll be arrested for breaking and entering! You'll lose your job!'

Celia turned to him briefly before putting her hand through the broken pane and turning the key. 'And we could lose our daughter. Come on.'

Celia opened the door and walked into the dark house. She was determined to discover everything she could about the man who thought he was her daughter's brother.

She took the torch off Paul and flashed it around the room. They were standing in a kitchen. 'There's bound to be something here that will help us.'

Paul stood in the open doorway, looking at her with a horrified expression.

'We can't break into someone's house and walk around it, Celia! For God's sake – think what you're doing?'

Celia angrily flashed the torch in Paul's direction. 'I could be saving our daughter's life. Are you going to help me or not?'

Paul blinked in the torchlight. 'What do you want me to do?' he whispered.

'Follow me!' Celia said, marching off into another room.

They walked through small, revealing flashes of light: a small narrow corridor; a small anonymous bedroom and then they came to a long room full of reflected light. In the middle of the room was a large shape. Celia flashed the torch on it and they both gasped; a large painting leaning on an easel; it was stunning in its colour and subject matter. Two bare-foot children walked along a vivid shore line and above them three swans flew as if guiding them.

'Good God. That's incredible,' Paul said.

Celia flashed the torch around the walls, she wanted to find the light switch; she wanted to see the painting clearly. She closed the curtains, found the light switch and suddenly the room was blazing with reflections; they saw themselves endlessly reflected in the mirrors on four walls; it was a highly disturbing vision.

'Good God!' Paul said. Why would anyone want so many mirrors?'

'To see themselves endlessly reflected, I suppose,' Celia answered.

'But why?' Paul asked.

'I don't know, but I'm sure Max will.' She looked at the painting again. 'Or perhaps it's the children he wants to see reflected again and again.'

'This isn't helping us find Anna,' Paul said desperately.

'There'll be something. We have to keep searching.' Celia snapped the light off and they walked out.

They discovered a small door in the hall and opened it. Celia flashed the torch inside, found a light switch and switched it on. A steep staircase descended. Celia shuddered; visions from the film *Psycho* suddenly shot in her head; Norman Bates' mother's desiccated remains lay in a room at the bottom of the stairs.

'You go first, Paul,' she said to her alarmed husband.

The room at the bottom of the stairs was totally unexpected; it was furnished with stylish Art Nouveau furniture and lit by three yellow and blue Tiffany lamps on occasional tables which made the room glow with muted light.

'Why is the best room in the basement?' Celia wondered.

'I don't think my heart will cope with this stress, Celia,' Paul whispered. 'What if he comes back and finds us?'

'I'll think of something,' Celia answered. Then she saw the photographs. 'Look!'

There were hundreds of small photographs arranged artistically around the room, depicting the lives of three people: Anna with two children in various stages of growing up. Celia shone her torch around to see the photos better in the muted lighting. Each photo scanned the lives of the children; a baby boy gradually grew into a tall, sensitive-looking thirteen year old with copper hair; a chubby baby girl transformed into a beautiful fairy-like child with a halo of copper hair; in almost every photo of the children they were either holding hands or he was holding her and the little girl had her arms around her brother's neck. There were photos on the beach; at the fun-fair; in Art Galleries and Museums. The three of them looked happy until Celia and Paul looked at the last wall; here the mother and children stared at the camera without smiling.

What could have happened to transform three happy people into the unsmiling ones in the last photos, Celia thought? If only Max was here to help them.

'Celia - we must get out of the house.' Paul was holding his heart.

Celia glanced at him; he looked grey.

'All right,' she said, but try to memorize everything we've seen.'

They heard a noise from upstairs and Paul closed his eyes. Celia held his arm as the letter box suddenly rattled and something dropped onto the floor.

'Dear God,' Paul groaned.

'It's just some junk mail.'

'This is the most stupid thing I've ever been forced to do,' Paul said, climbing the stairs.

At that moment, Celia saw a brown leather trunk, half hidden behind some cushions; she rushed over and opened the heavy lid; lying in front of her was a heap of diaries. She picked one up and opened it.

I saw her again today with Max Paris. He has far too much influence over her. It must be stopped. I haven't thought of a way yet.

Celia took out her mobile and dialled a number. It went immediately to voice mail. 'Max,' she said. It's Celia Baker. Ring me as soon as you can please. It's urgent. There's something you and the police should see.'

Chapter 46
MAX

Max was sitting in Tim's house, listening to Tim's complaints about his work load. He'd turned his mobile off because he thought Tim was worried about Anna and wanted some help. He was drinking heavily. Max watched him, knocking back the whisky and wondered what Anna had found attractive about him. He'd been there for hours and Tim had only mentioned Anna's disappearance once – she'd rung him to say she was safe, but she was unhappy about his obsession with genetics. 'I'm not obsessed, Max, I've given her everything I can. She's only a student, but look at the house she lives in? The life-style she has? How many other students live like this? I certainly didn't,' he whinged. 'I had debts up to my arm-pits as a Med Student.'

Jesus – what self-pity! Max thought. Why the hell did Anna stay with him? Perhaps it was just sex. Sex caused so many problems. If only an elixir could be invented that conjured up the person who'd bring someone happiness and little pain. He thought about the multitude of problems his clients created for themselves every day because they'd married a partner who gave them much pain and little happiness. Max almost laughed; even if people had the elixir – they'd still opt for sex! He sighed, thinking he couldn't take much more of Tim's whinging. He'd listened to problems all day.

'Your new partner must lighten your work-load, surely?' Max cut through Tim's monologue.

Tim stopped speaking abruptly and knocked back another whiskey.

'Have you got work tomorrow?' Max asked him.

Tim shook his head and stared at the floor. 'I've got a problem, Max.'

I know, Max thought. Your wife is distraught about losing her identity; she's pregnant and she might be with a highly disturbed man.

'I've been having an affair. I've ended it now, of course and I didn't know Anna was pregnant.' He looked at Max as if this lack of knowledge justified his affair.

'Does Anna know?'

'Good God, no. Not good for her to find out in her condition.'

'It's not good for anyone to find out, whatever their condition,' Max said. He had a sudden, alarming urge to slam his fist into Tim's self-centred face. He concentrated on Anna to calm himself. How could he help her best?

'So what's the problem if you've ended it, Tim?' Max spoke evenly.

'She doesn't want it to end. That's the problem and she's my new partner in the practice. Jesus, what a shit-hole, I'm in.'

'You've been having an affair with your new partner?' Max said, in astonishment. 'You've got the unbelievable nerve to ask me here - not to talk about your pregnant wife who's missing and might be with a potentially dangerous man – but your own self-inflicted problems about which I couldn't care a fuck!' Max shouted, jumping up from his chair, shaking with anger. 'You're the most self-centred bastard I've ever met! You're a fucking doctor – have you no self-knowledge at all?'

And with that, Max stormed out of the house, slamming the front door, thinking, if I see that bastard again, I'll kill him.

He sat in the car outside Tim's house waiting for his heart-rate to slow down. He hadn't felt this much anger since the night of Sadie's accident. He was angry with himself. So much negative energy in anger. Within five minutes, he was calm again. He switched on his mobile and heard the message from Celia. Jesus Christ – what had she found? He rang her number. She answered immediately.

'Max, I know it's late, but could you come round? We found Stefan Peterson's diaries. They're very disturbing.'

Chapter 47
CELIA

Celia and Paul were exhausted. Celia had called the police, although Paul hadn't wanted her to. A young police officer, about Anna's age had sat in their kitchen for an hour, taking their statement. Celia wondered whether she'd go to prison. If she did, she'd lose a job she loved. But before she could confess to breaking into Stefan's house, Paul had said it had been all his idea and he'd forced her to go with him.

Dan, the young officer had looked at him, startled. Celia knew what he was thinking: how could this mild-mannered man force anyone to do anything.

'You'll understand when you have children of your own,' Paul told him. 'Anna is our only child. You do anything if you think your child is in danger.'

He smiled at Celia and in that moment, she loved Paul more than she had ever done before. She got up and kissed him. Dan was embarrassed, but soon, after Celia had showed a real interest in his life, he was telling them about his hopes for promotion; his fiancée; his parents who were worried about him being attacked.

By the time Max had arrived, Celia knew that Dan was worried about what would happen to Paul if he reported the break-in, but also worried about what would happen to him, if he didn't. Celia was immensely relieved to hear Max's ring on the door-bell. She walked into the hallway, closing the kitchen door; she didn't want Dan to hear what she was going to say.

She was surprised by the exhaustion on Max's face when she opened the door.

'I'm sorry, Max, but I had to call you. We tried calling Tim, but he's not answering his mobile. Paul and I broke into Stefan Peterson's house tonight.'

The exhaustion on Max's face was instantly replaced by incredulity. 'You did what?'

Celia put a finger over her mouth and pointed in the direction of the kitchen. 'There's a policeman in the kitchen. Paul told him it was his idea.'

'And it was yours. Like mother, like daughter.' Max smiled at her.

Celia smiled back at him. 'What a lovely thing to say.' Her smile suddenly disappeared. 'Oh, Max. How are we going to find her?' Celia's mouth trembled in exactly the same way as Anna's did. Max touched her shoulder.

'We'll find her, Celia. Now give me some of your coffee. I need to stay awake.'

Max sat in the kitchen, drinking coffee and persuading the police officer that nothing would be served by Paul's admission; it would be much better for his future promotion to concentrate on finding Anna; far more kudos, than a mere break-in.

'But I'll have to report the break in,' Dan said, 'and I'm sorry, but Mr. Baker will have to go the station for questioning.'

Paul closed his eyes; suddenly, he looked very old and ill.

Celia knew she must tell the truth; she had brought this on a kind and loving man; a man who was prepared to take the blame for something he didn't even approve of. Her heart was thumping, she felt sick, but she was going to do it. Max was staring at her.

'Actually,' Celia swallowed hard. 'It wasn't my -'

'What about this?' Max said to Dan. 'You had an anonymous phone call about a break in. Nothing's been stolen so your

210

superiors are going to be far more interested in Anna Nash than in a broken piece of glass; especially when they find the fake photographs and diaries. In fact, who's to say that Stefan Peterson didn't break in himself because he forgot his key?'

Dan looked at him for some time, then suddenly smiled; obviously delighted with this idea.

'Concentrate on Anna, Dan, and tell your boss that I'll give the police all the help I can.' He gave Dan his business card. 'We'd all be grateful if you could make sure that they realise that this isn't just a missing person case. This guy has been stalking Anna for months and he's unbalanced.'

Celia and Paul stared at him in alarm. 'Then we should do something tonight, Max,' Celia said. 'We can't just sit here.'

'Stefan thinks that Anna's his sister, Celia. He's there to protect, not harm her.'

'So, she's not in any immediate danger, then?' Paul asked, wanting reassurance.

'No,' Max said. 'But she might be if something triggers a flash-back to the trauma of his sister's death.'

Celia and Paul stared at him, their faces drained of colour. 'His sister's dead?' Celia said. 'Then how-'

'It's too traumatic for him to remember so he's pushed the memory deep into a part of his brain that he doesn't want to access.'

'What will happen if he does remember?' Dan asked, glancing apologetically at Celia and Paul.

'I don't know, that's why you must get your superiors to realise how urgent this case is.'

'Case?' Celia said in a small voice. 'Anna's a case?'

Dan left, assuring them that he'd ask his boss if he could get a search warrant for the house in the morning. They wouldn't do anything this late at night.

'I've got to get some sleep,' Max said. 'I'll go to see the police in the morning and get them galvanized. Try to get some sleep too, if you can. I'll phone in the morning.'

Celia walked him to the front door and gave him a small package, knowing that she would now be classed as a thief.

'I took one of Stefan Peterson's diaries. I know I shouldn't have, but I thought it might help you, and the police will never know, will they?' she whispered, worried that Max might think less of her by her action.

But Max simply took the package off her and put it in his coat pocket and said 'I'll read it tonight.'

'Do you know where Tim is? We can't understand why he didn't tell us that Anna had gone away immediately.'

'I think…Tim's too busy to notice at the moment,' Max said in a neutral voice.

'You don't like him, do you?' Celia asked, knowing that Max was hiding something.

'No,' he answered. 'I don't.'

Celia took a deep breath, terrified that his answer might be the wrong one.

'She will be all right, won't she, Max?' She stared up at his exhausted face.

'Yes,' he said quietly. 'I'll find her.'

Chapter 48
MAX

Max could hardly keep his eyes open as he read Stefan's diary; he'd been dealing with problems for over twelve hours, but he knew the diary would reveal more about Stefan's mind and he needed that information.

In the summer when I was thirteen, I rode on my bike all along the wild beauty of the Gower; drinking in the magical limestone caves and cliffs and ruined castles. I rode along ragged paths steeped with secrets, until I reached Pwlldu Head. Here I soaked up the stories in the long, yellow bays, the white cliffs and the wrinkled sand which lay like buried ribs below me. I sat in the wind and thought of the Bach Têgs - the Welsh fairies. I wanted to tell you the story of the Bach Têgs, Anna, but you were too young then. You will be ready soon.

What's he mean 'ready?' Ready for what? Max thought.

'Once upon a time, a young man went to see the fairies dancing in the moonlight on the cliffs and fell in love with the prettiest. Each moonlit night he returned to the fairy ring to watch her dance.

Until one night he could endure it no longer, he caught her and carried her back to his cottage and tied her to a chair. Only releasing her each night so that she could dance for him in the firelight. Each night as the fairy danced she became thinner and thinner, pining for her old life. Soon the man could scarcely see her at all.

213

"What can I do to make you better?" He said in a whisper, frightened that ordinary speech might blow her away.

"Release me."

"But then you will never dance for me again."

"Release me on the cliffs and I will dance for you every moonlit night. Release me."

Even as she spoke the man could see her fading in the firelight and knew he would have to free her. He picked her up and put her in his deep dark pocket and walked towards the cliffs, tears spilling over his shirt. He only lived to see her dance. Gently he took her from his pocket and placed her inside the fairy ring. But the fairy had been in a mortal's house and had lost her magic. The man sobbed as she faded into the moonlight until there was nothing left of her at all.'

Nothing left at all? He couldn't mean… Max's eyes were closing; he was too tired to analyse it. He fell into a deep sleep with the Bach Têgs resting on his chest.

Chapter 49
ANNA

Anna was lying in bed, wide awake, running the meeting with her mother over and over again in her head. She had an intelligent, talented mother! A mother who hadn't wanted to put her children into care; she'd been forced to because of her illness. Anna could understand the depth of her trauma after her husband's accident. Renate had told her, she had seen him fall off a cliff to his death. *Would I ever recover if someone I loved suffered a similar fate?* The poor woman had been living in Institutes for twenty one years. What Anna couldn't understand was why she was still there. Some of Max's clients were more unbalanced than Renate and they were working in the City and no one seemed to notice. She spent the night thinking about the future. Perhaps the authorities would view her case differently now she had a son and daughter who could look after her; especially as one of them was almost a Certified Clinical Psychologist.

A thin band of light suddenly appeared at the bottom of the thin curtains in her small bedroom. Dawn already and she hadn't slept. What did it matter? She could sleep later, after she'd seen her mother again. She and Stefan were staying overnight at a Guest House near *Bryn Dail*. We can't travel all that way just for one visit, Stefan had said. At first she'd been annoyed; thinking of all the work she needed to do on her thesis. Now she was glad that she was only four miles away from where her mother was sleeping.

Today, she was going to tell her she was going to be a grandmother! Anna stared up at the awful artexed ceiling and joy spread through her body like a wave.

The Guest House was nothing like the beautiful hotel on the Gower Coast that Anna and Tim had stayed at, but it didn't matter and she could tell by the radiance on Stefan's face that it certainly didn't matter to him. They were having breakfast together in a narrow dingy dining room with windows so small that the sun had given up trying to find a way in. The low-wattage lights only increased the gloom.

Neither of them was eating much; both too excited by the future.

'I can't believe it, Anna.' Stefan's face was ecstatic. We're having breakfast together as we used to when you were a little girl. The only difference is that now you're a beautiful woman and the surroundings aren't as beautiful.'

They looked at the garish yellow plastic table mats on the table and suddenly laughed.

'I've got something to tell you, Stefan,' Anna said.

Stefan's face immediately lost its radiance.

'It's not bad – it's good. You're going to be an Uncle,' Anna smiled at the puzzlement on his face as he assimilated the information.

'An Uncle? So… you must be pregnant!'

Suddenly he was on his feet. Kneeling beside Anna, hugging her. 'Oh, Anna,' he said.

The owner of the Guest House came in at that moment and frowned. 'I hope you both had a good sleep,' he said in a tight voice.

'Wonderful,' they said together.

'Are you… relatives then? You look similar.'

Stefan beamed at him. 'Anna's my sister. My beautiful sister.'

The owner stared at them curiously, but they ignored him.

Anna had never seen so much pride on anyone's face before.

The trauma about her adoption was fading fast.

Half an hour later they were walking through the hall-way of *Bryn Dail*; this time Anna wasn't nervous; just elated. It wasn't until they got into the corridor near Renate's room, that Anna heard strange discordant sounds.

Stefan stopped walking. 'She's playing Stravinsky. He held Anna's shoulders. 'Remember what I told you, Anna. Sometimes, she's not herself. Sometimes she forgets things. Sometimes she invents things, but she's still our mother.'

They walked forward, but now Anna was frightened by Stefan's words.

Sunlight flooded over them as they opened the door; momentarily blinding Anna; she only heard discordant sounds crashing on the piano – sounds that paralysed her.

'Mutti, wir sind gekommen, Dich zu sehen! Please stop playing like that. Bitte!' Stefan shouted over the noise.

But Renate kept playing louder and louder until Anna put her hands over her ears, trying to block out the awful sounds.

Suddenly Stefan grabbed his mother's hands and whispered in her ear and gradually she relaxed.

He turned to Anna. 'Close the piano, will you?'

Anna crept over and closed the piano, worried of Renate's reaction. But she seemed oblivious to both of them. She got up and stared out of the long window at the beech trees.

'Explain them to me,' she said to Stefan. 'What is their meaning?'

Anna looked at Stefan. How could you explain a tree?

'A tree is a symbol of grace and magic. It gives shelter when we're cold or hot; berries to eat; flowers to nourish our spirit –

Renate interrupted him angrily. 'Yes, yes, yes - and fire to cook with and timber to build with… I know all this, but what do they mean? That's the question I asked you.'

'Trees mean life,' Stefan answered quietly.

Renate sighed deeply. 'Life? Is that all? I am so weary of life. Leave me now.'

Stefan looked heart-broken. 'But we've only just come.'

Renate frowned at him as if she'd only just seen him, then turned to Anna and said. 'She can stay. You go.'

Stefan turned to Anna. 'I'll wait for you outside,' he whispered and went to kiss Renate, but she pushed him away.

He walked dejectedly out of the room and Anna felt such pity for him. She wondered at this strange mother of hers; wondered how she could create so much pain in such a little time.

Renate sat on the piano stool and studied her. Anna wanted to run and hide; feeling like a small child again.

'Thoughts expressed by music are more precise than words can ever be. Listen.'

Renate opened the piano and Anna tightened, thinking of the awful sounds she was going to play, but the music she played now was magical; Anna could see people in a forest dancing, incredibly happy. She closed her eyes and let the beautiful sounds wash over her.

Renate stopped playing. 'Haydn,' she said as if that explained everything.

'It's beautiful,' Anna answered.

''You see, what I just said about words being more vague than music? What is beauty? Is it the same for you as it is for me? I do not think so.'

Then Renate was playing again; Anna erased from her mind.

Anna listened to music that sounded like people bubbling with laughter, then the angry cascade of an argument, then suddenly, the music lightened and Anna was in a land full of moon-light. She saw these pictures in her head and wanted to dance.

Renate stopped playing. 'Chopin - such a deceptively simple, complex man.'

There was a long silence; Anna was afraid to break it, knowing her words would be too vague for Renate.

Then suddenly she turned to Anna and frowned. 'Who are you?'

Anna heard a loud buzzing in her ears and her body went completely numb. 'I'm Anna. Your daughter,' she whispered.

She was terrified by what happened next.

Renate's hands crashed down on the keys in an awful cacophony of discord. She screamed at Anna: 'How dare you say you're my daughter! How dare you say that! My daughter is dead! My daughter is dead! My daughter is dead!'

She started wailing; a low wail which pierced through Anna's skin and crawled inside her body. The wail grew higher and higher; suddenly the room was full of running people in white coats and Stefan was trying to stop them holding Renate down. He couldn't. A needle was thrust into her arm and the wailing stopped.

Anna fainted.

Chapter 50
MAX

Max had been sitting at the Police Station for an hour, trying to convince a middle-aged Sergeant, who seemed more interested in talking about fly-fishing than a trainee Clinical Psychologist, that this was not simply a case of a missing person, but an abduction. An abduction? The Sergeant queried, raising sceptical eyebrows. Had he any evidence of that? How long had Mrs. Nash been missing. When Max said five days, the Sergeant looked at him incredulously. Max explained the reasons why this case was urgent in clear and simple terms: a highly disturbed man had been stalking Anna for months. He'd followed her to Wales. He thought he was her brother. Now she'd disappeared. Again the question: had Dr. Paris any proof of an abduction? Of course, he hadn't any proof! Max had snapped. But if the police went to Stefan's house they'd find his diaries; they'd find photos that he's doctored. All proof of a disturbed mind.

Interesting, the Sergeant had said. And how did Dr. Paris know about his house? There'd be a break-in there the previous night. And how did he know this? Max looked at the Sergeant calmly and said that one of his clients was a policeman and had mentioned it. If only he could have shown the Sergeant the diary Celia had given him, but he couldn't; it would implicate her. But anyway, Max doubted whether he'd understand the diary's obliqueness. And the video tapes wouldn't support his belief that Stefan had abducted Anna either; they'd only show his mastery of manipulation and his belief that he was Anna's brother.

If we arrested everyone who came in here saying that someone had been adducted, Sir, the Sergeant had said, looking at Max as if he thought he was more far more disturbed than Stefan, our police cells would be full.

Max felt like screaming. Nothing he said would convince the Sergeant that he was dealing with anything more than a woman who'd quarrelled with her husband and had gone away, perhaps just to annoy him. When Max had argued that Anna wasn't the sort of woman who walked out of people's lives because she was annoyed; she was empathetic, thoughtful and responsible, the Sergeant had looked at him oddly. If that's true, it's strange that her husband hadn't reported her missing, then, isn't Sir? Max couldn't help himself. No, it wasn't strange. *He'd actually shouted.* Her husband was a self-centred bastard! The Sergeant had closed the file on Anna at that point and Max realised that he thought the three of them were involved in a ménage à trois.

'I'm sure she'll turn up when she's good and ready, Sir. Don't you worry. We'll wait to hear from her husband,' The Sergeant had said pointedly, as he showed him out.

Max strode out of the station, wanting to punch a nearby wall. He hadn't been dispassionate enough and the Sergeant wasn't intelligent or imaginative enough to be able to understand the potential danger to Anna.

He rang up Marie on his mobile and told her to cancel all his appointments for the next three days. Something serious had happened and he had to sort it out. Marie calmly informed him that she would deal with everything. Thank God he employed her, he thought as he walked down the street towards a small café on the corner. He had to work out how he could get inside Stefan's head; to think what he would do next.

The café was as bleak as Max's thoughts. He sat at a plastic-topped table drinking something that tasted like saw-dust and stale water and stared unseeingly out of the window until he suddenly realised what he must do: ring all the Institutes for Psychiatric Patients to see whether Stefan and Anna had gone to one of them. He grimaced, thinking how time-consuming that would be.

Max got up, gave his saw-dust drink to the tramp sitting at the next table, and rushed out of the café.

Chapter 51
ANNA

Anna was sitting silently beside Stefan as he drove along the M4. She didn't register the road; she was too numb with shock. She realised now why her mother had been in Institutes for twenty one years – she suffered from schizophrenia! *That's why she thought I was dead.* Anna closed her eyes as it hit her: schizophrenia could be in her genes too! Or her baby's! She groaned loudly.

Stefan turned to her, concerned. 'Are you all right? We can stop at the next service station if you want. Don't be upset, Anna. I told you that mother sometimes isn't herself. She didn't mean to send me out of the room or to shout at you. She loves us.'

Anna glanced at him. He really believed that, she thought, even after what one of the nurses had told her about Renate's frequent mood swings and the way she treated him. She tried to recall what she'd learned about schizophrenia from her lectures, but she couldn't remember - there were so many classifications.

She suddenly noticed a large sign for Swansea. He was going the wrong way! 'What are you doing, Stefan? You said you were taking me home.'

Stefan pressed his foot on the accelerator. 'I *am* taking you home, Anna. We're going to our house on the cliff. It's near where you stayed with that man. It's been waiting for us.'

'I want to go back to London. I have work to do. I can't -'

'No, of course you can't. We're staying together now, Anna. Just the two of us until Mother gets better and then we'll bring her home and she can see the baby. What shall we call him? Do you think it'll be a boy? You'll have to get a scan soon, won't you?

223

I don't know much about scans. But I know about babies. I looked after you, Anna. Most probably I know more about babies than you.' He smiled at her before turning his attention again to the road.

Anna felt blood pounding into her temples. How did he know where she'd stayed in Wales? He must have followed them everywhere. He must have been planning this for weeks; a trip to see Renate, followed by a trip to the coast. That's why he left the photo in his file the first time she opened it. He'd planted a photograph of that hotel on the cliff-top in his file to get her interested in Wales. No, she mustn't think like that. He was her brother. Of course he'd try to get her interested in a place they often visited before she was adopted. But why couldn't he have just told her? Why had he played games with her for weeks? Dear God – what if her brother had the same condition as her mother, but was controlling it through medication? Anna started her deep breathing exercises, thinking how to control her stress levels. Stress wasn't good for babies, Tim had told her. Where was Tim? Why wasn't he helping her? Where was Max? Where were her parents? Her parents… tears started running down Anna's cheeks. She wanted them to be her parents so much.

'Don't cry, Anna. I've told you. I'm going to look after you from now on. We'll never be apart again.'

Then he started humming a tune that Anna couldn't recognise.

'This is one of Mother's favourites,' he said as he sped along the motor way. 'Chopin's Etude in A Minor.'

Chapter 52
CELIA

'Yes, that's right. Dr. Paris. Please get someone in authority to speak to me. Yes, this very urgent. ... yes, I'll hold.'

Celia looked at Max's tense face as he spoke on the phone; they had been making calls to Institutes for half-an-hour, but the only person any one would speak to was Max. Celia wasn't a religious woman, but she'd spent most of the night lying awake praying to a God she wasn't sure existed. She prayed so hard that her finger-nails had dug into the palms of her hands and she hadn't noticed the blood on the sheets.

Max drummed his fingers on kitchen table while he waited.

'We've got four more numbers for you, Max,' Celia pushed the telephone numbers towards him.

'One of them *must* be the right one.' The desperation in Paul's voice was disturbing.

'Hello,' Max said into the phone. Celia thought her heart would burst out of her chest as she listened to Max trying to convince the person at the other end of the line that yes, he really was Dr. Max Paris and he did have a well-known clinic in Wigmore Street. It was only after he'd embarked on a detailed monologue on Personality Disorders that suddenly he gave them a thumbs up. It was the right Institute!

Celia and Paul hugged each other as they listened to Max explaining how urgent it was for him to see Renate Peterson as she might have information that would help them find her son and the woman he thought was his sister. Max stopped speaking and frowned as the woman spoke to him.

Celia and Paul held their breath.

'How long ago? I see. Thank you.' He put the phone down and swore.

'She's with him, isn't she?' Celia asked nervously.

'They were there only half an hour ago! Damn! If only we'd found the number earlier!' Max jumped up and started pacing around Celia's kitchen.

'How long will it take us to get there?' Celia said.

'Three hours,' Max whispered.

***

Celia was alarmed; Max was driving his Peugeot down the M4 at nearly 100 mph. She turned to Paul who was sitting on the back seat and opened her eyes wide, meaning: say something.

'Max, could you drive a little slower?' Paul said. 'We'll be picked up by the police and that's not going to help Anna, is it?'

Max slowed his speed to 80 mph. 'Sorry. This is all my fault. I should never have allowed Anna to treat him.'

'You weren't to know he was so … difficult,' Paul said.

Celia was thinking about Anna. God knows what was happening to her daughter. She remembered the moment they'd seen her in the orphanage in Sevenoaks; they'd been living in Tunbridge Wells then and she remembered the drive up the A21 as if it was yesterday; it had been a clear, blue day in May. The trees were full of vibrant green leaves; the gardens flanking the road were a kaleidoscope of flowers. She'd looked out of the car window and thought: on this perfect day I'm going to see my daughter for the first time. She remembered walking up to the yellow door of the children's home; the kindly-looking woman who'd answered it. She'd showed them into a room where a copper-haired child, who looked as ethereal as a fairy, was dancing to *Mary Mary, Quite Contrary* on an old record player. She stopped dancing and turned to smile at her. Celia had crouched down on the floor, opened her arms and Anna had run into them. She had known that Celia really was her true mother, even then.

And now, because of one terrible lie, Anna wouldn't speak to her.

Celia looked at the road rushing past them and willed herself to be strong. 'How much further is it?'

'About five miles. We turn off at Junction 21,' Max answered.

'Concentrate on the road signs, Celia. We can't miss the turning,' Paul said.

Celia and Paul concentrated with every fibre of their beings on seeing the number 21. It was getting dark; it could easily be missed.

'There is it!' Celia shouted; she suddenly spotted the number in a gap between two lorries.

Max expertly manoeuvred the car in between the lorries and turned left onto the slip-road.

Celia prayed that Renate Peterson would somehow help them to find her daughter; the consequences of not finding her were too terrible to contemplate.

Chapter 53
ANNA

Anna concentrated on how she could get a message to Tim and Max as they drove along the dark, bumpy road; they'd know what to do. She was completely exhausted from lack of sleep and shock; the only reason she was still awake was fear; fear for what her brother would do when he found out that she couldn't stay with him. How would she tell him? He had been so badly traumatised that he wouldn't even speak about his father's death; wouldn't even tell her that their mother was too ill to be taken out of an Institute. How could she inflict more pain on him?

'We're nearly there Anna. Are you excited? This is the first time you will have seen our home for twenty one years! I can't begin to describe how happy I feel. Lighter than air! Higher than the stars!' Stefan laughed with such joy that the fear Anna felt was replaced by sorrow; she wished she could bring him happiness.

Stefan stopped the car. All Anna could see were giant shadows thrown by clumps of gorse on rough grass caught in the headlights. Stefan switched them off. They sat in darkness. Anna wondered what was going to happen to her. She must protect herself for the baby's sake.

'Look up when you get out,' Stefan said.

The moment Anna got out of the car she heard the distant roar of the sea and smelt the ozone in the air. Above her, the panorama of the night sky spread out in all its splendour; she had never seen such vastness before; she'd always had light in her life and suddenly felt incredibly small and insubstantial.

'That's what you get from living here, Anna. Peace. No people trying to destroy your life. No light pollution trying to destroy the stars. I only lived in London so that I could find you.'

He switched on a large torch and held her hand, his eyes wild with excitement. 'Come, we have to walk now. It's too difficult in a car.'

The path was treacherous to walk over; there were stones and small rocks and depressions all along it. Anna stumbled beside Stefan, holding onto a hand which held hers in a firm grip.

'It's all right. I won't let you fall. I know every inch of this area. I used to walk here every night when they thought I was in bed.'

'Our parents, you mean?' Anna asked. This was the first time he had used 'they' when talking about his past. She knew she must get him to talk about their father; it might help him heal. But not tonight. Tonight she had to sleep. The baby needed her to rest. She stumbled along automatically, too tired to think. Would the path never end?

At last, a large white house loomed up in the front of them, ghost-like in the torch-light. It looked like a Spanish villa with a wide balcony which ran along its length.

'Welcome to Bach Têg,' Stefan said. 'Wait until you see inside the house.' Stefan released Anna's hand and ran towards it. 'I can't believe it! I can't believe it! Come on, Anna. I have so much to show you.'

Anna walked towards the light of Stefan's torch and touched the mobile in her pocket.

Chapter 54
MAX

Max charmed Miss Haigh immediately by complimenting her on her article in *The Journal of Child Psychology and Psychiatry*. He had researched the article on the Internet and memorized a few facts from it. He picked out a few salient points to show her how interested he was; Miss Haigh was delighted.

They stood in the large white hall of *Bryn Dail*. Celia and Paul were completely ignored after Miss Haigh discovered they were not Dr. Paris' colleagues and therefore of no importance. She explained what had happened when Stefan and Anna visited and couldn't vouch for what Mrs. Peterson's behaviour would be like this evening.

'I'm sure I don't have to worry, Miss Haigh with you in charge of the staff.'

Miss Haigh beamed at Max and he realised he was overdoing the flattery.

'Of course,' she said, turning to Celia and Paul. 'Only Dr. Paris can be allowed to see Mrs. Peterson. 'In fact, she said coquettishly to Max, 'if it had been anyone apart from you, Dr. I wouldn't have let him in!'

She laughed and Max realised he'd have to raise a smile. God, the woman was flirting with him. 'Could I see her now please? As I explained on the phone it is urgent.'

He glanced at Celia and Paul's tense faces. 'I'll try not to be long.'

'Of course, Dr. Paris. Follow me.' She looked at Celia and Paul and said imperiously. 'Wait here, please.'

Max walked off with Miss Haigh, worried that he might be

wasting valuable time. Stefan and Anna could be hundreds of miles away by now.

He walked through the door that Anna and Stefan had walked through four hours earlier. And all the time Miss Haigh kept up an animated conversation about the next article she was writing. Perhaps Dr. Paris would like an advance copy. Max told her he'd be delighted to have one, thinking of ways to deal with Renate Peterson. He had to discover something!

He heard the music from the corridor, and, like Anna, was stunned by its beauty. How tragic that a concert pianist should be locked up in her mind. He was searching through his memory banks for the name of music she was playing. One of his Professors at University played it constantly.

Miss Haigh opened the door. Renate sat at the piano, immaculately dressed in a long blue evening gown as if she was giving a public performance; her back ramrod straight. Again Max was struck by the tragedy of mental illness. Why couldn't they have helped this talented woman lead a life outside the Institute?

Miss Haigh waited until the music finished. Perhaps she loves music, Max thought. 'She flies into a rage if she's interrupted,' she whispered to him.

'Here's the visitor I told you about, Mrs. Peterson. He knows Stefan.'

'I'd like to see her alone, please.' Max smiled at Miss Haigh, knowing she wanted to watch him at work.

She looked annoyed and walked off.

Renate stared at him. Max thought she must have beautiful once, but now she was faded; as if weary of life.

'Who are you?' She said sharply.

'Chopin's Concerto, number 2,' Max answered.

'In F,' she answered. So you know Chopin?'

'Not really,' Max said. 'Just that piece.'

She started to play again and the music was so full of pain and yearning that all the sadness in Max's life surfaced; he started to cry for the first time since Sadie's death.

She turned and saw his tears. 'Chopin was unhappy too.' She got up from the piano and stared out of the black window. 'I know why you have come.'

The moment she said those words Max's training took over: 'Why?' He asked, his heart thumping. Was she going to tell him something important?

She walked towards him and circled around him. It was unnerving.

'You want to know my secret in the white house, don't you?'

'Yes, I'd like to know your secret in the white house,' Max said quietly, frightened she'd stop talking.

'How much would you like to know?' Renate said, still circling round him.

'A lot,' Max whispered. He suddenly felt as if his life depended on her answer.

She stopped circling and said. 'Well, I won't tell you.' And suddenly, she was laughing hysterically.

Max knew he had to get her calm quickly or Miss Haigh would be there with her entire staff.

'I have a secret too,' Max shouted over the hysteria.

Her laughter abruptly stopped as if she'd turned off a tap.

'What is it?' She looked up at him, full of excitement.

'If you tell me your secret, I'll tell you mine,' Max said in a child-like voice.

Renate walked around the room, staring at Max, considering

the offer.

At last she said. 'I'll tell you a little. You'll have to guess the rest.'

'All right,' Max whispered.

'They never found out.' She started giggling.

'What?' Max felt sweat drip down his back.

'What he did.' She giggled again.

'What who did?'

Anger suddenly transformed her. 'Don't ask stupid questions! They asked stupid questions so I told them nothing!'

'What Stefan did?' Max asked, trying to keep his voice steady.

Renate giggled. 'That's what you've got to guess.'

Max's head whirled around all the incredible scenarios he could think of; then he looked at her with sudden - awful understanding.

'He killed someone,' Max whispered.

Renate clapped her hands in delight. 'Oh you clever, clever man. But you'll never guess who.'

Max ran out of the room, feeling nauseous as Renate screamed after him: 'You haven't told me your secret, you wicked, wicked man! You lied! You lied! You lied!'

Chapter 55
ANNA

Anna couldn't believe what she found in the large sitting room; it was as if three people had just stepped out for a walk twenty one years ago and never come back; the things they loved were everywhere: every wall was lined with hundreds of books; an immaculate black Steinway grand piano was angled across two walls with open music on it, waiting for Renate to play; an open child's colouring book lay on a thick deep blue carpet near the piano; on top of it were three fat crayons: yellow, blue and red.

'Your favourite colours, Anna,' Stefan told her.

Anna was staggered. Her colouring book was still on the floor after twenty one years! Beside the book was a large open drawing pad with a picture of a little girl dancing. She looked at Stefan. He smiled at her.

'That's one of the drawings I did of you. You were dancing to Mother's music.'

He took her hand and guided her around the room as if they were in a museum; explaining a past Anna couldn't remember. In one corner there was a pile of classical records and an old record-player; every night Mother told them odd facts about the composers: Mozart liked playing jokes on people; J.S Bach married his cousin and had twenty children; Beethoven, Schubert, Brahms and Wagner were all under 5 foot tall; every night they learned something new. In another corner was a small heap of children's games and a rag doll with red and white striped legs – your first doll, Anna. Stefan showed her the games they used to play; the jigsaws they used to make; the books they used to read.

234

'This is our past, Anna. Isn't it wonderful? Waiting for us to reclaim it. *A house with a door – windows - 1,2,3,4, - ready to play – what's the day? It's Tuesday!* Do you remember 'Playschool'? I watched it with you every time it was on.'

Anna felt claustrophobic; she couldn't breathe with so much past in the room; the present didn't exist here. But unlike Miss Havisham's room in *Great Expectations*, here nothing was faded by the decay of jilted disappointment; this room had simply waited without aging. There was no dust and yet everything was scattered around as if it had just been left!

Before she could ask Stefan how that was possible, he was guiding her up the wide staircase covered with expensive olive-green carpet. Her parents obviously had money. At the top of the stairs there was a long gallery with six cream-coloured doors; each door had four panels painted light green, decorated with much care.

'Mother's room,' Stefan said, pointing to the door at the end of the gallery. 'And that's my room.' He gestured towards the door in front of him. 'And that's the door to your bedroom.' He pointed at the door next to his.' And as he opened her old bedroom door, Anna wondered who and what the other rooms were for.

Stefan walked into the room and flicked the light-switch and Anna gasped: a child's bedroom lay in front of her; the bedroom of a much-loved, pampered child. She walked in and looked around the pink and white walls covered with sea paintings and drawings of the house that must have been drawn by Stefan as a teenager; family photographs; a child's naïve drawings. Her drawings. She looked around in wonder. A child's bed stood against one wall, covered with soft toys and over it hung an exquisite glass blue and white butterfly mobile that was tinkling in the draft from the door. She put her hand over her mouth; this was the mobile Stefan had bought her as a baby. Stefan dimmed the lights and Anna saw hundreds of small stars on the ceiling.

'You used to stare up at them at night when I read you a story,' Stefan said.

And suddenly, Anna was crying. Giant sobs which tore out of her body and Stefan was rocking her gently in his arms and stroking her hair.

'Shhh, liebling. Don't cry. We're together now. You're tired. You need to rest. Lie down and sleep in your old bed while I cook dinner.'

Then he left her, lying on a child's bed, staring up at the stars and soon she was asleep.

Chapter 56
CELIA

Celia and Paul were sitting on two hard seats in the hall as Max ran past them, shouting. 'Come on!'

They jumped up and ran after him; terrified by his urgency.

'What happened, Max?' Celia shouted as they dashed off after him.

'It must be bad, Celia,' Paul could hardly articulate the words.

'He's got some information. Could be good.' Celia wanted to believe her words as they ran towards the car where Max was already waiting with the car doors open.

Celia got into the back with Paul, worried that Max would drive too fast. The moment they had their seats belts on, Max sped off with the gravel peppering his car.

'Where are we going?' Paul wheezed.

'To the Gower Coast,' Max said. 'He's taken her to a white house.'

Celia looked at Paul. 'The Gower Coast stretches for miles.'

'You mean the house in the photograph,' Paul said, excitedly, his breathlessness forgotten.

'Yes, try to remember every detail you can,' Max said. 'It's vitally important.'

Paul dug into his pocket and brought out a folded photo. 'Don't have to. I brought it with me, Max.'

Celia and Paul lurched forward as Max slammed on the brakes and screeched to a halt at the end of *Bryn Dail's* long drive.

Dear God, Celia thought. We're not going to survive the journey.

'For crying out loud, Max!' Paul was actually shouting. 'We can't help Anna if we're dead! Drive more carefully!

Celia looked in amazement at her husband. She'd only ever heard him shout once before – when he discovered a boy kissing Anna in the tree-house.

Max looked apologetically at them. 'Sorry. That's brilliant, Paul.' He took a torch out of his glove compartment and passed it to him. 'Could you and Celia study it while I drive? Look for anything that could help us identify the area.'

Celia and Paul poured over the photograph in the torch-light. Now that Celia knew it was a fake she didn't mind looking at it. It was uncanny how Stefan Peterson had managed to superimposed Anna's head onto another woman's body. She would never have known it wasn't genuine. She looked around the house for any clues, but all she could see were gorse bushes and grass. Nothing to identify where it was.

'Hang on. Can you stop a minute, Max,' Paul said. 'Slowly this time. I can't read properly in this light. There's something on the gate.'

'I can't stop here.'

Celia and Paul looked up; they'd been so intent on the photograph that they hadn't noticed they were back on the M4.

'Well, whenever you can,' Paul said. 'Do you see, Celia? There's some letters on the gate.'

'I must be a house name!' Celia said, excitedly. If they had a name they could find it. For the first time since they'd set out she felt positive; now they had something helpful to focus on. 'Give me the torch. My eye sight is better than yours.'

'The enlargement has made some of the letters very fuzzy. All I can see clearly is a B.'

Celia took the torch off Paul and peered at the letters

238

carefully. 'I think that's an A after it.'

'B. A...' Celia said. 'Anyone think of the name of a house beginning with B A. '

'Don't be ridiculous, Celia. We have to have more information than that. Blast! The next letter is far too blurred to read.'

'But the next one isn't. So it's B – A – something - H.'

The car swerved slightly and Max said. 'Bach! The house is called Bach Têg!'

Celia and Paul stared at him in surprise. 'How on earth did you get that from three letters?' Celia said.

'Stefan wrote a story about a Bach Têg in his diary. It means Welsh Fairy,' Max said in a tight voice.

'What a strange name to call a house,' Paul said.

'Look at the little girl in the photograph,' Celia answered.

Paul peered at the little girl's face and gasped. 'Good Lord. I was concentrating on Anna's face. I hardly noticed the child. She could have come from a fairy tale. They must have named the house after her.'

Celia and Paul didn't notice Max increasing his speed; they were concentrating on the beautiful face of a three year old child who must have died soon after the photograph was taken.

Chapter 57
ANNA

Anna woke up and for a moment had no idea where she was; then she saw the stars on the ceiling and the butterfly mobile above her head. An eleven-year-old boy had bought these things for her when she was a baby! So much devotion. Part of her wanted to embrace Stefan's love completely, but the other part was frightened; his love was too obsessive. She sat up, suddenly hearing the faint strains of music from downstairs and knew she must find her mobile in her coat. Her heart thumped as she looked on the chair – the coat was gone! *He's trying to stop me contacting anyone*, she thought in a sudden panic. *Dear God, what I am to do*?

What would Max do in such a situation? Would he try to persuade Stefan that he really needed to overcome his past to move forward? Or simply explain that he could still have a relationship with his sister, even if she wasn't living with him; even if they didn't see each other every day? Anna shook her head, knowing instinctively that Stefan wouldn't agree to a separation.

A small knock on the door. It suddenly opened. Stefan stood there smiling at her.

'Are you feeling better?'

Anna nodded, forcing herself to appear happy as she got up from the bed.

'Good. We'll eat in half an hour, but first I want to show you something.'

Anna tensed; what would she see? Stefan guided her out along the gallery, past numerous paintings of Vienna; past three closed doors to the room at the end of gallery. Anna realised with a sudden shock that she had seen no evidence of their father in the house at all! It was as if he had never existed. Did one of the rooms contain his belongings or had Stefan simply got rid of everything? If only she could get Stefan to talk about him, he might come to terms with his death and not be so obsessed with her. But how?

Stefan smiled before opening a door.

'You'll like this, Anna.'

He pushed the door back and Anna breathed in sharply as she saw a large room lit by dozens of candles and mirrors; Renate's early life, lit for her to enjoy. The reflections from four large ornate Viennese mirrors made the room enormous and reflected the candles endlessly. A mahogany four-poster bed stood in the centre of the room, covered with gold sheets and drapes which shimmered in the candle-light. On the bed, a long shot-silk dress had been arranged as if for a fashion shoot; its colour mutating from azure to sapphire in the flickering light. Sapphire silk shoes waited beside the dress for someone to wear them. Again, Stefan took her like a museum-guide around the room, showing her posters and programmes of all the Viennese concerts that Renate had played in; the ornate Viennese furniture that had been shipped from Vienna and arranged artistically around the room; the sumptuous array of evening dresses in a wardrobe; the harpsichord angled near the bed. Mother liked playing late at night, Stefan told her. The harpsichord is a quiet instrument.

'Everything is yours now,' Stefan said, smiling at her, his large brown eyes glowing in the candlelight.

'What do you mean?' Anna whispered. This room was unnerving; it was a shrine to Renate.

'Everything Mother has is yours.'

Anna closed her eyes, trying to work out what he meant. Their mother was still alive so why would he say Renate's possessions were hers? The grand piano and harpsichord alone must be worth a fortune and she couldn't even read music! She opened her eyes and looked at him. She had to say it.

'How can they be mine, Stefan? She's not dead.'

Stefan looked around the room as if he was in pain.

'She'll never wear these beautiful dresses again, Anna. They are made to be worn, not to hang in a wardrobe, waiting for moths to eat them.' He looked at her intently. 'Will you do something for me? It's important.'

Anna squeezed her hands together, dreading what he might ask her to do. 'Do what?'

'Will you wear this dress and shoes tonight … for me?'

Is that all? Anna thought with relief. Wear a special dress and shoes? 'Yes, I'll wear them, but they might not fit me.'

Stefan looked as her and said. 'The dress will fit you perfectly.' He walked over to the bed, picked up the dress as if it was the Holy Grail and gave it to her. 'I'll wait outside while you change.'

Stefan walked out and closed the door. Anna was left in the past and all the mirrors reflected her.

She pulled off her green tunic top, unzipped her short skirt and stood in her bra and pants, staring at the dress; it was so beautiful; how did Stefan know it would fit her? Anna picked the dress up reverentially; it felt as soft as moonlight. She lifted it over her head and it slid effortlessly down her body. Did her mother really wear this dress? Each movement of her body changed the colour of the silk in the mirrors; it was like watching a mirage shimmer. Anna closed the zip at the back, but the small

242

hooks at the top of the zip were impossible to fasten. She was contorting her arms into impossible positions behind her back when Stefan knocked on the door.

'Can I come in?'

'Yes,' Anna said, softly. The room possessed the seductive stillness of a Catholic church; she didn't want to disturb its tranquillity.

The door opened and Stefan moved silently towards her. He was wearing evening dress and looked incredibly handsome.

'I'll fasten them,' he whispered. 'Turn around.'

'Why are we dressing up?' Anna said, doing as she was told and feeling like a small child.

'We're celebrating.'

His hands were feathers on her back as he fastened the hooks. Each small movement of his hands on her back made her body quiver. This wasn't how it should feel; Stefan was her brother! She remembered what Max had told her about genetic sexual attraction and silently groaned. She was pregnant – how could she be attracted to her brother?

'Turn around,' he said.

She turned to face him and his smile was so loving she suddenly wanted to cry.

'I knew it,' he said. 'I knew you'd look as beautiful as she did in that dress, but there's something missing.'

He walked over to an ornate dressing table, opened one of its drawers and brought out a long blue velvet box. He opened it and Anna gasped; in front of her was the most incredible necklace she had ever seen; an opal sapphire pendent surrounded by diamonds. Underneath the pendent were two sapphire earrings and a sapphire ring. Stefan took the pendent out of the box carefully and walked behind her.

243

'Our grandmother gave these to our mother. Lift up your hair.'

Anna lifted her copper hair off her neck and trembled slightly as Stefan fastened the necklace gently around her neck. He leaned forward and his lips feathered her back.

'Don't, Stefan,' Anna whispered.

His hands lightly touched her shoulders and he turned her round. 'I have found my Bach Têg. My fairy in a winter wood.'

Anna didn't know what he meant, but she didn't care; she could see herself reflected infinitely in his eyes. Her eyes couldn't be that brilliant, could they? He picked up her right hand and placed the earrings and the ring in it.

'Put them on,' he whispered.

She put on each beautiful item feeling as if she was stepping into someone else's life.

'And now the shoes.'

Anna found the shoes a little tight, but not uncomfortable.

Stefan's eyes swept over her in admiration. 'You are perfect, Anna. Now we'll have dinner.'

Hundreds of elegant people dressed for a Viennese opera shimmered in the mirrors of the candle-lit room as they walked out.

***

Anna and Stefan sat at a round white damask-covered table, listening to *Debussy's Prélude à l'après-midi d'un faune* and eating Wiener Schnitzel and Erdäpfelsalat which Stefan told her was a marinade of potatoes, red onion, vinegar and oil. It was delicious. Greta, their housekeeper had taught Stefan to cook when he was a small boy. Anna thought how different both their lives would have been if Renate hadn't become ill. Stefan opened a bottle of champagne and poured her a glass, but when she refused because of her pregnancy, he said:

'A sip – to celebrate our reunion. Prost!' He leaned over the table and tinged his glass against Anna's in a toast. 'To the first day of the rest of our lives, Anna.' He drained his glass and poured himself another. 'Listen to that beauty. It's Debussy's response to a Stephane Mallarmé poem. A faun goes to sleep and dreams sensual dreams. Can you see the images?'

She nodded. Everything was becoming dream-like for Anna; the man, the music, the clothes; it was like being inside a fairy tale.

'This evening feels unreal, Stefan.'

'And what is reality?' He asked her. 'A mirage is a mere phenomenon of light, but I have photographed it. A house on the horizon looks no bigger than a matchbox.'

Suddenly Stefan jumped up and pulled Anna up from the table, towards a mirror.

'Where are you standing? A long way behind the glass. How can that be? You're in front of it! Do you see how perception is delusive?'

Anna was back in her childhood with her father explaining the metaphor of Macbeth's dagger of the mind. Her father! Who was he? She was losing her sense of reality.

Stefan was as clever with words as their mother with music. What was she clever with? She used to think people, now she wasn't sure. But she was sure she'd have to tell this intelligent, disturbing man that she wasn't going to live with him inside a fairy-tale world. But he was still talking about the illusion of perception. How people felt a phantom limb long after it had been amputated; about sticks looking bent in water; about the Müller-Lyer illusion of simple lines deceiving the eye.

'People are diseased by tunneled vision, Anna. They can't see

245

the impossible. They would say that it is impossible to discover a sister after twenty one years but I have proved them wrong. I will prove that a brother and sister can live in perfect harmony without other people.'

He laughed; then walked over to the table to drink his champagne and pour himself another.

Anna walked away from the mirror. 'We all need people, Stefan.' She tensed, knowing he'd hate what she was going to say. 'I'm married to a doctor.'

'That man in the theatre? The one who became angry with you because you disagreed with him.'

Anna clenched her hands together under the table – he was at the theatre – watching her!

'I was sitting behind you. He doesn't deserve you, nor does Max Paris. They want to use you. All men will want to use you, except me, Anna. My love is the most selfless you'll ever experience. I only want you to be happy with me.'

'I *am* happy with you, Stefan, but…' His face darkened on the word 'but'. She wasn't sure how to explain how their relationship could continue in the future without making him angry and she definitely didn't want to do that; memories of Renate's outburst were far too raw.

'But?' Stefan asked in a strange voice as he walked towards her. 'There can't be any conflicting conjunctions, Anna.'

Chapter 58
MAX

All the time Max was driving at high speed down the dark motorway, Renate's words were rolling round his head like a ball - Stefan had killed someone! Stefan had killed someone! Who the hell had he killed? If Stefan was a killer, finding Anna was as imperative as breathing and he was finding that difficult to do. From the back seat, Celia and Paul were asking him questions he couldn't answer or concentrate on; he had to block them out. He'd never felt so helpless and yet he knew he had to think rationally; it could save Anna's life. She would be protected unless she tried to regress Stefan back to the time he'd killed someone. She'd remember what he'd told his students, surely? Patients suffering from schizophrenia, bipolar conditions, suicidal tendencies or manic depression were not good candidates for hypnotherapy. What would she do if Stefan had a psychotic episode? God forbid she'd talk to him about his past! He wanted to shout out to the wind to carry the message to her. Don't take him back to the past! Talk to him about the present; reassure him about the future! Don't touch on the past!

'Junction 42, Max. Turn off!' Celia was shouting at him.

He slowed the car and turned off the M4, realising that Celia and Paul must be terrified by his speeding.

'Sorry about the driving.'

They didn't respond. Suddenly the strain of driving at high speed hit him; he'd been driving for hours without registering the road at all. Momentarily, he closed his eyes easing the strain of the aggressive glare from on-coming car halogen lights. Gradually, they were diffused by the softer sodium of Swansea's street lights. But he was still on automatic pilot; he had to reach Anna before Stefan discovered the truth. Nothing else mattered.

It took them over half an hour to reach the sign for Rhossili, but they still had to find the white house.

'Someone is bound to know a house called Bach Têg, Max,' Celia said in a quiet voice. 'There aren't too many houses around here, are there?'

'I suggest we all knock on as many doors as we can find,' Paul said.

Max drove into the dotted lights of Rhossili village, desperately hoping that someone would know the house.

'Stop here!' Celia commanded, almost getting out of the car before it stopped moving.

'For God's sake, be careful, Celia!' Paul warned her.

They had knocked on ten doors before Celia shouted to them.

'This gentleman knows the house!'

Max and Paul ran over to where Celia was standing in a pool of light outside a small cottage.

'Could you tell us exactly how to find it?' Celia asked him.

The man seemed as ancient as the village. Max tried to contain his frustration as the man droned on about how many years the house had stood empty and how it was haunted by secrets.

'Yes, but where it is!' Max shouted.

The old man's face closed like a clam. 'There's manners for you. Shouting at an old man.'

After Max had apologised and explained how urgent it was that they find the house, the old man brought his middle-aged daughter to the door; she explained how difficult it was to reach the house by car as it was on the cliffs. They'd have to walk to it for about half a mile. She drew them a complicated map and Max wanted to strangle her for her unbelievable lack of imagination.

Chapter 59
ANNA

Stefan had finished the bottle of champagne and was staring at Anna with an inscrutable expression.

'What do you mean – you can't live with me? This is our home, Anna. It's been waiting for us to return. Where else can our baby be born?'

Anna tried not to reveal how disturbing his words were: *our* home; *our* baby. He was treating her more like a possessive husband, than a loving brother.

'I could come here at weekends to see you and we could go for walks together.'

Anna watched in horror as Stefan squeezed the fingers of his right hand around his wine glass harder and harder until the glass shattered and blood dripped gently over the white table-cloth.

'Oh, my God,' she whispered.

'And what am I to do when you're not here?' Stefan said, opening his bloody hand and staring at it as if it belonged to someone else. There were slivers of glass embedded in his fingers, but he didn't seem to notice.

Anna's heart was thumping hard. She had to find her mobile, but where had he put her coat? How could she leave the room when he'd just cut his hand with glass particles?

'We must clean your hand, Stefan. I'll get some water.'

Anna ran to the kitchen and looked around frantically for her coat. It wasn't there. There wasn't a phone either; then she realised that she hadn't seen one in any of the rooms. She leaned against the kitchen sink, thinking what to do. Clean his hand that's as far as she could think. She opened one of the cupboards, took out a small bowl and filled it with water. What could she wipe his hand with? A small green tea-towel hung on the back of the kitchen door. She picked up the bowl and tea-towel and walked back into the sitting-room. Stefan was sitting like a statue; staring in fascination at his fingers while a small pool of blood spread over the white table-cloth.

She leant beside him and took his hand in hers. He smiled at her so gently she was amazed she could have been frightened of him. How could so much kindness engender fear? He allowed her to bathe his hand to wash off the blood; smiling at her with wonder.

'No one has ever bathed my hand before, Anna. No one. Now can you see how we were meant for each other?'

The mahogany Grandfather clock in the corner chimed melodically into the silence before Anna answered.

'Yes, I can see that now, Stefan.'

His face lit up. 'You can? You don't want to leave me again?'

'I didn't want to leave you before, did I? I was forced to,' Anna said, gently.

'Yes, you were. They were terrible people who took you away from me, but they won't do it again, will they?'

'No, they won't, Stefan. I won't let them.'

Anna hated herself when she saw how much joy her words gave Stefan; her words had the power to bring this man more happiness than most people felt in their entire lives and yet she knew she'd have to leave him. But there must be a way to help him overcome his traumatic past. She had helped Kieran overcome a dominant father. Could she help Stefan overcome his?

'I've got to get the glass splinters out of your hand, Stefan.

251

I've got some tweezers in my bag upstairs. I'll go and get it. All right?'

Stefan nodded. 'I'll put on Pavarotti singing *Recondita Armouria* from "Tosca". You'll like that, Anna.'

Anna walked out into the hall, looking for her coat. There was a coat-stand underneath the stairs. She crept over and found her coat beneath Stefan's. Her mobile was in her pocket! She took it out and ran lightly up the stairs, listening to the powerful voice of Pavarotti singing. How could she betray Stefan when such music was playing?

She went into the child's room she'd slept it and closed the door, but the faint strains of poignancy could still be heard. Why couldn't she ignore it? She opened her mobile, switched it on and waited… there was no signal! Shuddering, she put her mobile inside her bag and brought out her make-up bag. The only person she could rely on from now on was herself. She had to be strong for the baby.

Stefan was sitting with his eyes closed listening to the music when Anna walked in. He immediately opened his eyes and smiled at her.

'You're here,' he said. 'How is it possible that some men can compose such music and others only create war?'

'I don't know, Stefan. We're a strange species.'

She knelt beside him and painstakingly took the glass slivers from Stefan's hand while he watched her face.

'Don't look at me like that,' she said at last.

'Why not? I love looking at beauty.'

He was stroking her hair rhythmically; hypnotically. Anna closed her eyes, relaxing into the strokes, but she knew she must break free. She opened her eyes and propelled herself away from

252

him. Stefan looked startled.

'Will you let me help you?' She said.

Stefan looked at his hand. 'You already have.'

'I don't mean your hand. Do you trust me enough to let me help you with therapy?'

Stefan looked at her with all the innocence of a child. 'I trust you with my life.'

'Then let me hypnotize you. You're suppressing so much, Stefan. Remember what I said about wanting you to be the person you were meant to be. Let me help you become that person.'

Stefan stared at her and a shudder ran through his entire body. Anna knew the cost of what she was asking him to do: relive a terrible trauma to overcome it.

'I don't think I have the courage,' he said quietly.

'I think you do, Stefan.'

As they listened to Pavarotti's voice fade away, Stefan gave her a small nod.

Stefan did everything she asked him to do; take off his jacket and shoes and lie on some cushions on the floor. He looked up at her so trustingly that Anna was overcome by a powerful urge to protect him; to stop him from feeling any pain.

'I want you to focus on the painting of Renate on the wall, Stefan, and start breathing in through your nose and out through your mouth. In... and ...out...in ...and ... out... in ...and ...out.'

Stefan was relaxing because he trusted her. Anna realised that this was the most important moment of her life; she had to get it right.

'Your eyelids are becoming heavier and heavier.' Stefan's

eyelids descended slightly. 'Your eyelids feel as if heavy weights are pulling them down.' His eyelids started fluttering. 'Soon they'll be so heavy they'll close.'

Stefan's breathing slowed down as his body relaxed. 'Relax …and let go, Stefan. Relax …and let go.' Anna watched Stefan's jaw drop. 'Breathe slowly and smoothly. Let all your muscles become loose and limp… that's very good, Stefan. Now I want you to take a deep breath and hold it for ten seconds… and exhale… … now you're stepping onto a descending escalator, a long, slow escalator that will take you into a state of deeper relaxation. You're going deeper and deeper into relaxation with every breath you take. Deeper and deeper into relaxation. As you go down, I want you to count backwards from 10 to 1 and when you reach 1 you'll be in a deep state of relaxation.

Stefan counted backwards and Anna watched him go into a trance, his fingers and legs twitching slightly. She repeated his descent twice to ensure that he would be able to access the deepest recesses of his mind.

'Now you're feeling more relaxed that you've ever felt before and you're going back to the day your father died. What happened that day, Stefan?'

Stefan's head started moving back and fro. 'We were going to have a picnic on the beach.'

Anna was finding it difficult to breathe. What if she asked the wrong questions? 'Who's 'we', Stefan?'

'Mother, Anna, me and Greta.'

She suddenly realized that he'd said Anna, not you. What did that mean?

'Where was father?'

Stefan's head trashed back and fro.

'Where was he, Stefan?'

'Standing at the top of the stairs, shouting. Always shouting.'

'What was he shouting about?'

'Anna had left some toys on the stairs and he was shouting at her and she was frightened.'

He was still talking about her in the third person!

'So what did you do?'

'I told him to stop shouting, but that made him angrier and he started throwing the toys down the stairs and one of them hit Anna and I screamed at him and he ran down the stairs towards us and -and - and...' Stefan started groaning; a low animal sound. It made the hairs on the back of Anna's hair stand up.

'What happened next, Stefan?' Anna said gently.

'Anna ran out of the door and it slammed behind her and I shouted to mother that I'd unlocked the gate because we were going on a picnic. And we all ran out of the house and saw Anna running towards the cliff, but the more we shouted, the faster she ran because she saw that bastard running after her and suddenly she slipped and fell – ' Stefan screamed as if someone had severed his arteries.

Anna held onto the table for support. *Dear God in heaven. I'm not his sister. His sister fell off the cliff!*

'And that bastard was still running towards her so I ran behind him and punched him off the cliff and mother screamed and screamed and screamed!'

Stefan was rocking back and fro and moaning; crushed with the pain of reliving his memory. Anna never imagined his past was so traumatic. She should never have hypnotized him. Dear God - how could she help him recover from this? She held him tight and whispered to him.

'Anna didn't die, Stefan. I'm here.' She rocked his body. 'Anna's here with you. It's all right. She didn't die. I'm here,

Stefan. Your sister is here. I want you to close your eyes and breathe in and out. In and out...' His breathing was ragged. 'A slow breath in... and ...out... in... and ...out.' Anna repeated the instructions in a soothing voice until his breathing became a little less erratic and his body a little less tense. 'Now you're going up an elevator and when you reach the top, you'll relax. I'm going to count from 1 to 10. When I get to 10, you'll go on another elevator until I reach 20.'

It wasn't until Anna got him ascending the second elevator that he began slowly to relax. As they reached the third, Anna willed him to forget; some memories were better for being buried, she thought. She blamed herself for attempting the hypnosis. Why should he remember the trauma of pushing a man like that over a cliff? Stefan was now lying flat on the cushions, completely relaxed.

'When you reach the top of the elevator, you'll wake up, Stefan, very happy and so relaxed that you won't remember any trauma from the past at all. 28... 29... 30. Now open your eyes, Stefan.'

Anna's heart thumped as his eyes opened. Would he remember? Would he remember that she couldn't be his sister? And if he did, what would he do to her? Anna held her breath as Stefan opened his eyes and looked around in amazement. He suddenly smiled at her and said 'I feel wonderful. What did I tell you?'

'You told me our father fell off a cliff. It was an accident.' Anna said calmly.

'He was a terrible man, Anna. He used to drink and make us all very unhappy.'

'Well, he can't anymore, can he? He's not here.' Anna was euphoric; she felt that she'd scaled Mount Everest. She'd done it!

256

She'd helped him forget!

Stefan jumped up from the carpet full of excitement. 'No! He's not here! Let's go for a walk along the cliffs.' He rushed to get their coats.

Warning signals suddenly flashed through Anna's body. The cliffs at night? After what he'd just told her! But, of course, he couldn't remember little Anna's death, only his hated father's. He still wanted to protect her.

'It'll be dangerous at night, Stefan.'

He was putting on her coat. 'Not with me beside you, Anna. Nothing will be dangerous ever again.' He was putting on his coat. 'I'll leave some lights on to guide us home.'

And suddenly, Anna was outside the house; outside the gate walking towards the cliffs.

Chapter 60
MAX

It had taken them half an hour to find the right path and the torches they carried only picked out small circles of grass in front of their feet. Max felt monumental anger. Why weren't the police helping them? A woman had been abducted and no one would believe him; even after all the information he'd given them about Stefan's stalking; even after reading his diaries. Fanciful, the Police Sergeant called them; not proof of intent. He'd be the laughing stock of the station if he brought such 'evidence' to the attention of his superior. Max hoped the Sergeant's balls would drop off.

Celia and Paul were holding hands tightly as they stumbled behind him. Max felt desperately sorry for them; they shouldn't be here. Tim should, but he'd never responded to the numerous text messages he'd left him, telling him where they were. Max knew why; Tim was appalled at the thought that his baby might be genetically inferior in some way. What a bastard, Max thought. He hadn't told Celia and Paul. They had enough to worry about. They reached a bend in the path and as they turned it, Celia shouted:

'There it is!'

And there it was. A large villa, dimly lit, standing 200 yards back from the cliff.

'Oh, no… I feel a little faint.' Celia leaned against Paul.

'Oh, my dear love. We'll rest a minute.' He looked at Max and Max knew he wanted him to go on alone.

'I'll check the house. Wait here,' Max said, walking off before Celia could stop him.

As he reached the side of the house, he suddenly felt a sharp pain in his chest; he was terrified he might have a heart attack before he reached Anna. Tension, he told himself. Tension creates pain. He forced himself to breath slowly and the pain eased. He crept up to one of the windows; his heart hammering so loudly he thought Stefan would hear it from inside the house. He looked into a large, elegant room; the table was laid for two, then he saw the blood over the table-cloth and groaned. Jesus Christ. What had he done to her? He had to get into the house.

Max was walking around to the front of the house when he heard a man's excited voice in the distance. He immediately switched off his torch. Anna and Stefan were walking towards the house, hand in hand. Suddenly, Stefan's large flashlight swept over him and held him frozen in its beam.

'Noooooooooooo!' Stefan screamed at him. 'Leave us alone! Run Anna, run!'

'It's all right! It's all right, Stefan!' She was saying, but Stefan wasn't listening; he was pulling Anna away from Max, back along the cliff path.

'You're not separating us again! Go away!'

'I don't want to separate you, Stefan. I want to help you.' Max shouted, holding his chest; the pain was back. He switched his torch on and saw Stefan pulling Anna harder and harder away from him.

'Anna!' It was Celia's voice in the distance.

'We're here! Paul shouted.

Their torch jerked over the ground as they tried running towards her. Max groaned. God knows what Stefan would do if he felt under attack.

'Keep still!' Max shouted to them. They stopped at once.

Max shielded his eyes from Stefan's flashlight playing over

his face.

'Leave us alone!' Stefan screamed again. 'Leave us alone.'

'Are you all right, Anna?' Max shouted.

'Of course, she's all right – she's with me! Go away!'

His tone of voice brooked no opposition. Max knew that somehow he'd have to make it look as if he was leaving. 'All right. We'll leave!' Max shouted.

'We're not leaving!' Celia shouted back.

'Shut up, Celia! We are!' Max walked towards Celia and Paul who were standing helplessly near the house.

Chapter 61
ANNA

Anna watched her parents and Max walk away and wanted to shout for them to stop. She wanted to go home and sleep; to escape from this shattering stress. Stefan was screaming and waving the flashlight manically, making the sky and grass oscillate around her. The tenderness she'd felt for him had been replaced by nausea. How could she pretend to be the sister of such a manic man?

Suddenly, his hand was wrenched out of hers. The flashlight arced into the sky as a body hurtled itself at him. Stefan grunted as he fell heavily on the ground.

'You bastard! What have you been doing with my wife!' Tim shouted as he punched Stefan repeatedly.

'It's all right, Tim! Don't hit him! I'm all right!' But Tim wasn't listening. He kept punching Stefan, but Stefan was now prepared and punched him back hard in the face. Tim fell backwards. Anna ran to get the flashlight which was pointing towards the sea. The world wobbled wildly as she picked it up. Her head was exploding. Running feet! Voices! Violence! She started running away from the terrifying noise.

'Anna! Stop!' Stefan's voice in the distance, but Anna kept running.

'Anna!' Tim's voice, but she kept running, away from the violence, towards the cliff.

She didn't see them running after her, trying to block her path; she couldn't see anything because her eyes were blurred with tears. Someone was racing behind her, breathing heavily.

She suddenly tripped.

And the shocking scream of a man falling over the cliff echoed in her head as she lay shaking on the grass.

Chapter 62
MAX

Max was sitting in an anonymous room at the Gower Police Station giving a statement to Inspector Williams; the others had gone with Anna to hospital. She'd started bleeding after her fall and when they'd carried her into the house, she'd had a miscarriage. At least Tim was able to help her with something, Max thought bitterly. Even as he told the Inspector what had happened, he found it difficult to believe himself. If Tim hadn't intervened Stefan would never have died and Anna would still be pregnant. What terrible irony, Max thought.

'We've had a number of deaths on those cliffs.' The Inspector was saying. 'Too many people don't treat them with caution. They take risks. I remember the deceased's father's death in 1991. I was a young copper then. First death I'd ever seen. Terrible for the family. Heard Mrs. Peterson never got over it. Didn't know the son had come back. House's has been empty for years now.'

There was a knock on the door and a young policeman came in.

'Excuse me, Sir, but Mrs. Owen is here. She wants to see Dr. Paris.'

Max was startled. He didn't know anyone called Mrs. Owen, so why did she want to see him, especially here?

'Show her in here, Clive.' The Inspector leaned on the table and got up. 'I'll call you if I want any more information, Dr. Paris. You look as if you need a good's night sleep.'

'I do. Who's Mrs. Owen?'

'She worked for the Peterson family for years. We all know Greta Owen here; her husband used to work for the force.'

Another knock on the door and a small woman dressed in black entered the room. The Inspector put his hand on her shoulder before leaving the room. She sat down opposite Max, her face twisted with grief.

'I know you must be tired, but I have to know what happened.'

Max rubbed his eyes with the balls of his palms; tiredness wasn't an adequate word; he felt shell-shocked; it was the same numbness he'd experienced after Sadie's death. But he explained how Stefan raced after Anna to stop her from falling, but when she tripped, his speed propelled him over the cliff. Tears ran down Mrs. Owen's face as Max spoke. He marvelled at the depth of her grief.

'I watched Stefan grow up in Vienna,' she said. 'He was like a son to me.'

'You worked for them in Vienna?' Max was too tired to take it all in. This small Welsh woman worked in Vienna.

'I worked for Renate's family before she was married. So when she married an English man, I went with her to London.'

'So you're Austrian?' Max said in amazement. 'I thought you were Welsh.'

'I've lived here for over twenty years, Dr. Paris. Accents change with time, but it wasn't a good move for anyone, except Mr. Peterson. He was a tyrant who was jealous of his wife's talent; he tried to destroy her before he died. He would have destroyed Stefan and Anna too, but...' She put a hand over her mouth.

'How did Stefan's father die?' Max said; his numbness had miraculously vanished.

Her eyes fluttered away from him. 'He fell off a cliff. History often repeats itself, Dr. Paris.' Her body suddenly shook. 'He was running after little Anna. Frightened out of her wits, she was. He

263

was a nasty, nasty man. If ever a man deserved to die it was him.'

Max suddenly wondered if she had pushed him, not Stefan. How could he trust what Renate said?

'What happened to little Anna?'

'Stefan ran like the wind to stop her from falling. He caught her just before she reached the edge.'

'So how did she die?'

'What?' Mrs. Owen said, confused.

'How did Anna die?'

Mrs. Owen stared at him for a long time. 'You're getting confused, Dr. Paris. Anna's not dead.'

Max's heart thumped very hard.

'Stefan's dead, not Anna. There isn't a God, is there? To think he's only just found her.' Mrs. Owen brought out a large white handkerchief and wiped her tear-filled eyes.

Max was finding it difficult to make sense of what she was saying. 'But Stefan's sister died so Anna can't be his sister.'

Mrs. Owen suddenly glared at him. 'Who says she died?' She blew her nose loudly. 'I knew she was Stefan's sister the moment she walked into the hotel.'

'The hotel?' Max suddenly felt as if he was in Alice in Wonderland.

'I run a hotel in Rhossili. Stefan gave me the money to buy it. Anna stayed there. It's not far from Bach Têg. I rang up Stefan to tell him I'd seen Anna and he said not to say anything to her about Back Têg as he wanted to be with her the first time she saw it. I've been looking after the house since that awful night.' Her mouth trembled. 'I told the authorities I'd look after the children after Renate's illness, but all they saw was an unmarried, foreign woman, so they put them into care.' She started crying noisily. 'Oh, my lovely boy. I'll never see him again.'

Max's head was throbbing. This woman really believed Anna was Stefan's sister. She must have recognised something about her that made her believe that. But what about the file in the children's home that stated little Anna had died at three! Why would someone write that if it wasn't true? And then there were Stefan's photos. Max's head was pounding.

'I'm sorry. I'm very tired, but why would Stefan fake photos to make Anna look as if she was Renate if she's his sister? It doesn't make sense.'

'I imagine Stefan thought that Anna wouldn't believe him if he didn't, as you say, fake the photos. And he was right, wasn't he? You still don't believe he's her brother.'

Her mouth trembled as she realised she'd used the present tense.

Max closed his eyes, trying to think. John Peterson fell off a cliff; then his son falls off the same cliff twenty one years later. What was the likelihood of such an improbable coincidence? He dragged himself up from the chair, swaying from exhaustion.

'I'm sorry, but I have to see Anna; then find somewhere to sleep.'

'You can stay at the hotel.' Mrs. Owen twisted the handkerchief repeatedly in her fingers. 'Can I see Anna?' She whispered. 'She's the only one I've got left now, you see. I've no children of my own and my husband died three years ago.'

'No, she's too ill.' Max spoke too harshly and the woman broke into tears again. 'When she's better, I'll tell her you'd like to see her,' he said more gently.

When Max got to the hospital Anna was in a deep sleep after being anaesthetized. Celia and Paul sat together on one side of the bed, holding hands and staring at Anna's waxen face. Max wanted to kneel down beside Anna and sob.

Chapter 63
ANNA

Anna woke up feeling groggy and stared up at a white ceiling. Something was in her arm. A drip. She had cramps in her lower stomach and the insides of her body felt as if someone had scraped it.

Tim was sitting beside her, looking concerned.

'Is it over?' She said.

'Yes, don't worry. D & C is only a minor op; it won't affect your ability to conceive again.'

'That's not what I'm worried about.' Anna answered in a flat voice.

'You'd be surprised how common miscarriages are in the first trimester.'

'Really?'

'Yes, although no one knows exactly why they happen, but it's more likely to be due to random chance than to any underlying problem with us. We can always try again.'

Anna heard him talking about miscarriages as if she was a medical student, not his wife who had just suffered one. They could be caused by a problem with the genetic material from the egg or sperm during fertilisation, or an imbalance in hormones or problems in the immune system. As if such facts bore any relationship to what had happened to her. Tim had killed her baby as much as if he had aborted it. If he hadn't attacked Stefan she wouldn't have nearly been killed on the cliff and Stefan wouldn't have died. She stared up as he continued talking, remembering Tim's face in the hotel when she told him she was pregnant. He'd looked... what was the word? Anna noticed two brown water stains on the ceiling… cornered. Yes, that was it. As if she'd used her body against him.

She turned to look at him, still talking, and said. 'Go away.'

Tim was momentarily speechless. 'You're bound to have strange reactions after a miscarriage. It's only –'

'Piss off!' she screamed at him. 'This is not a strange reaction. It's a normal reaction! Go away! GO AWAY!'

Anna tried to curl up in a ball, but pain tore up her arm. She'd forgotten the drip. As she turned her head towards the wall, she heard his retreating footsteps echoing down the ward and felt as remote as a river. She had become what Max had always wanted her to become …detached.

Chapter 64
CELIA

Celia felt the warmth of a September sun on her back as she trowelled the earth; summer was stealing days from autumn, but she didn't care. She stopped work to stretch her back and looked across the garden; it was such a delight: the delphiniums and peonies and poppies she'd planted in February were colour-washing flower-beds; the green leaves of the horse-chestnut trees threw huge canopies of latticed shade across the bottom of the garden and yellow and red butterflies flitted over the bushes like flickering flecks of sun. Anna sat at a small white garden table, her face dappled with the shadows of leaves, frowning at the book she was studying. It had been a long recovery after the miscarriage and the accident on the cliff, but she had come through it stronger, Celia thought. She had helped Anna recover from the miscarriage because she knew exactly what the pain felt like; she had had to endure it three times; this shared knowledge bonded them so completely that Anna had forgiven them. But Celia felt ashamed of her happiness; happiness created by the death of a child.

A cloud suddenly eclipsed the sun and she thought of that terrible night on the cliffs. Thank God Max had been with them. Tim had nearly cost Anna her life and yet, what would they have done if he hadn't come at the last moment? Would Anna have escaped from that man? Celia was still baffled by the fact that Anna seemed to be grieving as much for Stefan as for her lost child. Celia felt sorry for the man; it was a terrible way to die, but look at the fear he had created, especially in Anna and she wasn't even related to him. They'd adopted Anna from a children's home in Sevenoaks, and Stefan and Anna had been put into care in Wales. The poor man had had mental problems. What a terrible waste of talent, she thought, remembering the wonderful painting she and Paul had seen in his house.

'Mum – fancy a cup of tea?' Anna called over to her.

Celia felt such joy. She had become her mother again. 'Love one, darling. How's the studying going?'

Anna put the book down, her face suddenly shadowed by sadness. Celia wanted to rush across the garden and hug her, but Max had told them not to cosset her too much; she needed work to centre her in the present.

'Not bad. What time is it?'

'Almost 3 o'clock, so you haven't got any more time to impress Max with your research. He'll be here in a minute.'

Anna made a face at her. 'As if I could impress Max!' She sprung up out of the chair. She had only just started to be vigorous again. 'I'll make the tea.'

Anna's slight body moved across the lawn. She had lost a lot of weight since that night, but she was a fighter, Celia thought; she'd soon be back to normal. Anna's nervousness and inner preoccupation had lessened in the last month; she'd started taking an interest in life and studying again; all good signs for the future.

Celia stood up and massaged her neck, wondering what Anna was going to do about Tim. There was a huge rift between them since that night. Why did he have to act the hero at the last moment? And why had he seemed relieved rather than upset by Anna's miscarriage? Max knew something, she could tell, but he wouldn't speak about it.

A ring on the door bell. Max. 'I'll go.' She called out to Anna as she stepped towards the terrace.

Celia looked forward to his visits because Max made her feel so positive about life; the guilt she'd felt about not telling Anna about her adoption had almost vanished once he'd showed her how to concentrate on the positives in her life, not the negatives.

She knew that he loved Anna as much as Paul and she did and it amazed her that Anna didn't. But then, she'd not been aware of much, except grief, during the last five months.

Celia hastened down the hall and opened the front door. Max stood there, smiling at her.

'You're looking more like Monty Don every time I see you.' He looked down at her feet.

Celia laughed as he walked in. She'd forgotten to take off her gardening boots in her hurry to see Max before Anna did. 'She's in the kitchen making tea. The bad dreams seem to have stopped,' she whispered.

Max raised his eyebrows as if to say it's too soon to know.

Anna had woken them up frequently after the accident, shouting as she relived the memory of the cliffs, but she hadn't had one for a week. At first Celia thought she would never recover, but since Max's weekly visits to supposedly talk about Anna's thesis, she was slowly healing.

'She's been reading a lot this week. Research for her thesis. Come into the garden and tell me what you think of it. Bring a cup for Max, Anna.' She called to her as she and Max walked out into the sunshine.

'It's a haven of tranquillity, Celia. I could rent that tree-house and live here.'

Celia smiled at the image of an eminent clinical psychologist living high in a tree like Tarzan.

'Where's Paul?' Max asked.

'He's buying more photographic equipment. As if he hasn't

got enough.'

'Everyone needs a hobby,' Max stated.

'What's yours, Max?' Celia shaded her eyes with her hand as she looked up at him.

Max walked over to look at the book Anna was reading and didn't answer. Celia wondered what he was thinking.

Anna walked across the lawn towards them, carrying a large tray of tea and biscuits. Max raced across the grass to take it off her.

'I might have the body of a weak and feeble woman but -' Anna said.

'You have the heart and stomach of a clinical psychologist,' Max answered.

Celia held her breath, looking at the softness on Max's face as he smiled at Anna. Why couldn't Anna see how much he loved her?

'Remember how many psychologists it takes to change a light bulb?' Max said, looking at her intently.

Anna smiled up at him. 'Only one, but the bulb must really want to be changed.'

'I think you're ready to come back to the clinic.' Max said.

Celia didn't understand what they were talking about, but they were smiling at each other and suddenly, in that moment, she knew Anna would divorce Tim.

Chapter 65
MAX

Max knew he shouldn't be driving; he wasn't concentrating, but thinking how to ask Anna to marry him once her divorce from Tim was absolute. His training told him to wait until after Christmas, but his heart told him to ask her now. He wanted her to know how he felt; wanted her to become used to him as a lover, not as a supervisor. He'd never felt this happy with a woman before, remembering every angle and expression on Anna's face as they'd sat each week in her parents' garden; whatever the weather. Anna wanted to be outside all the time; as if being inside tied her to the past. And yet, she was living in the past by being in her parents' house. She'd never returned to Tim after the accident and now their house was being sold. Max had never told her about Tim's affair and she'd been far too preoccupied with grief to wonder at his frequent house calls.

Celia had told him she'd seen Tim's car driving at high speed the night Max had got drunk and they'd had to take him home. Where was Tim going? She'd asked him as she was pruning some flowers. So Max had told her about Tim's affair and Celia had dead-headed her glorious crimson-purple Flagstaff roses, saying she wished they were Tim's neck. Max smiled as he checked the rear mirror and turned into Bond Street. Anna's directness had been nurtured by Celia's. Amazing how nurture can overcome nature, Max thought.

Anna was reunited with her parents, so he hadn't told her about Mrs. Owen's belief that she was Stefan's sister. He'd contacted the children's home to ask them to check the Peterson children's file again and they insisted that it stated that Anna

272

Peterson had died, but there was no record of what she'd died from. Max was going to travel to the children's home to see the file himself, but one day as they were sitting in the garden together, Anna had said that she didn't want to know about her birth parents any more; the past was gone; she wanted to live in the present; to qualify as a clinical psychologist and perhaps get a job in a good clinic. Max had loved the way she'd looked at him when she said that; a cross between an innocent child and a coquette. She was such an alluring woman, but it wasn't simply desire that fuelled him; this time he wanted someone else's happiness far more than his own. It had taken Anna months to overcome the double bereavement; mainly because of the guilt and anger that stalked her every day once the numbness of shock had lessened; guilt that she had created the conditions for each death, and anger that she had allowed the deaths to occur. It had taken Max nearly a month to convince Anna that she hadn't caused either death, but the anger remained: who then was to blame if it wasn't her fault? Tim? God? Fate? The fact that she had shouted out her pain had helped her to heal. She's my greatest success, Max thought with immense pleasure, but only Celia and Paul knew how much he'd helped her recover.

Today was her birthday and she was coming to the clinic to give him her thesis. He'd asked her to come because he'd arranged a surprise celebratory lunch at Luigi's for her. As he drove along Wigmore Street, he wondered if the 26th September was the day he'd have the courage to ask her to marry him.

He slammed on the brakes as he saw a halo of copper hair in the distance; Anna was crossing the square. The man in the Audi behind him screeched to a halt and leaned on his car horn angrily; Max held up an apologetic hand in an effort to calm him down. He wiped his hands on his trousers before starting the car again; they were clammy with sweat. As he drove down the ramp of the Cavendish Square car park, his stomach knotted; he was experiencing the same nervousness he'd felt when he was a sixteen-year-old teenager asking his first girl-friend out.

Marie was patiently explaining to a client that he had come on the wrong day when Max walked into the client. She excused herself diplomatically from the man, came up to Max and whispered.

'One of Anna's old clients came to see her. You remember Kieran O'Reilly?'

Max reluctantly dragged his memory back to a nervous woman with a dependency problem. 'Yes.'

'Well, she's training to be a teacher and she wants to thank Anna for her help. I thought it would give Anna a boost. She's got a secret admirer, I think.'

Max wanted to run up the stairs to ask Anna out to lunch, but he forced himself to be polite. 'Who - Kieran?'

'No, Anna. A big special delivery package came for her this morning. Beautiful writing all over it. I've put it in the room she used to use before...' Marie shied away from words like nervous breakdown. 'She looks almost back to normal, doesn't she?' She glanced up at Max's face. 'Sorry, not a good choice of words.'

Marie bustled back to her desk, unaware of the devastating effect of her words on Max. A secret admirer! His earlier happiness evaporated like mist. What was he thinking of? She was a beautiful young woman. She could have any man she wanted - why would she want him? He didn't want to see her excitement as she opened the package. It was bound to contain something that he would never be able to compete with.

But as Max walked up the stairs, he reprogrammed his thoughts: why should there be a secret admirer just because

Marie thought there was? There could be many other possibilities. What other man had been seeing Anna constantly for five months? What other man had helped her overcome two traumatic events so she could restart her training and live again?

Max suddenly smiled as he strode along the corridor. There were voices coming from Anna's old office. Excited voices. Kieran must have had a metamorphosis, Max thought. Anna's door was open. Max stared into the room and saw Anna opening a large package, her face radiant with excitement.

'I don't know who the present is from,' Max heard Anna say in a child-like voice that wasn't hers.

'I wonder why it was delivered to the clinic,' Kieran asked.

Suddenly both women were ripping off the packaging until the floor was covered with ribbons of packing paper. Then Anna laughed as she saw the uncovered present.

Max desperately wanted to walk into the room to see what she was looking at, but something held him back. He saw a letter lying forgotten on the floor, addressed to Anna in a large, artistic hand and he immediately knew.

'Oh...' Anna whispered. 'It's us.'

Both women were staring at the opened present in awe; as if they'd discovered a priceless work of art.

'I've never seen anything so beautiful, Anna,' Kieran said. 'Who are the children on the beach?'

Max watched Anna's beautiful face turn with delight to Kieran and felt his heart breaking as he heard her say:

'My brother and me. We often walked on Rhossili Beach when we were children. My family had a house there on the cliffs, you see.'

Max shook his head as if he could shake the words away. Such words weren't possible. He'd been seeing Anna for months;

she'd recovered. She couldn't say such words.

'It's amazing. Who painted it?' Kieran asked Anna with wonder in her voice.

Max leaned against the corridor wall for support and slid slowly towards the ground as he heard Anna's answer.

'Stefan…my brother,' Anna said. 'He painted it for me.'